Explosion on the Sound

On the Sound Book One

Gemma Christina

Jpenname Publishing LLC

Copyright © 2023 by Jpenname Publishing LLC

All rights reserved.

No portion of this book may be reproduced, stored in a retrieval system, or transmitted in any form or by any means, electronic, recording, or otherwise without written permission from the publisher or author, except as permitted by U.S. copyright law.

All characters in this book are fictitious and any resemblance to actual persons living or dead is purely coincidental.

Cover by Stuart Bache

Contents

Dedication	VI
1. Chapter 1	1
2. Chapter 2	8
3. Chapter 3	18
4. Chapter 4	27
5. Chapter 5	32
6. Chapter 6	39
7. Chapter 7	42
8. Chapter 8	46
9. Chapter 9	51
10. Chapter 10	54
11. Chapter 11	60
12. Chapter 12	71
13. Chapter 13	77
14. Chapter 14	84
15. Chapter 15	91
16. Chapter 16	94

17.	Chapter 17	103
18.	Chapter 18	107
19.	Chapter 19	115
20.	Chapter 20	120
21.	Chapter 21	123
22.	Chapter 22	130
23.	Chapter 23	140
24.	Chapter 24	150
25.	Chapter 25	157
26.	Chapter 26	159
27.	Chapter 27	165
28.	Chapter 28	175
29.	Chapter 29	184
30.	Chapter 30	188
31.	Chapter 31	200
32.	Chapter 32	208
33.	Chapter 33	214
34.	Chapter 34	222
35.	Chapter 35	226
36.	Chapter 36	232
37.	Chapter 37	237
38.	Chapter 38	242
39.	Chapter 39	248
40.	Chapter 40	254

41.	Chapter 41	263
42.	Chapter 42	274
43.	Chapter 43	280
44.	Chapter 44	287
A Letter from the Author		289
Thank You		290
Also By Gemma Christina		291

To my husband, Dwight, the one person who always believes in me more than I believe in myself. There would be no novel if there were no you.

Chapter One

Eighth-grade teacher MJ Brooks tried not to look at the clock again. The parent meeting started an hour after school, and another agonizingly fruitless hour had passed. The conference room desperately needed a release of the stale air and the tension. All the faces gathered around the oval table were tense and washed pale by the fluorescent lights. MJ longed to be outside, even if it was still raining.

"Like I said, I don't even know why you called me here," complained Angela Lawrence, the mother of Ethan Lawrence, an eighth grader with twenty discipline referrals in one quarter and not one passing grade. "He obviously hates school," she continued, gesturing toward Ethan with a flourish of her tattooed arm. "And you all do nothing about it. He's bored, so it's no wonder he is entertaining himself." She viciously tucked her long hair behind both ears and folded her arms tightly across her chest.

Ethan sat slouched in a chair next to his mother with the hood of his well-worn navy Seahawks sweatshirt pulled over his head and his sandy bangs in front of his eyes. A flimsy camouflage backpack similarly slouched at his feet, obviously not full of books or his binder.

MJ looked over at Jay Butler, the dean of students. He nodded sympathetically at Mrs. Lawrence. "I'm sure we could do more to engage Ethan in his classes."

The room went quiet. MJ stared at Jay Butler in his yellow tie, which did nothing for his sallow complexion. How could he be so self-seeking? He knew his comment flew in the face of the truth.

Science teacher Sean Wheeler shifted in his seat. His tall frame always made him look uncomfortable in these settings, but that comment by Butler was sure to get his blood boiling. MJ risked a glance at Sean. She knew he'd be furious; and sure enough, his lips were a tight line of frustration.

The eighth-grade team had spent hours discussing how to help this student. Sean, in particular, invested a lot of time and energy into working with Ethan, bringing him in at lunch for homework help. Ethan sometimes came to MJ's room as well, but that usually ended with Ethan eating his lunch and not getting much work done.

This was the first time Ethan's mom had agreed to meet with them.

Mrs. Lawrence continued. "I'm just tired of getting email after email, phone calls home . . . Ethan's failing, Ethan threw a pencil, Ethan keeps sleeping in class. Ethan won't put his phone away. I just don't know what you want me to do about it?" She shrugged, looking at them defiantly.

"We understand how frustrating that can be," conceded Shannon Davis, the school counselor, her long blond hair gathered up in a neat bun. She wore her thick, black-framed reading glasses propped on her head. "But the team is very concerned about Ethan's progress at school. That is why we'd like to put Ethan on a behavior plan that we all agree to, as we outlined earlier. This way we can all be on the same page, and Ethan knows how to best communicate what he needs to avoid any further discipline issues and improve his academics."

Mrs. Lawrence glared across the table at her. "I will sign nothing that makes Ethan seem like a retard."

Ethan's head shot up, and for just a second, his eyes met MJ's. They were wide with surprise, or fear. She couldn't tell which. He glanced away and then pulled his hood further down on his head.

MJ seethed inside. This needed to end. It was going nowhere. Unfortunately, the principal had been called out of the meeting to help with a frantic parent phone call. Assistant Principal Carrie Chadwick was out sick, and Butler lacked the people skills to put the meeting back on the rails and bring it to a close. His attempts at being popular with students' parents meant he usually told them exactly what he thought they wanted to hear.

MJ fought the urge to speak, or at least she told herself she was fighting it. This happened to her a lot. Unlike Sean, who would die from the stress of not speaking his mind, MJ usually gave it a cursory effort, and then boom, almost before she knew it, her thoughts were out there.

"Mrs. Lawrence," she said, her voice calm despite a slight shaking in her hands. She clenched them under the table to keep the rising frustration with Butler in check. "Ethan," she said to get his attention. "Do you mind if I share a personal experience?"

Ethan shrugged without looking up at her. Mrs. Lawrence shrugged one shoulder. "I guess."

"So, bear with me, because you might wonder what this has to do with anything, but I'll get there, I promise."

Mrs. Lawrence eyed her suspiciously, but her shoulders relaxed a little. "Go ahead."

She took a deep breath. "So, my first job in high school was at this little coffee shop in my hometown. Here's a little secret, I don't drink coffee and never have. Do you think I knew how to make good coffee?" She directed this question at Ethan, who had decided to look at her now. He shook his head.

"Right. Nope. But did I think I knew how to make coffee?" she smiled. "Yep. I sure did. So, I went into this coffee shop, and even though they had posted the directions on how to make each of the specialty coffees, I just kind of threw stuff together." She smiled and shook her head. "Anyway, after a bunch of complaints from customers and my fellow employees, the boss—who was my grandma, by the way—took me aside."

Mrs. Lawrence and Ethan were both eyeing her warily.

"She said, 'Hun, we gotta come up with a plan because I love you, but not your way of making coffee.' At first, I was mad, maybe even embarrassed. I mean, how hard was it to make coffee, but it seemed like I was failing at it.'"

Everyone at the table was staring at her, including Jay Butler, with unconcealed disapproval. "Ms. Brooks, I'm sure . . ."

"Almost there." MJ continued. "My grandma could have just kept me on trash duty or fired me, but she cared enough to make sure I learned from the experience. I won't bore you with the details of the plan," she said with a wave of her hand. "But bottom line, I became a pretty decent barista."

She turned to Ethan. "Do you see what I'm saying?"

He smirked. "You want me to make coffee?"

"Yes!" she exclaimed. Then, much more calmly, "Well, no. I'm saying that plans just allow us to understand each other and agree on what we are trying to do together. And for you, that means success as a student. And for us, that is how we can help you get there. Understand?"

Ethan nodded slowly.

MJ looked at Mrs. Lawrence, who was studying Ethan with defiant but tired eyes. MJ inwardly pleaded with her to end this meeting.

Suddenly, Mrs. Lawrence unfolded her arms and sat forward. "Fine. Let's sign this thing. I need to pick up Ethan's brother anyway."

The entire room exhaled in unison. They passed around the requisite paperwork for signatures, and in just a few minutes, Mrs. Lawrence gathered her bag and her son and rushed out without a look back.

Sean looked across at MJ with a crooked smile. "A barista?"

MJ laughed. "It was all true. I swear." She stood up. "Anyway, I have got to get going."

"You know, MJ," said Butler as he gathered up his notes, "She just signed it to get out of here."

"Probably," replied MJ. "And I don't blame her a bit. We could've gone around for another hour if you prefer."

He smiled thinly. "I prefer you keep your stories out of the meeting. Thanks to you, we have about zero percent chance of this plan working. And, of course, you'll expect me to deal with it when Ethan goes off the rails."

MJ dug her fingernails into her palm to keep herself from telling Jay Butler everything she really thought about him. Instead, she stared straight into his eyes and said with calm conviction, "I wouldn't dream of it, Jay. Don't worry, I will make this plan work, as will the rest of our team."

He looked slightly taken aback by the confidence in her tone. He quickly recovered, however, and shook his head like a disappointed parent.

Jay Butler and MJ did not see eye to eye on much of anything. He was all about the policies and procedures that made him look good, but in MJ's opinion, he didn't see the people behind all those rules. MJ liked to think unconventionally. She had faith that by being creative, they could solve nearly every problem, even if they had to think beyond the policies and procedures. Butler found her attempts at trying new things irritating. He disliked her; he especially disliked that she had the principal's ear.

Just then, Principal Troy Danielson poked his head in the door. "I take it we're all done?"

Shannon Davis sighed, "Yes, thanks to—"

"Yes," said Butler, cutting her off. "It was a tough conversation, but we eventually worked it out and Ethan's mom agreed to the behavior plan."

Danielson nodded his approval. "Excellent!"

Davis glared at Butler before giving MJ the slightest eye roll.

MJ shrugged. Yes, Butler was a glory hound and control freak. As the dean of students, Butler's job description did not include being the boss, but that didn't stop him from trying. Let him have it. She would forget about Butler as soon as she was out the door.

"Hey MJ," said Danielson, "I'll see you at city hall tonight?"

MJ gave him the look she usually reserved for students; that "teacher look" that says, "Now would be a good time to quit talking."

"Really, you don't have to come," she said, looking anywhere but at Troy. She suddenly really wanted to exit the conference room. "It's not a big deal."

"What?" exclaimed Danielson. "Of course it is. And I wouldn't miss it, so stop trying to stop me." He smiled his broad, white-toothed grin. MJ always thought his smile made him look a bit like a mischievous elf. Danielson was easily the best principal she'd ever worked for. He was a smallish man with thick white hair and an athletic frame that spoke of his membership in the cycling club. He and his partner Kevin, a teacher in a neighboring district, often spent their summers cycling in exotic locations around the world.

Troy hired MJ after her disastrous first year of teaching at OHS, the district's one high school, also known as Orca High School. MJ had jumped in with both feet, and she really thought her American Literature class would mesmerize students. She quickly realized that passion for a subject is not all you need to be a brilliant teacher. The kids ran circles around her. She almost quit teaching altogether. Troy convinced her to come to Mariner Middle School, where he took her under his wing. She never looked back.

"Oh yeah," remembered Sean. "You're getting that award tonight, teacher of the century or something..."

"Teacher of the month," MJ said emphatically, "and by giving an award every month, I'm pretty sure the city intends to recognize every teacher, so your time's coming, Sean." She picked up her laptop, notepad, and pen off the table. "See you all tomorrow."

"You mean tonight," said Danielson.

"Fine. Tonight," she agreed, smiling as she passed by him and went out the door.

Chapter Two

MJ locked up her classroom and headed out to her Ford Bronco.

Her Bronco.

She still felt a bit of wicked joy every time it roared to life. It had been Justin's baby... a little hers, but mostly his. It was the only thing she asked for in the divorce. She just wanted the 1987 Ford Bronco II, red with a broad white stripe on the sides, 2.9L V6 automatic, lovingly restored whenever Justin, an Army Ranger, wasn't deployed to somewhere in the Middle East or Asia. He loved that rig, but not enough to fight her for it.

She might have felt guilty if she ever gave herself time to think about it. Justin hadn't wanted a divorce, and he parted with everything he loved, including her. And the dog. She insisted on keeping Edgar. The whole mess was complicated. No one really understood her split from Justin, and even she found it difficult to explain. She was happier; she knew that.

When she reached the Bronco, MJ pushed the hood of her jacket back and glanced up at the sky. Tiny bits of rain hit her face with soft, icy pats. She sighed as she thought about Edgar and the waning light in the sky. The sun disappeared so fast this time of year. There were things to love about fall in the Northwest. Disappearing sunlight was not one of them.

MJ climbed behind the wheel, cursing herself for promising Claire—her landlady, neighbor, and friend—that she would pick up some eggs from the Hamblins on her way home. The Hamblin Homestead, a farm owned by Dominick and Meredith Hamblin, was sort of on her way, but it was just enough off of her route that it would really press her for time. Poor Edgar would not get much of a walk before the day faded away and she had to head to city hall.

She waved to Sean as she pulled past him in the parking lot. He waved back as he slid the door of his minivan open to throw his bag in. It was his job to pick up his daughter from daycare after work.

Mariner Middle School was a two-story building sitting in an area of dense forest. MJ thought the school looked under constant threat of the forest creeping in and overtaking it. At night, it could be downright creepy with quiet, a fact she knew all too well from working weekends at the school alone.

One lonely, two-lane highway provided access, etching its way through the evergreen thickness with a haphazard winding that made it beautiful and dangerous. When she wasn't in a hurry, MJ loved her commute, awed by the stoic splendor of the place.

She used to find the walls of trees stifling. She grew up in Las Vegas, where you could see into the distance for miles. But here, the surroundings are full of secrets she would never know, even though she passed by them every day. In time, she learned to love it. Sometimes, the sun and clouds commingled to create ribbons of color that begged her to stop and grab her phone for a picture.

Today was not one of those days.

MJ needed to turn left onto the highway, but a bus waited to turn left into the parking lot, its yellow bulk standing out against the gray-green day like someone had painted it into the scene. The lettering on the side said, "Eagle Ridge School District," showing they were the opponents for tonight's boys' basketball game.

MJ groaned as car after car flew by in a wet rush, and the bus waited and waited. She knew and appreciated the driver's care with the student cargo, but that didn't mean she wouldn't tap her steering wheel impatiently.

The logjam finally cleared, and MJ headed toward the Hamblins. She loved going to the farm. The older kids were her students a few years ago, and their youngest, Diana, had MJ's language arts class this year. Diana was such an old name for a young girl. Not old enough to be posh again, but old enough that it seemed odd. Her mother loved Princess Diana, hence the name.

Diana danced to the beat of her own drum. She was quirky and deep-thinking at the same time. Her siblings were the same way. MJ regretted she didn't have time to linger as the conversations were always thought-provoking. No, today she hoped the eggs were ready to go and she could make it a quick stop.

Once away from the school, traffic was light, and MJ reached the Hamblins in good time. She turned onto the farm's badly rutted lane. The Bronco labored back and forth over water-filled craters. She pulled up next to the house just as Diana came flying out of the back door.

MJ stopped and turned off the engine, waving through the windshield at Diana. The girl was wearing a bright pink poncho, the hood of which kept falling in her eyes. Meredith Hamblin came out carrying a carton of eggs. She stood next to Diana with a serene smile. MJ found her to be one of the most intelligent, calm women she'd ever met. The pair of them looked so happy to see her that she had to get out of the car.

"Ms. Brooks!" shouted Diana, leaving her mother's side to wrap her in an enormous hug. She stepped back and looked up at MJ. "I finished my essay." She stuck her chest out proudly.

"Did you?" MJ said with surprise. "Well, that was fast."

"I did it on the bus on the way home."

MJ laughed. "That's one benefit of a long bus ride." She looked at Meredith, who was nodding in agreement.

"And it is long. You usually beat the bus here." She handed MJ the carton of eggs.

"I know. Long meeting after school."

"That's too bad. I've got your favorite tulsi mint tea on hand," she said, motioning with her head toward the house, "but I bet you're eager to get going after a long day."

"That sounds wonderful, but yes, you're right. I need to get going. Poor Edgar needs to get out."

"Ooh, Edgar!" Diana loved Edgar. MJ brought him over a few times to play with the Hamblin's two golden retrievers, Zeus and Athena. "I miss Edgar."

"I will make sure he knows that."

"And be sure to give our love to Claire," Meredith added. "I hear she's off in Arizona again. That would be nice on a day like today."

"Yes. She'll be back later tonight."

"And with fresh eggs for her breakfast." Meredith smiled.

"Ms. Brooks," Diana interjected, "Mom says you are getting an award for teaching from the city tonight."

MJ smiled knowingly. "I wonder why I'm getting that award?" she said, looking Diana in the eye.

The girl beamed. MJ loved how much happiness sat permanently on Diana's face. She had an uncharacteristic amount of positivity for an eighth-grade girl. MJ hoped middle school and eventually high school would not beat it out of her.

"We couldn't have nominated a better person," Meredith said, putting an arm around Diana's shoulder. "Unfortunately," she said, squeezing Diana's shoulders, "this girl has a piano recital tonight, or we would love to be there."

Diana pouted. "I tried to talk Mrs. Gourde into changing it, but she already booked the church and there wasn't another day, or so she said."

"Diana," said her mother gently. "You know Mrs. Gourde would change it if she could."

"I know," Diana admitted. "I just wish I could go."

"I would love for you to be there," said MJ, "but you are such a beautiful pianist, I wish I could be at your recital."

"Maybe the next one," smiled Meredith. "But you better get going. Those meetings start at six, I think."

"Yep. We'll catch up more next time. Thank you for the eggs."

"No problem."

"Bye, Ms. Brooks, see you tomorrow," Diana called as MJ walked back to the Bronco. "Drive safely!"

She waved, smiling to herself at being reminded by a 13-year-old to drive safely.

***

When MJ finally got home, she could hear Edgar whining from the driveway. How he knew it was her, she didn't know.

She placed the carton of eggs carefully in the insulated box outside Claire's door, as she did almost every Wednesday.

Claire's part of the house was in the back and took up most of the main floor and the second level. MJ's place was a smaller portion carved out of the bottom level in front. The view made up for any lack of square footage.

As soon as MJ opened her door, Edgar jumped up for the dog version of a hug.

"I'm sorry, buddy." She ruffled his fur and hugged his neck. "Long day followed by too long of a meeting."

He appeared to forgive her instantly when she put her bag down and walked to the closet that held his dog food. Edgar just knew things. A mix of Border Collie and Australian Shepherd, the dog seemed to understand her more than people sometimes.

After feeding Edgar and putting on her Hunter's rain boots, she switched out her light rain slicker for her warmer Columbia coat and grabbed the leash. It rained all the way home, and a quick look out her window told her it hadn't stopped, though it had relented to a lighter drizzle.

She apologized to Edgar again because it would have to be a short walk. She figured they had time for a quick jaunt down to the beach. The extra work of going up and down the beach access stairs would help tire the dog out. MJ also badly needed the movement.

Living on Stanton Inlet, MJ had beach access the city would not allow today. West Sound zoning laws forbid new homes from being built within 50 feet of the shoreline, but the 1939 Cape Cod that MJ and Claire called home claimed historical significance and had its own share of legal protections.

Claire's father built the house, and Claire grew up there. She had never married but had a wide circle of friends, and she had grown fond of MJ. The feeling was mutual. They shared a love of the outdoors. In fact, Claire, a retired park ranger, kept two kayaks down at the beach that the older woman used almost daily. One or two Saturdays a month, she and MJ paddled up the inlet to the greater Puget Sound.

Even though the rain had slowed some, the wind whipped MJ's long dark curls around her face and in her eyes as she negotiated the stairs with Edgar pulling ahead of her on the leash. The tread of her boots offered little grip on the wet, moss-covered stairs. She looked down at the beach, positive she wouldn't see anyone else on a day like today. Sure enough, not another living thing seemed interested in visiting the blank slate of wet, dark sand. They had the low-tide beach to themselves for Edgar's enjoyment. She reached down and unclipped Edgar. He bounded the rest of the way down the stairs, ecstatic to be set free.

As MJ walked, she threw a mangled tennis ball. Edgar retrieved it and brought the sand and slime-covered ball back to her, which she threw again. They repeated this method of exercise as the daylight slipped away, like someone sneaking away from work. Long summer nights in Washington exacted the heavy price of short, dark days in the fall and winter.

MJ hardly noticed as she mulled over the meeting with Ethan and his mother. She hated those types of meetings. So often they felt dishonest, like no one wanted to say what was really going on. Ethan had little structure at home. There was no father in the picture, and his overworked mom was unequipped to provide the limits Ethan craved. Teachers and other staff were trying to work miracles with limited time and resources to meet Ethan's needs during the school day. Worst of all, Ethan wasn't the only one. Similar stories made up the lives of too many of her students.

She shook her head, feeling deflated. Teacher of the Month. If she was so great, why did she feel so useless in helping kids like Ethan?

Edgar dropped his ball at her feet again and then bounced with anticipation. She picked it up and threw it, suddenly realizing that it had gotten too dark for her to see where the ball landed. How had the minutes flown by so fast? She cursed herself for not paying closer attention to the time.

"Edgar!" she called. The dog ran up to her with the ball in his mouth, ready to chase it again.

"Time to go." She grabbed the ball and held it gingerly between her figures. No way was that sandy, slobbery mess going back into her pocket.

She headed toward the stairs. Edgar trotted with her, jumping at her side every few steps, trying to get his ball back.

Once inside, MJ raced to make herself look presentable again in ten minutes. The email from the city manager asked her to be fifteen minutes early so she could meet all the council members and the mayor, but MJ already knew she'd be lucky to make the meeting on time. After a little mascara refresh and smoothing of her hair, she changed her clothes and flew out to the Bronco.

MJ usually drove with as much zip as her Bronco allowed and within the legal speed limit, meaning nine miles over, just enough to feel dangerous but not enough to attract attention. Tonight, she pushed it to a full eleven miles over until she got closer to the city hall; she didn't know the one-way, two-way quagmire of downtown West Sound well enough to ignore the signs. Slowing down was completely necessary to find a place to park. Without too much time lost, she spotted a car leaving a prime street-side parking spot. MJ lurched the Bronco ahead, determined to get to the spot before anyone else could claim it.

She slammed on her brakes.

A young man, hands in his pockets, darted in front of her. He stopped as her brakes squealed, then turned and gave her an angry glare from under his gray stocking cap. A streetlight illuminated him just enough for her to see limp, jet-black hair hanging below the cap, almost covering his eyes and stark against his skinny, pale face. One gloved hand left the pocket of his grungy tan jacket to flip her off; then he continued to the other side of the street.

MJ ignored the gesture and pulled into the parking spot, her heart pounding at the near miss and yet annoyed by the apparent homeless jaywalker.

The growing homeless population caused a contradiction of opinions for the population of West Sound, and MJ was no exception. It is inhumane to allow people to live outside without proper shelter. Yet, there were many tax-payer-funded programs and resources available to the homeless that many refused to use. As a result, the problem persisted with much political handwringing and unsustainable programs, but no proper solutions.

She could relate.

Grabbing her bag, she flung the car door open. As she did so, her phone buzzed. She swiped the screen quickly and saw a text from Troy Danielson. "Where are you? :)" She knew he'd beat her there.

She jumped out of the car and locked the door, running to cover the block and a half to the two-story, white building that was West Sound City Hall.

Bounding up the steps, she paused at the door to catch her breath. Just as she grabbed the door handle, a ferocious noise rushed to her ears. She could feel herself being pushed back by a wave of heat. Her right side collided with something metal as she fell to the sidewalk, her shoulder hitting first.

Confused, she lay on her back, staring up at the sky. Thick, black smoke floated up to meet the dark gray mass above. She reached up to her ears. They felt full of cotton.

A man in a suit was suddenly standing over her, reaching his hand out. She noticed his tie had pumpkins on it and she remembered it was almost Halloween.

The man was saying something to her, still holding out his hand. She heard nothing but buzzing or ringing, something in her ears. There was something in her ears. The man turned and looked behind him. She followed his eyes. Flames and smoke spilled through the doors of the city hall.

Chapter Three

MJ opened her eyes. The lights were dim, and she recognized nothing. She tried to sit up, but a jarring pain in her side convinced her to lie still.

Someone jumped up from a chair to her right. "Hey," said the soothing voice.

MJ squinted up at her, still feeling groggy. It was Shannon Davis, the school counselor and one of the few people she was friends with outside of work.

Shannon pulled her chair closer to the bed. "Hey," she said again. "Just lay down and relax, MJ."

MJ laid her head back on the pillow and closed her eyes. She was in the hospital.

"When . . . how long have I been here? What time is it?" Her mind was foggy. Or was it smoke? She remembered pieces of the night. She hit the ground, fire, and the man who reached out to her. Sirens and the ambulance played somewhere in her memory, but not with any clarity. She definitely did not remember getting to the hospital.

"It's about 5 a.m. You've just been here for the night," Shannon assured her. "They say you were in a pretty terrible state of shock, and they were a little worried about a concussion as well. The police went around to your house and talked to Claire. She called me." She paused and tucked a few errant strands of blond hair behind her ear. "As far as what happened," she sighed and looked down at her hands. "They're not saying much right now." She said, looking up again. "Just that there was some kind of explosion." There was a catch in her voice. She looked away.

MJ looked back at her and noticed the red around her eyes.

"Why have you been crying?"

Shannon bent her head down and took a breath.

"Shannon," she said with forced control. "Tell me what happened."

Shannon still didn't look at her. MJ could tell she was trying to get her emotions under control.

Panic grew in MJ's chest.

When Shannon finally looked up, she struggled to keep her lips from quivering. A silent tear rolled down her cheek. She took a deep breath.

"They are saying there are three dead, several more people are in the hospital, some in critical condition, but Troy . . ." A silent sob swallowed her words.

MJ sat up, ignoring the pain in her side. "Is he injured? In the hospital?"

Even as she said the words, she knew the truth from the anguish on Shannon's face.

Tears spilled over Shannon's cheeks. She shook her head and said in a whisper, "He didn't make it."

MJ stared at her. This couldn't be happening.

"I'm sorry, MJ." Shannon, fully crying now, laid a hand gently on her arm.

"No. They have to be wrong." MJ covered her face with her hands. "No! No, no, no!" She couldn't stop the sobs that now came quickly. She slammed her head against the pillow. "I told him not to come," she said through gritted teeth, ignoring the wetness from her eyes and nose. She turned her head away from Shannon and wept into her pillow. She made sobbing sounds that she didn't know could come out of her.

"I know," Shannon said, rubbing MJ's shoulder.

It seemed like they sat that way for a long time.

When MJ finally tried to wipe her face, her right side screamed at her like she'd been hit by a truck. She turned back to face Shannon. Without having to ask, the other woman handed her a tissue.

MJ stared ahead, trying to think of words to say, or even think. Her head felt foggy, and she struggled to believe the reality that Troy and others were dead, and she was almost one of them.

Troy was dead. Too many emotions coursed through her like streams of anguish that overflowed. She didn't know how to comfort herself.

She was angry at Troy for insisting on going, and grieving for him, taken in an instant. But she also felt guilt. It was her fault Troy was gone. She thought of Troy's partner Kevin, the other teachers, and her students . . . she couldn't bear it. And she'd been late. If she'd been on time, at least they might have died together. A stupid thought, she knew, but it was true.

She put her good arm over her eyes, trying to hide the tears that wouldn't stop. Crying was not something she usually did. But this crying, she couldn't control it.

Shannon stood up. "The nurse asked me to let her know if you woke up, so I'm just going to step out for a minute."

MJ nodded without removing her arm. She heard Shannon's light steps leaving the room. Regardless of whether she actually needed to talk with the nurse, MJ appreciated having a few minutes to herself.

She attempted to control her breathing. This helped to calm her wildly beating heart and give her a clearer head. The anguished tears slowed, but the ache in her heart continued to grow. A yawning black hole was opening in her chest. She felt ill.

A few minutes later, as she lay with her arm still covering her eyes, she heard the door open again. It wasn't just Shannon coming in.

MJ pulled her arm down to see two men in white shirts and ties entering the room, followed by Shannon.

"May we come in?" asked the older of the two, a tall bald man with intense blue eyes and a salt and pepper goatee. "We're with West Sound PD."

MJ nodded, wiping her eyes and nose.

Shannon returned to the bed and grabbed her gigantic bag beside the chair. MJ knew her for the bottomless bags she insisted on carrying around. Shannon wanted to be prepared for everything at all times, in case a student or staff member needed something. She carried bandages, granola bars, gum, hair ties, markers, sticky notes, and sometimes even socks.

She bent over and touched MJ's arm. "I have to head home for a shower and then go over to school. Everyone wants to know how you are doing, and I've promised I would keep them updated so you don't get a barrage of visitors." She smiled and squeezed her hand. "And don't worry about your classes. We've closed for . . . I don't know how long. That's another reason I'm heading back to the building. All the counselors need to be on hand for students, in case they want to talk about what's happened."

"Of course. Thank you for being here, Shannon." A few more tears escaped her eyes.

"I wish I could stay." She took the hand of MJ's good arm, gazing down with concern in her eyes, which were more red than brown from crying. "Claire will be here later to visit and possibly take you home if the doctors say it's okay," she said, smiling gently and squeezing her hand.

"Oh, she doesn't have to do —"

Shannon put her hand up. "MJ, just stop right there. She would be here now, but I convinced her to wait. So let her help you. She really wants to."

MJ nodded, too spent to argue.

"Alright, I will let these guys do their thing," she said, glancing back at the two waiting detectives. Then she squeezed MJ's hand before heading toward the door.

"Oh," Shannon said, pivoting to face MJ again. "I almost forgot. Your mother is on her way from Vegas."

MJ's eyes flew open, and she shook her head, "No, that's unnecessary."

"Too late. I tried, but there was no stopping her. She's renting a car, so no need to worry about someone picking her up at the airport. She'll be here sometime today. I don't know when exactly."

MJ looked up at the ceiling. She loved her mother dearly, but her idea of visiting was to clean MJ's house incessantly, complain about the liberal politics of Washington, and repeat the many reasons MJ should move back to Vegas, in her mother's opinion. "You can teach anywhere," she could hear her saying. This would only strengthen her case. MJ wasn't sure she could handle that right now. Sighing, she decided to worry about her mother later.

"Okay, thanks again, Shannon."

"Follow the doctor's orders, MJ. And try to rest," she said, eyeing the officers as she opened the door.

"We won't be too long. We promise," the bald guy said kindly.

The two officers moved closer to the bed. The other officer, an attractive Hispanic man, stood just a bit shorter than the older one and looked to be at least ten years his junior.

The older one spoke first. "I am Detective Greg Larson with West Sound PD, and this is Detective Jaime Mendez."

MJ nodded, unsure what she should say.

"We know you have been through quite an ordeal," Larson continued. "So first, we offer our condolences for your loss. I've met Principal Danielson a few times over the years, and he was a great man."

A few fresh tears rolled down as MJ nodded.

Detective Larson cleared his throat. "We just need to ask you a few questions to make sure we have your information correct. Are you okay with that?"

"Yes, but . . ." MJ tried to sit up more but could not move without causing pain that emphatically reminded her of her injury. She gave up. "Do you know what happened? I mean, was this an accident?"

Larson's face held the same expression, but MJ sensed the slightest change in the way he looked at her. "Do you have reason to believe it wasn't an accident, Ms. Brooks is it?"

"Yes," she replied. "Wait, no!" she said, shaking her head frantically. She took a calming breath before speaking again. Her next words were slow and measured and laced with irritation. "I mean, yes, that is my name, and no, I don't have any reason to think it wasn't an accident." Her hands curled into fists as she fought to stay calm. "But I would like to know what the heck happened. My principal died in there." The tears started afresh, and she couldn't reach the tissue box.

Larson motioned for Mendez to sit in the chair Shannon had vacated. The younger detective sat down, grabbed the tissue box, and held it out to her. With angry and tear-filled eyes, she snatched a few while glaring at them both. Why didn't they just tell her what happened?

"We are investigating all avenues, so we can't really answer that for you at this time, but we are so sorry for your loss," said Mendez, setting the box of tissues down. He took out a pen and pad of paper. "This will be a very important investigation, and I'm sure you can understand that it is extremely important that we get information as soon as possible." He had the slightest accent, and his copper eyes, framed in heavy lashes, were kind and patient.

He made perfect sense, but MJ was struggling against her all-too-natural impatience. She wanted answers, not questions. Nevertheless, she mopped her eyes and took a breath, willing her face to relax and look more cooperative.

"Good, we have just a few questions for you. We are told you will be released as soon as the doctors are satisfied that your injuries are not serious, and we want to make sure we, or another agency, can contact you later. Good," he said again as she waited for his questions. "Okay, so your full name is Melissa Jo Brooks?"

She nodded, and he continued.

"You are a teacher at Mariner Middle School?"

"Yes," she said. "I teach eighth-grade language arts and history."

He wrote that down. He continued to get all her general information down.

"Okay, Ms. Brooks," Mendez continued. "It is our understanding that you were attempting to enter the city council meeting when the explosion occurred?"

"Yes, I was running a bit late because of a long after-school meeting, and then I had to pick up eggs at the Hamblins and go home and feed my dog, Edgar. We probably spent too long down at the beach." She inexplicably felt the need to spill every sin. "I drove as fast as I could. I mean, I sped a little, but then I couldn't find parking. I almost ran over a homeless man. He flipped me off, by the way. Then I parked and got a text from Troy." She swallowed hard. "He was wondering where I was." She stopped and looked down at her hands to steady herself. "He knew me well. He probably wasn't surprised that I was a bit late." She sighed, trying to keep back new tears. "When I finally got out of the car... Wait, where is my Bronco?"

The two officers exchanged looks. "I'm sure your Bronco is where you left it," said Larson. "Nothing is leaving the scene at the moment."

She nodded. "I only got a few steps when it happened. I don't remember much after that, except the guy with the pumpkin tie who was trying to help me up."

"Pumpkin tie?" Mendez raised an eyebrow.

"Yes, he was in a suit, and it was a Halloween tie, black I think with jack-o'-lanterns on it."

"Did he say anything to you?" Larson asked.

"Yes, but I couldn't hear anything," she said, squinting at the memory. "He had his hand out like he wanted to pull me up, but then I saw the flames and smoke, and that's pretty much all I remember."

She eyed them quizzically. "You don't think he did it, do you?"

Larson smiled patiently. "We are investigating everything right now. The exact cause of the blast has not been determined yet, and we can't rule out accidental or criminal possibilities. But most likely he was just a Good Samaritan."

MJ nodded. "Well, you can get some security footage, right? I mean, city hall must have cameras, and the businesses and traffic cameras..."

Mendez looked down at the floor, and MJ could tell he was hiding a smile. Anger flared in her chest, and she could feel her face growing hot.

Larson fixed his eyes on her, and while his smile was friendly, it was clearly an effort.

"I assure you all available investigative tools are being employed."

They all looked toward the door as a nurse entered.

"I'm sorry, gentlemen, but it's time for the doctor to come in. You need to wrap it up," she instructed.

"No problem," said Larson. "I think we are done for now." He turned to MJ. "It is highly likely someone will contact you again, either West Sound Police or another agency, perhaps the FBI."

"The FBI?"

"If we find the explosion is a criminal act, the investigation will involve many more law enforcement agencies. We don't know for sure that will happen, but we want you to be prepared for the possibility of being requested to make a formal statement when you are feeling better."

"Okay," she replied. "I guess that makes sense." She didn't really think any of this made sense. Her life felt shattered into a million pieces.

Larson gave a slight bow in her direction. "Thank you, Ms. Brooks. We hope you heal up quickly."

Mendez nodded in agreement. "And again, we are so sorry for your loss."

MJ only nodded as she felt the tears rushing to her eyes again.

Chapter Four

West Sound Detective Jefferson Hughes pumped the last couple gallons of gas into his Audi Sportback, a car he loved but which currently needed severe cleaning inside and out. He rubbed his face and felt the rough baby stubble beginning to grow. Unfortunately, he would not have time to shave.

He listened as a man and woman at the fuel island in front of him discussed the explosion while they waited for their own cars to fill up.

"Did you hear about city hall?" the woman asked.

"Hear about it? I heard it!" the man replied. "I was two blocks over. Nearly gave me a heart attack."

Jefferson glanced over to see the man, who looked old enough to worry about such things, shaking his head. "Those poor people. I can't believe the mayor is on life support. I hope he makes it."

Lack of sleep and caffeine consumption were catching up to the detective. His hand shook as he pulled the gas nozzle out. He did so too hastily and a leftover gush of fuel landed on his Berluti Oxfords.

"What the . . ." He slammed the nozzle back into the machine. The two conversationalists looked over at him, the woman with a disapproving, sour face.

Jefferson ignored them and grabbed a paper towel from the windshield cleaning station. He sat in the car and attempted to wipe the gasoline from his shoe. An ugly wet spot persisted. He threw the paper towel away with disgust. Today would be hard enough without a bad mood to get him started. And now his hands smelled like supreme unleaded.

Last night, he jumped in the car as soon as Chief Carlson called him with the news. Then he drove throughout the night because he was more than 800 miles away.

He'd taken a rare week off to attend his father's funeral in Redding, California. His father's death still felt unreal, and if he thought about it too much, the guilt at being so far away from his parents for so long crept back into his thoughts. He played a persistent refrain in his head. He should have moved back home a year ago, right after his father collapsed in the garage after a massive heart attack.

He knew his older brother, George, and his mother thought the same thing. They never actually said it outright, but they made poorly concealed remarks along those lines.

On some level, he agreed with them, but the time never seemed right. He'd had a long night of endless highway to beat himself up about it. He'd been horrible company for himself.

At least he could claim to be better than Alex, his younger brother. He only showed up long enough to go to the funeral and try to bum money off every relative in attendance. Jefferson finally threw him out of their parents' house when he caught him rummaging through their dad's things for anything valuable.

He'd never forget the anger and sorrow that combined in his chest when he found Alex, standing in his father's study, a gold watch in his hand. The face that looked back at him, for a brief second, had the same wide-eyed innocence of his little brother from years ago. Just as quickly, it vanished, and Alex looked every bit the petty thief that he was.

Jefferson felt the hurt again as he remembered the scene. It was just one day after the funeral.

He'd roared in anger, grabbed Alex by the collar, and dragged him to the garage. He threw him in the car and drove him to the bus station without speaking a word. Alex knew better than to protest. George would have beaten the crap out of him.

Jefferson gave him enough money for a bus ticket and a meal. And then he drove away. He did not know where he was now.

His mother cried all night. The whole family had tried to get Alex clean for so many years. Jefferson spent years searching for him every time he did a disappearing act. Alex had exhausted everyone's pity. Well, everyone except his mother. And now with Dad gone . . . Jefferson shook his head at the thought. His mother was no match for Alex's desperate manipulation. He loved his brother, but he had long ago run out of patience for his pillaging of their parents' resources.

Drugs. Drug dealers. Scum of the Earth, and just plain evil in Jefferson's opinion. Alex's addiction and the drug dealers who preyed on him were the reason Jefferson became a cop in the first place, a decision that no one in his family understood.

The plan had been for Jefferson to be a big-time corporate lawyer. He loved law school at Cal Northern, but something never felt quite right. He sat for the California bar exam, which he passed. By that time, Alex was in his first treatment facility trying to get clean.

He was so angry that his little brother was struggling with drugs and being manipulated by filthy criminals that he changed his career course completely. Getting drug dealers off the streets might not save his own brother, but it could save someone's.

Now he needed to get to an early morning briefing, and he would just make it on time. He expected it to be full of a variety of local and federal law enforcement agencies, including other members of the Joint Terrorism Task Force, or JTTF, which included officers and agents from local police departments and federal agencies like the FBI. Jefferson trained with this regional team for large-scale operations. He'd pushed himself to get a place on this team because of their work investigating drug trafficking.

The team assembled mostly for training and to learn what the feds knew about potential threats in the area. Most of their work was intelligence sharing. They had definitely never needed to be called up for a crime in West Sound, a small but growing city on the Puget Sound.

The destruction of city hall by an explosion was still hard for him to fathom. He knew very little at this point. They could rule it an accident—a gas leak, or something similar. But whatever the cause, it would be devastating to this close-knit community. Jefferson knew firsthand that West Sound had its share of crime, but people still felt safe. Until now, security at city hall was pretty much just a few cameras. Even if the explosion was an accident, that would change.

As he ducked back into his car, his cell phone buzzed on the seat. The name "SSA Wells" popped up on his screen. Chief Carlson had shared Jefferson's situation with Amber Wells, the FBI's supervisory special agent in charge of the JTTF.

"Hughes here."

"Ahh, Hughes. Are you close? We're about to start."

"Just a couple of minutes away."

"Great. I'm saving you a seat, if you don't mind sitting amongst the feds."

He smiled. "Of course, I do. But save me a seat anyway," he quipped.

"See you soon."

His drive to the WSPD station took him close enough to city hall to get a first-hand look at the scene. He drove slowly by the cordoned-off area. That was enough to see the charred entrance of the building. Forensics teams in white jumpsuits moved in and out of blackened areas like moths fluttering in the dark.

He knew right then that whatever happened, this would consume his life for the foreseeable future.

Chapter Five

At the station, Jefferson stepped into the restroom to wash his hands, straighten his tie, and try to appear as polished as possible. He took pride in presenting a groomed appearance, something he took a lot of ribbing for, but he didn't care. Everybody has their thing.

The briefing room usually worked just fine for accommodating the officers at WSPD, but as Jefferson entered, he had to squeeze by several officers standing against the wall near the door. The area was little more than an oversized conference room with one long table surrounded by chairs. A few extra seats lined the walls on either side, for overflow like today.

SSA Wells waved her hand to get Jefferson's attention.

Seated near her were other local FBI agents: Special Agent Ron Benton, Special Agent Julia Liufau, and the newest, youngest member tech guru and special agent, Jared Hill. WSPD Detective Rory Jackson, Jefferson's partner, sat on the other side of the seat Amber saved for him.

As Jefferson made his way over. Amber moved her raincoat off the chair next to her. Jefferson shook hands and patted a few shoulders of the team before he sat down.

Amber moved her coat to the back of her chair. "You're just in time." She tilted her head toward the front of the room.

West Sound Chief of Police Keith Carlson sat at the head of the table. He nodded at Jefferson. "Welcome Detective Hughes. It's good to see you made it. I'm sorry we had to tear you away from your family."

"It's all good, sir. This is where I need to be right now. My family understands." Even as he said it, he knew it wasn't quite true. He pushed the thought out of his mind. This is where he needed to be, even if they didn't quite understand.

The chief gave a slight smile, but it took effort. He was all business with his neat, slicked-back silver hair. He looked polished as usual, but bruising circles hung beneath his eyes, making him look years older than a week ago.

Detectives Larson and Mendez sat to the side of Rory. Jefferson, Rory, Larson, and Mendez made up the detective unit of the West Sound PD along with the uniformed officers they peeled away when necessary. Larson, the longest serving of the four, was also a sergeant and the lead detective in the department.

"Glad to have you back, Jeff," said Larson.

Mendez nodded his agreement.

"Good to be back."

Several other WSPD officers, State Patrol, Rainier County Sheriff's deputies, and fire officials sat around the table, stood, or sat in the chairs against the wall. The room held a palpable mixture of exhaustion and restlessness. Jefferson knew the men and women around him were eager to know their next steps. Everything hinged on the information about to be shared.

"Alright everyone, let's get started," began Chief Carlson. "It's been a long night for all of us, so I appreciate your patience with me and the various teams as we let you know what we've learned so far. I know you're all anxious for the results of the fire investigation, so we'll just get to it." He looked to his right. "Tom."

"Thanks, Keith," said a silver-haired man with a neatly trimmed beard that contrasted with the black shirt of his uniform. "Good morning, everyone. For those who might not know, I am Tom MacGregor, fire chief for the City of West Sound. I first want to express, on behalf of the entire department, our deepest condolences to all those who have family or friends injured or killed in the explosion at city hall. We are all shocked and deeply saddened by this devastating event suffered by our city." He faltered for a moment and stopped to take a deep breath, looking down at the table.

Rory leaned over to Jefferson and whispered, "You remember Tonya Eberle?"

Jefferson nodded. "The city manager."

"Yep. Also his sister-in-law. She's in intensive care."

Jefferson shook his head in disbelief. The magnitude of the loss mounted with each bit of information.

MacGregor gained his composure and raised his head to continue. "Our investigative team has worked non-stop to determine the nature of this event, and they have come to some important conclusions. First, and most important, we have ruled out an accidental explosion."

MacGregor looked around the room, fully expecting this to cause an angry buzz.

He was right. Most of the attendees turned to their neighbors, expressing shock in a variety of expletives or intense whispers. Many people began casting furtive glances toward Amber.

This changed things. The FBI would most likely run this investigation.

Chief Carlson locked eyes with Amber, the agent who would direct the FBI's efforts. She met his gaze with an almost imperceptible nod.

Jefferson didn't envy her in situations like this, when emotions are so high, but he trusted her leadership completely, and he knew the chief did as well. She'd earned respect in local law enforcement circles. Few had Amber's ability to create a functioning team from a patchwork of organizations without creating territorial in-fighting.

The five-foot-three dynamo Amber Wells exuded confidence and strength, and not just because she had the lean build of a gymnast, something she did competitively in college. She had a sharp, curious mind and an amazing ability to understand people better than they understood themselves.

At fifty-five, her blonde hair was growing white, a fact she did not cover or hide in her tight, low ponytail, the same way she'd worn her hair her entire career. In fact, the only change in her appearance in the seven years Jefferson had known her was the recent addition of a slim-framed pair of glasses over her hazel eyes.

MacGregor waited for the din to die down. "We have also concluded that three people perished in the blast, including city council members Jonathan Silva and Sheila Cochran, as well as the principal of Mariner Middle School, Troy Danielson. Paramedic crews transported several people to the hospital, including the mayor of West Sound, George Sully, who is currently on life support at St. John's Hospital. Five other individuals, including four city employees and one member of the public, are also hospitalized with serious injuries. Outside of the building, one civilian suffered non-life-threatening injuries. The blast occurred when no one occupied the upper offices of city hall, and there were no victims in those areas. Property damage outside of the building is limited to a few broken windows of nearby businesses and vehicles."

Another fire official, sitting at a computer, stood as MacGregor gestured toward him.

"Now I will turn the time over to our lead fire investigator, Nick Hernandez, to explain the evidence used to determine the cause of the blast. Nick."

A projector screen slowly descended from the ceiling.

"Thanks, Tom," said the man, picking up a laser pointer from the table. He wore closely cropped jet-black hair and stood ramrod straight, all the former Marine.

"Before I begin, I want to thank Maury Appleton and his crew over at ATF for their expertise and assistance in our investigation. Their help has been invaluable." He nodded toward Maury, a tall black man standing with his back against the wall. Maury tipped his head in acknowledgment.

Hernandez turned back toward the screen. "This is a diagram of the council chambers," he said, waving the red pointer over the screen on which an image was coming up to full brightness. "This is the door the public enters. And these are the doors, one on each side of the council seats, that lead to the offices and conference room behind the public meeting room." He clicked the pointer to advance the slides, revealing an image of the council chambers. "This shows the council chambers prior to the blast." He clicked forward to the next slide.

The horrific image struck the room silent. A few people shifted in their seats. Chief Carlson stared ahead without looking at the screen. Anger radiated from him. He didn't need to see the images again.

Jefferson looked away. Who could do that to people?

He forced his eyes back to the screen. The charred room looked like a war zone, the thing you expect to see in terrorism-ridden countries, not West Sound, Washington.

Hernandez waited for the room to absorb what they were seeing before starting again. "I won't go into too much detail as your agencies all have a copy of our full report, but there are a couple of important findings we want to highlight."

He moved the laser dot on the screen to the area of the council seats. "We found a high level of explosive residue in this area. That evidence, added to our analysis of the trajectory of blast material, leads us to conclude that the device used was in the vicinity of the council seats, specifically on the side occupied by the mayor and Council members Silva, Cochran, and Forsberg, with Forsberg being absent because of a family vacation. The worst damage is confined to this area," he said, pointing again to the council seats, "and this is also where we saw the loss of life and most serious injuries."

Hernandez advanced the slides again. "This image shows recovered fragments of the explosive device, including what appears to be pieces of what we believe to be a duffle bag that may have contained the device. An analysis of the fragments and other material in the area is consistent with the use of a fairly sophisticated IED. Even more troubling is the fact that the explosive material used was C4, not an easy thing to come by."

Jefferson heard Amber blow out a breath next to him. He glanced at her. "What the heck?" she whispered incredulously, meeting his eye. "Who could've done this?"

He shook his head. "I don't know, but I'm ready to get this thing going. The sooner we get moving, the better chance we have of finding out."

She nodded and returned her gaze to the front of the room.

"That's where we'll leave it for now," Hernandez was saying. "I am available, along with the folks at ATF, to answer questions and go over details in our report. Back to you, Chief Carlson."

"Thank you, Nick," Carlson said. "We appreciate the extraordinary work by your department, and in a short amount of time."

The fire investigator returned to his seat, and the chief continued. "Thank you, everyone, for coming to this part of the briefing. We appreciate all the work, late hours, lack of sleep . . . your dedication. As I'm sure you are all aware, but I must repeat, do not speak to the press or share this information." He looked around the room, his eyes boring into each face. "All press statements will come through official channels," he added sternly.

"We will take a quick break and then hold the law enforcement briefing for WSPD and our FBI partners back in this room in ten minutes."

With that, the low hum of conversation and movement began filling the room, but it was quieter than a normal end-of-briefing. The shock of what they'd seen was new, but Jefferson expected it wouldn't take long for all of them to bottle up their shock and anger. They had to. It was the only way to get to work.

Chapter Six

Jefferson sat back and ran a hand through his blond hair, derailing a bit of its perfection. "Holy—"

"Don't say it," Amber warned. She was tough as nails, but foul language annoyed her. She believed the public should be able to tell the difference between the criminals and the professionals bringing them to justice. If she caught anyone on her team swearing, that person would be the next one buying takeout for the team. It had become a bit of a joke whenever the group met for training, as they found other words to fill in for the common curse words.

"Cow," Jefferson finished with a crooked smile.

"Just what I was thinking," chimed in Rory, pointing at Jefferson. "Those were definitely the words going through my mind." His unruly ginger beard contrasted with his neat gray suit. Rory said he enjoyed dressing up because he'd spent too many years covered in dirt chasing terrorists in the Middle East.

Ron stood up, all 6'7' of him.

"I'm going to go get some coffee. Apparently, the Northwest Bean brought in some good stuff in the staff room. Anybody else want some?"

"Please, yes," answered Julia, looking like she'd already worked an all-nighter. She'd stuffed a Mariner's cap over her curly black mane and wore a Seahawks hoodie and jeans. Julia put the rest of the team to shame in her knowledge of Seattle sports and all terrorist attacks against the United States' interests. She was also the mom of a two-year-old boy. "I'll come with you. I need to move."

Jared had his laptop open, reading and tapping intently, ignoring their chatter.

"What's up?" Amber said, looking over Jared's shoulder.

He answered without taking his eyes off the screen. "I'm just going through the inspector's report, double-checking all the images for possible searchable items."

"Found anything yet?"

He shook his head, his mop of brown curls falling just shy of being in his eyes. "Just started."

Jefferson didn't know this new techy well, but what he knew was impressive. The young man was intense and didn't engage in small talk, but nobody could debate his skills with a computer or any other technology. It did not surprise Jefferson that the young man already had his nose on the screen, looking for investigative avenues.

Amber, Ron, Julia, and Jared worked in the small FBI satellite office in West Sound. They investigated federal crimes in West Sound and surrounding areas and as far south as Portland, Oregon. More often, they assisted local law enforcement when their resources were stretched. Now that they knew the blast was criminal, it became an act of terrorism and a federal crime. West Sound had nowhere near the resources needed to investigate it.

And the city was wounded. Someone had almost decimated city leadership. Having the federal agencies involved provided much-needed stability.

Jefferson checked his phone. He had a text from his mom. "Let me know when you make it home."

Jefferson smirked. Home. He didn't know when he would get to his house, or when he might get to sleep. It didn't seem likely to happen soon. But even if the chief sent him home right now, he doubted his ability to relax. He knew his mind was too full for that.

He texted his mom a quick, "Made it." Worry would consume her if he didn't respond.

Amber leaned over so their shoulders were touching. "How are you doing, Jeff?"

He shrugged. "I'm good, you know, considering. But I'm ready to go." The last thing he wanted anyone to think was that he couldn't do his job right now. This was going to require all hands on deck. He wanted to find out who did this as badly as anyone else.

She nodded. "I am sorry to hear about your dad."

"Thank you."

"Jerry lost his dad last year. It's such a tough time."

They were quiet for a minute.

"How is Jerry?"

"Oh, he's enjoying retirement a little too much. He's visiting Carolanne and the kids in Texas right now, probably playing a round of golf every day. So yeah, he's fine." She gave an affectionate smile reserved for talking about her husband, kids, or grandkids.

"Lucky guy," smiled Jefferson. "We are about to be consumed."

She nodded. "We'll get him," she said flatly.

"Yes, we will." He knew it was true. Whatever it took, they would find whoever did this, and sooner rather than later.

Chapter Seven

Chief Carlson returned to his seat, and the rest of the officers and agents began doing the same. Ron and Julia returned with their coffee.

The meeting now included just the FBI agents, WSPD detectives, and Chief Carlson.

"Let's get started," the chief began. "I'm going to turn it over to Sergeant Larson to share the video footage. Then we'll discuss our cooperative strategy."

Larson stood up and walked nearer to the projector screen. "This video represents what we see as our best lead on a suspect."

Jefferson sat forward in his seat as the clear, color video began. The footage started outside of the city hall.

"Of course, this camera is facing Center Street, near the main entrance. Keep your eye on this guy," Larson said while pointing at the screen. A slim white man in a tan winter jacket and gray beanie was making his way up the sidewalk to the entrance. He was carrying a black duffle bag. He reached for the door, and at that point, the video footage switched to the inside.

"This is the main lobby, and here is our guy again," Larson said, pointing.

The man walked into the lobby, still carrying the bag, and then disappeared through another door.

"It's at this point he enters the council meeting room."

The footage switched again, and Jefferson watched as the man made his way to the front of the room and approached one of the council members seated behind the council bench. He then handed the bag to a male council member, who accepted it and appeared to set it down on the floor.

A few people exchanged glances, but no one made a sound. Jefferson stared at the screen. The two men in the video exchanged a few words; the council member even reached a hand out to the slim man, who shook it and then turned away.

"For those of you unfamiliar with the city government," said Larson, "the man receiving the bag is Council Member Jonathan Silva, one victim in the explosion."

The video continued, showing the young man walking out of the meeting room, through the lobby, and out the front entrance. Jefferson noted several points in the video in which the camera caught a clear picture of the slim man's face—young, knit cap, white, unkempt . . . perhaps homeless. Why didn't he attempt to avoid the cameras?

The video feed switched back to the outside entrance. The man appeared again, walking through the door. He turned to the right, walked down the sidewalk, and then cut between two parked cars to walk onto Center Street without looking. Then he pulled up as a vehicle heading toward him slammed on the brakes. He lifted his right arm and flipped the bird to the driver before continuing to the other side of the street. The vehicle headed in the opposite direction and out of the frame. Jefferson thought the man's pace was purposeful like he knew where he was going, but not hurried. He continued walking toward North Beach Street and out of the camera's view.

"We are working on obtaining footage from local businesses to trace him beyond this point. This will take some time as we are not sure of his direction after this point," Larson said, pointing to the screen.

He looked out at the crowd, faces full of questions. "If it wasn't so horrifying, I'd call this footage a gold mine."

"So that's why the fire investigator is so sure it was a duffle bag," Rory said.

Larson nodded. "Yep, the bits they found matched what we see in the video."

"He seems unconcerned with being on the surveillance camera," Jefferson remarked.

"Yeah, that is curious. It's almost as if he didn't care." Larson seemed to consider what it might mean.

"Maybe he planned it as a murder-suicide," suggested Ron, taking a big gulp of his coffee. "Then he chickened out."

"It's worth considering," agreed Larson. "If nothing else, it should make finding him easier. We've run his face through facial recognition software, but nothing came up. Obviously, finding this guy is our top priority." He looked down and tapped his index finger on the table as if contemplating saying more. "We still have more questions than answers right now, so the sooner we chase this stuff down, the sooner we get this guy."

The chief thanked Larson. Then he turned his steely eyes on Amber. "There is a lot of evidence to comb through and follow up, and as SSA Wells here is calling the shots for the JTTF, she'll lead the investigation, so we don't end up stepping all over each other's toes. I will be directing our patrol officers through the door-to-door and finding more footage. I'll also be communicating with state patrol and the sheriffs from ours and the surrounding counties who are eager to lend a hand. Larson, Mendez, Jackson, and Hughes, you will take your direction from SSA Wells. She'll let me know when we need more officers."

Jefferson looked around at the team. Their faces were somber and focused. The earlier banter, which served as a way for the team to keep their spirits up during demanding investigations, was gone for now. The weight of the investigation rested firmly on their shoulders.

The chief seemed to sense the mood. He looked them over and took a deep breath. "I have all the faith in the world in you all. I know there is no better team out there to hunt down the monster that did this."

The chief had a close relationship with the mayor and may have lost other people he counted as friends. He hid it well. His eyes were dry and determined.

"We've trained for this, and I expect every officer of mine to be alert and ready to do whatever it takes to get the job done."

Amber smiled gently. "Thank you, chief. I can assure you U.S. Attorney Morgan has already demanded we employ every resource on this case. As we go forward, whatever we need, the FBI stands ready to assist." Her smile vanished. "So, let's go get 'em."

Chapter Eight

Wells stood up and pushed in her chair. Standing behind it, she looked down at her notes. "We need to sift through some of this evidence to determine all the lines of investigation. With WSPD and other agencies working the scene, doing door-to-door interviews and taking statements of those in the area, I would expect more information to act on relatively soon."

She touched her lip thoughtfully with her pen. "Can you also keep us updated on the state of the mayor and three injured council members, um . . ." she glanced at her notes, "Weinberg, Knight, and Olsen? It's my understanding they are all heavily sedated right now or in surgery."

The chief clasped his hands together on the table. "The hospital has been very clear that none of them are in a state to give interviews right now. We will continue communicating with the medical staff and let you know as soon as that changes."

"Thank you." She looked down at her notes and continued. "I've already requested more federal forensics specialists to help with combing the scene for evidence. As soon as my guy Jared cleans up an image of the beanie man from the video, we can begin circulating that with your officers for scouring the local area . . . businesses, bus stations, homeless camps, convenience stores, etc. Right now, he is a person of interest, and I'm of the mind that we don't publish through the press or social media just yet. Any thoughts on that?"

She looked around the room. Her tone wasn't challenging, but it was terse enough that no one would speak up unless their input was extremely relevant.

"Good. I'm not naïve enough to believe the picture will stay out of the press for long, but I hope we get the jump on this guy. Chances are he's already on the run, but you never know." She looked down at her notepad on the table.

"We need to know everything about the people in that room, specifically what was on the agenda that night, upcoming agendas, council member relationships with the public, any threatening messages or behavior from the public, that sort of thing. Julia and Ron," she said, pointing her pen in their direction, "I'd like you to canvas email, social media, council agendas, and minutes, and interview any city employees lucky enough not to be invited to the meeting."

The two agents nodded their agreement while making notes.

She looked at Chief Carlson, "I know you need the uniformed officers for the door-to-door, but can you spare a couple competent with computer searches to help mine all this information?"

He nodded. "Whatever we need, we'll get it. We have officers pouring in from all over the state to lend a hand."

"Great. Larson, your crew will work on investigating the relationship between Council member Silva, the duffle bag he seemed to expect, and our person of interest. You and Mendez should start with his wife. I'm sure it's not a great time, but waiting is out of the question."

Larson clicked his pen. "Do you want us to check with Council Member Forsberg as well? I believe she gets back in town this afternoon."

"No, I'd like you to interview the families of the injured council members. See if they know anything that may have been out of the ordinary--crazy constituents, threats, or personal issues. Let's have Jefferson and Rory look specifically at anyone who would normally have been at the meeting but was absent."

Larson nodded. "That works."

"Do we know how many people we're talking about?" Jefferson asked.

Larson put down his coffee that he was in the middle of sipping. "Currently we know of two people, but we have not had time to cross-reference the sign-ins, agenda, video, etc."

"Start with the names you have," Amber said. "I'll have Julia work the cross-referencing and pass on names and info to you as she gets it."

"Got it," said Julia, scribbling with speed.

"To start," said Larson, "there is the vacationing council member, and the only other name we have is the teacher, Melissa Brooks. She was supposed to be there for some teacher award. I guess that's why the principal was there. We spoke to her as soon as she was awake. She wasn't in the meeting but just outside and took a pretty good bruising to the ribs when the blast went off." He sipped his coffee.

Jefferson raised an eyebrow, wondering why her principal made it in, but she didn't. "What was her state of mind when you talked to her?"

"Well," started Larson, "upset as you'd expect. A little confused at first, but she definitely got a look at the beanie boy, so I'd get that picture in front of her as soon as possible. She seemed quite put out about him flipping her off." He gave a devilish grin. "You'd think a middle school teacher might be used to that kind of thing. At least mine should've been."

Larson lifted his coffee to his mouth but stopped midair. "One thing she seems used to is taking the lead. I'm not sure who got interviewed, us or her." He flicked his eyes toward Jaime Mendez as he finished with a sip of coffee. "Am I right?"

"She was upset and really wanted answers for why her friend died," Mendez said diplomatically. "Who knows if she's always that way? She may have been on something, too. Who knows?" He lifted one shoulder in a noncommittal shrug.

"Why wasn't she in the meeting?" Jefferson asked. He considered whether she could have been faking. She wouldn't be the first person to hate her boss.

"Late," said Larson. "Something about walking her dog after school."

"The old 'I was walking the dog' alibi," said Rory.

Larson waved his hand at Rory's sarcasm. "I'd be seriously surprised if she had anything to do with it. She's just a bit intense." He winked at Jefferson. "You'll see."

"She may have nothing to do with it," said Amber, "But until we know, we assume nothing."

Jefferson agreed wholeheartedly. He stood up. He had orders and wanted to get moving. "All right, Rory. Let's go. I'll drive. You call around to the hospital to see if she's still there."

Amber put her hand up. "Hold your horses there, Jeff and Rory."

Jefferson sat back down. Amber looked around at the group. "One last thing." She took a deep breath. "We have to answer some questions for the public. While I don't want to tip our hand about the video footage, this community deserves to know that this was no accident. The chief and I will make a statement to that effect, so don't hold that fact back during your interactions today."

They gave their agreement.

"Now, go get it done."

Jefferson and Rory jumped up, coats in hand.

"Keep us informed, and we'll do the same," said Amber. "And watch your phones for a picture from Jared."

"Will do," Jefferson said as he and Rory headed for the exit.

Chapter Nine

Did he do it?

Dylan Warren lay curled in a tight ball on his filthy sleeping bag. The rain had stopped, but all of his stuff was wet and would be for a long time. Right now, he didn't care. His ears still rang with the sound of the explosion.

He'd never questioned what was in the bag, and now the wads of cash hiding in his shoes made him sick to his stomach. He clutched his head tighter, pulling the beanie down hard and trying to keep the imagined mayhem out of his mind. He heard the explosion and saw the smoke. He ran without turning around. It wasn't long before people came into the camp with the news: an explosion at city hall. Something in him knew it was the bag.

Tears stung his eyes, and fear gripped him hard. The police would know where the bag came from, and they'd be coming for him.

Footsteps outside his tent made him freeze, his eyes wide and ears alert. Someone began unzipping the opening. He glimpsed purple fabric and relaxed. It was Rachel, his sometimes girlfriend and always high tent mate.

She dipped her head inside, her stringy blonde hair hanging out of a light blue Seattle Kraken winter hat she'd nicked from Target. The gray poof ball on top got stuck on the zipper. She pulled it out and looked him over.

"Some of us are going to shower at the Weston," Rachel said, referring to the nickname the homeless population gave to West Sound Services. "Wanna come? Well, I mean you should come. You smell like the sewer."

He shook his head.

Her eyes narrowed. "What's the matter with you?"

"Nothing. I just don't feel good," he said, not meeting her eye.

She was quiet before she said, "Want a hit? I got a little left."

"Go away," he said.

"Fine, be miserable, you little piece of—"

"Just go!" He flipped her off.

"Whatever, loser." She pulled her head back out and left without zipping the tent, allowing the wet autumn breeze to blow over him. He shivered.

After Rachel's steps faded away, he sat up slowly. He couldn't stay here. It was only a matter of time before they'd come after him. He'd done it. He was sure now.

Once he decided, it only took him a few minutes to pack everything he wanted into his backpack. He thought about taking down his tent but decided against it. Rachel didn't have anywhere else to go. He felt bad leaving her, but it was for the best.

As he threw his backpack over his shoulders, a few neighbors looked out from their soggy tents and junk-constructed shacks. He'd been in this spot the longest, a patch of thick fir trees in the right-of-way between the Cherry Street freeway exit and Donald Park. People came and went daily; it was considered rude to ask questions. Only Rachel might have said something, but she was off getting clean, in one way at least.

Without a word to anyone, he adjusted his pack, pulled his beanie down tight over his ears, and walked out of the camp.

Chapter Ten

When Rory called the hospital, a nurse informed him they had released the teacher from the hospital, with strict orders from the doctor to go straight home and continue resting. "I'm not sure she'll follow that. A bit of a firecracker, that one," the nurse warned.

"Could be interesting." Rory smiled as Jefferson steered them through the winding lane leading to Melissa Brooks' home. Rory, happily married, loved to play matchmaker for his partner, mostly because he knew Jefferson hated it. Relationships were trouble, and Jefferson knew he was not in the right mindset to start one.

Jefferson just shook his head. "She's, at the least, a witness, Jackson. I'll be keeping my eyes on my notepad, and so should you, as I'm sure Marissa would agree."

Rory smiled as they turned into the driveway. "Always, Jeffy. Always. Keeping it strictly by the book, just like you."

Jefferson ignored the remark. He and Rory had a good working relationship. They understood each other. Jefferson never took much of what Rory said seriously. It was just Rory being Rory. Jefferson stuck religiously to the rulebook, for good reason. As a young cadet, he came within a hair of losing his job and career because of a rule-breaking partner. He'd never let that happen again.

Rory suddenly sat forward. "Whoa, look at that view!"

Jefferson had already noticed. The house sat high enough on the bank to give a sweeping view of Stanton inlet and the evergreen shores that bordered it. The clouds gave way to a slice of sunshine, revealing bits of the silver and snowy Mount Rainier. On a sunny day, the view of the mountain must be stunning. The mixture of sunlight and gray skies gave the lawn an unearthly glow as it stretched to the edge of the bank. A low stone wall bordered the property with one iron gate signaling access to the beach.

It looked just nice enough to leave their warm overcoats in the car. "Let's go," said Jefferson, opening his door and breaking nature's spell.

The slate-blue house blended in with the landscape like someone formed it from the sky. A canary-yellow door faced the driveway. This appeared to be the side of the house but also the main entrance. Cobalt blue pots sat on either side of the door holding maroon Chrysanthemums.

Jefferson rang the doorbell. Almost immediately they heard the door unlocking, as if the person had been watching them. Both men were surprised when a wiry, older woman opened the door.

"Can I help you?" she asked with authority. The woman had short, spikey white hair and a fair but healthy complexion. She gazed at them through narrowed eyes.

"Yes, ma'am." Jefferson showed his badge. "I am Detective Hughes of West Sound PD, and this is Detective Jackson. We are looking for Melissa Brooks."

Her face relaxed slightly. "I see. I assume you're here about the explosion." She said this like a statement, but her stern face said she expected an answer. Jefferson wondered if she'd been a teacher too.

Rory nodded. "Yes, ma'am."

"Well, she's been through a terrible shock." She shook her head. "Getting injured and losing that wonderful principal." She looked at them with concern, crossing her arms tightly across her chest and leaning against the door frame. "You know she came within seconds of being in that blast herself."

The death of the principal wasn't new information, but until now Jefferson hadn't considered that perhaps the killer expected Brooks to be in the meeting. He tucked the information away mentally as he said, "We know this is a difficult time, but we need to speak with her. Is she inside Ms. . . . ?"

She looked back and forth between the two of them. She stuck out a hand. "O'Neil. Claire O'Neil."

Jefferson and Rory shook her hand in turn.

"She's my tenant. Her place is around the front." She stepped outside and led them to the end of the driveway. "If you take the stairs and the path around, it will take you to the entrance for her part of the house."

She smiled weakly. "Sorry about the frosty reception, officers. It's just that I've been down to see her several times since bringing her home. You know, making her tea and just talking and such to try and calm her. I am really concerned. MJ is one of the toughest young women I know, and I have never seen her so affected. She can't seem to sit still." She looked thoughtfully toward the sky and then back at them. "I think she may still be in shock."

Jefferson nodded. "That would be understandable. Thank you for letting us know. We will keep that in mind."

She smiled. "Thank you. I'm sure you know what you are doing, but I can't help but look out for her. She's alone right now, but I believe she is expecting her mother at any moment."

She took a step back toward the house. "Well, I will let you get on with it. I just saw the news conference with the FBI saying that they think it was a bomb. You need to find out who did this God-awful thing."

"Yes, we are doing our best ma'am." Rory smiled sincerely.

"Good. I'm sure that's the case." She crossed her arms against the cold. "The whole city is with you." Her eyes became glassy. She quickly looked away, gave them a small wave, and retreated toward the house.

The detectives looked at each other. Jefferson took a deep breath, "Shall we," he said pointing to the stairs.

The path took them around to an expansive front porch. As Rory knocked on the door, Jefferson glanced around him. A porch swing hung on one side of the door and a picnic table sat on the other. Both wore the same yellow as the doors. Rhododendrons skirted the porch and pots of purple and pink pansies were on each side of the stairs. Everything looked immaculate.

He turned his attention back to the door, realizing Rory had knocked again and no one had responded.

"Hmm, maybe our teacher slipped out past her pit bull keeper?" Rory looked around.

Just then, Jefferson's phone buzzed in his coat pocket. He pulled it out and quickly scanned the screen.

"Looks like the photo from Jared has arrived." He looked around the porch and then towards the beach. "Do you hear a dog?"

"Faintly."

"Can't sit still?" Jefferson said with a raised brow. He turned and followed a path of round concrete steppingstones that led to the gate at the edge of the bank. Rory followed.

Beyond the gate, steep wooden steps, green with moss, cascaded down to the beach. Jefferson opened the gate and started down.

Rory groaned. "Do you realize how much sand will get in your car?"

"Come on," shouted Jefferson.

As both men bound down the stairs, Jefferson hit a particularly slick piece of moss and lost his footing, landing on his backside on a squishy stair.

"I am not going to laugh." Rory's impish look said he might not laugh, but this would not be forgotten.

Jefferson glared up at him. He stood up and continued down with more caution in his step, feeling cold and wet in uncomfortable places.

When they reached the bottom, they'd only taken a few steps when a black and white dog came bounding toward them. A woman was running after him calling, "Edgar, no!"

The dog dropped a dirty tennis ball at Jefferson's feet. Then he jumped up, dirty paws aimed toward Jefferson's white shirt and inky blue tie. Jefferson jumped back, but too late.

Rory didn't hold back this time. He laughed and patted Jefferson's back. "Oh, Jeffy, you are having a day." He bent down to pet the offending Edgar.

The woman reached them, out of breath. "I'm so . . . sorry," she gasped.

Jefferson looked at his shirt covered in wet sand and then at the woman. Pink cheeks stood out against her pale complexion and dark hair. Her blue eyes, bright from exercise, matched the sapphire of her coat. She searched his face, waiting for him to speak. The intensity of her questioning gaze was both patient and insistent. He found it strangely disconcerting. Was that look a teacher thing?

He knew he should say the polite "Oh, no problem," but at the moment he didn't feel polite. When he just stared at her and then at his shirt again, her eyes narrowed in annoyed confusion. She turned to Rory.

Rory also glanced at his silent partner. Rather than wait for Jefferson to end the awkward moment, Rory smiled at the woman. "Sorry to disturb you, ma'am, but are you Melissa Brooks?"

"Yes," she said warily, petting the panting dog who was now resting against her legs.

Rory showed his badge. "I'm Detective Jackson and this is . . ."

"Detective Hughes," Jefferson finished, as he began wiping sand from his shirt. "We'd like to ask you a few questions."

She closed her eyes tight before opening them and meeting Jefferson's gaze. He expected to see sadness, confusion, worry, or the haze of someone in shock, as her neighbor had suggested. Instead, he saw something like defiance—against what he didn't know. He'd probably annoyed her with his reaction to her precious pooch.

This was not starting well. He knew the importance of establishing a positive rapport with an interviewee. In his ten years as a detective, he'd excelled at it, but today, Jefferson's normally competent skill in speaking with the public seemed to have abandoned him.

"Would it be possible for us to talk in the house, Ms. Brooks?" he said with an attempt at a more friendly tone.

She did not release her intense focus on him, and his awkwardness increased. He looked down at his shirt front, brushing at any remaining sand. In reality, he wanted to avoid her eyes.

Finally, she spoke, "I imagine you've had enough of the beach."

"You could say that," he answered, returning his gaze to hers.

She nodded. "To the house it is. And you can call me MJ."

She clipped a leash on the dog and led the way across the soggy sand and up the stairs.

Chapter Eleven

As they approached her door, MJ slipped off her sand-laden boots and set them next to the welcome mat. Rory followed suit, but Jefferson hesitated. He hated taking off his shoes in other people's homes. Walking around in stocking feet made him feel weirdly vulnerable, like only people he trusted should see his socks. Rory, on the other hand, looked comfortable enough to go rummaging through her fridge. Finally, Jefferson sighed and removed his shoes, grimacing at their condition as he did so.

MJ hung her coat on a hook by the door. She was dressed for comfort in a pair of sweatpants and a navy Mariner Middle School sweatshirt.

"Would you like a drink? Water, tea, coffee?" MJ asked as she put on a pair of slippers.

"No, thank you. We don't want to take too much of your time," Jefferson said as he sat on a tan leather sofa. He gazed out the windows. They were cased in dark wood and spanned the walls on both sides of the door. Even indoors, the inlet took the starring role.

The whole room felt like an extension of the outside. Nature's grays, greens, browns, and blues that surrounded the house also filled the walls and furnishings inside.

This part of the house was tiny, in fact, the living room, kitchen, and eating area seemed carved out of what should be one room. But considering the beauty of the surroundings, Jefferson thought the teacher had made out spectacularly with this place.

MJ went to the kitchen. "Well, I'm going to have some tea, so if you do want something, it's no bother."

"I'll take some tea," said Rory good-naturedly.

Jefferson gave him a hard stare.

Rory mouthed, "What?"

"I've got mint, a vanilla chai, or West Sound Fog. Which will it be?" MJ said from the kitchen.

"Oh, the chai, for sure," answered Rory.

Jefferson waited for all this pleasantry to be over. He probably should have taken a drink too, but he was impatient to get on with their questions. Sitting there in his stocking feet, he found it difficult to get back his . . . his what? Focus? Confidence? No, he had to admit that he wanted control of the situation, and so far, he felt out of sorts.

Was it the silly dog ruining his shirt? He looked across the room to see Edgar lying in his fluffy dog bed staring at him. Jefferson stared back. The dog did not flinch but instead lifted his head and looked even more intently into his eyes. Jefferson grew annoyed. What dog did that? Like owner, like dog. Don't dogs cower and look away when people stare into their eyes? The detective shook his head and reminded himself that he hadn't slept all night. Maybe he'd try to sneak a car nap at some point today.

MJ came over and set Rory's tea on the end table next to him. "I put a couple of sugars and a cream here, not sure if you want either, but there it is."

"Thank you, that's perfect."

MJ winced slightly as she slowly lowered herself into an emerald armchair. She held her mug between her hands with her elbows on her knees.

"You were injured?" Rory asked.

"It's just bruising," she said, waving it off. "It's already feeling a little better."

"And you probably wouldn't say it if it didn't." Rory smiled.

She flicked a quick glance at him. "Look at you. We've just met, and you already know how to imitate my mother." Her smile was faint, but it said he'd guessed right.

Rory chuckled.

Jefferson pulled out his notebook.

"Before you start," said MJ, her face set with the same determined look as earlier. "I haven't been watching the news. It's just too much right now, but I need to know." She took a deep breath. "How did this happen?"

As a detective, Jefferson was hard-wired to question every facial movement, every emotion. As he observed MJ, he wondered at her intense expression. He couldn't quite make it out. Was it an attempt to prepare herself for what she might hear?

He looked at Rory and nodded, indicating that he should tell her. Jefferson wanted to examine her reaction.

Rory put down the tea. "Fire officials and forensic experts have determined that the explosion was the result of an incendiary device left at the scene."

She stared at him.

"In other words . . ."

"I know what that is," she interrupted. "My ex-husband served three tours in Afghanistan." She set her tea on the coffee table in front of her and hung her head down. "You mean," she said looking up angrily, "that someone injured and killed those people, including my principal? On purpose?"

Rory nodded. "I'm sorry to say that is the case, according to the evidence."

Moisture sprang to her eyes, but her eyes were angry, and the teardrops never fell. "I'm sorry." She said dabbing at her eyes anyway. "So, what is being done to find out who did this? You must have some idea."

Jefferson watched her intently, but so far, he didn't see anything to make him believe she was insincere. He did, however, sense that MJ was used to being in charge, and she was turning the tables on them.

He remembered Larson's earlier comment, that Ms. Brooks likes to run the show. As much as he understood her shock at the news, he wanted to get back to detectives asking the questions.

"We are investigating on multiple fronts right now," he responded. "That's why it's important that we get as much information from you as possible, to help us narrow our focus." Without waiting or allowing any response, he continued. "So can you please tell us about your movements prior to the explosion?"

She sighed. "I already told the other officers all of that in the hospital, but here goes." She went through the day's events again, from the ending of her school meeting to when she almost ran over the homeless guy.

"This man who crossing the street," asked Rory, "would you recognize him if you saw him again?"

"Probably." She sat up. "Wait . . . is he the one? Did he do it?" Her eyes were wide and alert.

"I'm sorry, we can't share details of the investigation," Jefferson responded rigidly, as he reached into his pocket for his phone.

She narrowed her eyes. "But aren't you sharing them by asking me about them?"

Jefferson ignored the question as he looked down at the phone. He swiped at his screen until he found what he wanted. "Is this the man?"

She looked briefly at the phone as he held it up for her. "Yes," she said. "Yes, that's him."

"You seem quite sure," he said, lowering the phone to his lap.

"Well, he scared me to death and then had the nerve to flip me the bird."

She tilted her head to the side as if considering something.

"Wait, can I see it again?"

Jefferson looked at Rory who just shrugged. "Sure," answered Jefferson. "Have at it."

She took the phone and played with the screen, increasing and decreasing the image, turning it this way and that. This went on for a good minute and Jefferson was getting impatient. They did have other people to interview, and somehow this teacher kept taking over the process.

Suddenly she held the phone up to them. "I think I know this kid."

"Do you?" asked Rory. "That would definitely be helpful."

"I didn't see it at first," she explained. "Kids, especially boys, change a lot between middle school and adulthood."

"Can you tell us his name?" Jefferson had his pen ready. Getting a name would make this nightmare of a visit worth it. He'd ruined his shoes and a good shirt.

"Well, I don't know that. When I say I know him, I mean I've seen him. I'm sure he was a student at our school, but not one of mine." She examined the picture again before returning the phone.

"Okay," said Jefferson as he took it, disappointed. "Can you remember which teachers may have had him in class?"

"I'd guess he's about 20, so that would have been six to seven years ago, maybe longer if he's older. If I didn't have him for Language Arts, he would have had John Benson, who is now retired, or Tammy Schlattmann, also retired."

Jefferson wrote down the information. When he turned his attention back to MJ, he didn't like the look he saw brewing on her face.

"You know," she said. "I could talk to them for you and maybe ask around to the other teachers, especially if I have a copy of the picture." She smiled sweetly. "It would help me feel like I'm doing something."

Only over his dead body would Jefferson allow this woman or any member of the public to start messing around in their investigation. "We appreciate the offer, but it's important that the police carry out the investigations. It's a legal thing. I'm sure you understand."

She nodded, but those determined eyes were back, and he was sure she did not like his answer.

"And we have a few other questions, if it's not too much trouble," Rory added.

"Of course."

Rory referred to his own notebook, "You mentioned another man, one with a pumpkin tie that approached you after the explosion."

MJ took a sip of her tea. "I do not remember much about that. I think I focused so much on the tie that I didn't commit much else to memory. He had darkish hair. I might remember if I saw him again, but I'm not sure." She held the mug for a few seconds longer, warming her hands on the sides before setting it down again. She reached down to pet Edgar, who had quietly joined the conversation.

"Did he say anything to you?" Jefferson asked.

"I think so, but my ears were affected by the blast. In fact, they are still ringing constantly." She touched her hands to either side of her head then dropped them back in her lap. "I think he was just trying to help me out of the area."

Jefferson nodded. "These next questions may be difficult, but they are important to the investigation. Can you tell us about your principal?"

MJ looked down at her hands. "Troy was a good, good man. The best boss in the world, and he loved kids and his job." Her voice trembled slightly. "He was only there because of me."

Rory smiled reassuringly. "You're doing great, MJ, and we appreciate you answering all of our questions." He checked his notebook again. "Were there any difficulties with students, parents, or staff members recently, anyone you can think of that might hold a grudge against you or the principal?"

MJ's shock got the best of her. "You can't possibly think this had something to do with Troy or me? That's crazy, and I must say it's a serious waste of your time. Everyone loved Troy."

"And you?" asked Jefferson.

She glared at him for a second before a corner of her mouth lifted in a gentle smile. "Detective, I'm sure I upset eighth graders on a daily basis. But no, I can't think of anyone upset enough over lunch detention to go to this extent."

"How about your colleagues? Any staff members that might resent you or Principal Danielson?

She shook her head, but Jefferson sensed some hesitation. He decided to press a little. "There must be some bad feeling sometimes. Surely your principal has had to call teachers out or discipline them for one reason or another."

"Sure, but I don't see how anyone could plan for him being there. It wasn't common knowledge. I wasn't even sure he'd be there until that day. It's just not plausible that anyone would do this because of him."

He smiled briefly and tried a new question. "How was your relationship with the principal?"

She looked confused. "Excellent. Tory was not only my boss, but I counted him as a friend and mentor."

"Did Principal Danielson's personal relationships ever cause any concerning reactions from parents or students, threats or anything of that nature?"

"You mean because he was gay?"

"Yes, exactly."

"No, not any that I'm aware of, and I'd be surprised if there were any issues related to that. He's been the principal for twelve years. If there was anything, he didn't share it with the staff. You might ask Kevin, his partner." She paused. "Although this isn't the best time. The service for Troy is in a few days," she added quietly.

"There are going to be a few of those," Rory said.

MJ looked between them and then her eyes grew more gentle. "I'm so sorry. I didn't even think . . . You must have lost people you know."

The detectives were quiet, but Rory nodded while folding up his notebook. He looked at Jefferson.

Jefferson wasn't quite ready to leave. He had another follow-up question.

"Your husband."

"Ex," she reminded him.

"He's a soldier?"

"Yes, an Army Ranger."

Jefferson nodded, "And where is he now?"

She tensed. "Last I heard he was in the Philippines."

"So, you're not sure he is still there?"

"We don't really keep in touch."

"His name?" Jefferson asked, pen ready.

"Is that really necessary, I mean the last thing I want is for him to feel the need to contact me."

Rory's eyes narrowed. "Has he ever been violent with you?"

She looked confused. "Oh gosh, no! Quite the opposite. He's the sensitive type and will probably think I need his protection." She pushed a brown curl behind her ear. "I'd rather leave him out of it, but if you insist, his name is Justin Brooks."

Jefferson wrote the name down with a star next to it. No matter what MJ said, this guy could have the knowledge to pull off the attack. He wouldn't be the first ex to go nuts and do something violent to get back at his former wife.

"Thank you, MJ," Jefferson said cordially. "We know this hasn't been easy. We'll leave our cards and if you remember anything pertinent to the investigation, please give one of us a call."

The detectives stood up and handed MJ their cards. As she took them, she was looking at the couch with a curious expression. Jefferson looked behind him. To his horror, a wet spot darkened the leather where he'd been sitting.

He looked back at MJ, not able to keep the color from his cheeks. He cursed his Scandinavian ancestry. "The stairs," he sputtered. "I slipped."

Rory was looking everywhere in the room except at Jefferson and MJ.

For the first time, Jefferson saw humor in MJ's blue eyes. "Don't worry detective. Your secret's safe with me."

***

Jefferson couldn't get to the car fast enough. Rory walked casually behind him.

Then Jefferson stopped. "Great," he said between gritted teeth.

A black Range Rover was parked directly behind them. The back liftgate was open, and they could hear someone rummaging there.

"I'll get this moved," Jefferson said as he strode quickly toward the sound.

Before he got there, the back closed and a smartly dressed woman emerged. She walked forward rolling a suitcase behind her. She looked curiously at the detectives. Her dark hair was pulled back into a low ponytail. Jefferson would guess she was somewhere in her 60s, but her polished look gave her a youthful appearance.

She looked at Jefferson's car and then at her own. "Oh dear, have I blocked you gentlemen in?"

Jefferson forced himself to smile, regaining some of his composure as his frustration mellowed. He looked at the two cars and the driveway. "I think I can get around. No problem."

"You're sure? My daughter will already find me an odious house guest if I've upset her friends."

Jefferson put his hand up in protest. "No, no, ma'am, not a problem. And we are with the West Sound PD. MJ was good enough to give us some of her time today."

"Police?" She looked at them thoughtfully. "I guess that's to be expected." She glanced at the cars again. "If you really think you can make it, I'm going to head down to the house. My drive here from SeaTac took longer than my flight from Las Vegas, and I am ready to hug my daughter and rest my eyes."

Rory stepped forward. "While Detective Hughes here maneuvers the car, let me carry that bag down for you."

"Detective," she smiled. "Are you also a detective," she asked Rory.

"Yes ma'am, Detective Jackson," he said, taking her bag.

"And so polite. Thank you. I am Toni Devey, MJ's mom, as I mentioned." She smiled gently. "You boys have quite a job ahead, I don't envy what you must be going through." She shook her head. "So, I'll stop prattling on. I'm sure you have mountains of work to do." She nodded toward Jefferson. "It was nice meeting you." Then she and Rory headed down to MJ's door.

Jefferson watched her go, walking gingerly in her tailored pantsuit and heels. He couldn't help but wonder how two such different women could be mother and daughter.

Chapter Twelve

As soon as the detectives were out the door, MJ was rummaging one-handed through her bedroom closet for her box of Mariner Middle School yearbooks. The other hand held her side, trying to ward off the throbbing her movement was causing. She'd find that kid if it was the last thing she did.

Edgar began barking like the vicious guard dog he was not. She stopped and listened.

The front door opened, and she heard a woman's voice—correction, her mother's voice. She really came. MJ had only partially believed Shannon this morning. Was it this morning? Time meant nothing, and she'd lost all sense of it.

"Oh, Edgar dear, have you forgotten me already?"

The barking stopped and MJ could hear the clink of Edgar's paws on the wood floor as he clamored for affection. "Oh yes, yes, yes. There's a good boy. Thank you, detective, right there is fine."

MJ smiled to herself as she walked back to the living room. It sure sounded like the detective deserved a dog biscuit.

There was her mother, dressed to the nines as usual.

"Oh hun," she said, turning to look at MJ. "How are you?" She walked toward her with her arms out for a hug.

"I'll get going." The bearded detective was backing toward the door.

MJ's mother released her from a tight hug and thanked the detective again, watching him close the door gently behind him.

Toni looked sideways at MJ. "I didn't expect to be greeted by two handsome detectives."

MJ just shrugged.

"You mean you didn't notice the brooding good looks of mister tall, blonde, and handsome, or the endearing kindness of his ruggedly attractive partner? Serious Viking vibes from that one."

"Oh geez, mom. You know, I really wasn't paying attention to that."

Toni took MJ's face in her hands. "I know, honey. How are you doing?"

"I'm fine." MJ pulled back from her. "I mean, I'm sore, but nothing's broken."

Toni studied her face. "You know what I mean, MJ." She grabbed her hand and steered her around to sit on the couch.

"Look, sweetie."

MJ rolled her eyes. Her mother loved to use terms of endearment meant for children when talking to her.

"Okay, I see you're not in a place to talk. I'm just concerned because I know you and how you like to bottle things up, worry about everyone else, and pretend you're fine."

Toni led the list of top-earning Las Vegas real estate agents. She attributed her success to an innate ability to handle her clients' various emotional and family crises. MJ suspected her mother saw herself as some kind of untrained psychologist.

"I know why you're here, Mom, and yes, I'm sad, but I'm dealing with it." What she didn't say was how the guilt kept her from sleeping.

Troy's smiling face flashed through her mind. A pang of grief surged through her. She blinked it away.

Toni searched her face with the same blue eyes as MJ's. Only hers were framed in perfectly applied eyeliner and falsies under an expertly arched brow. MJ looked closer. She detected a trace of circles under her mother's expensive foundation.

Toni looked away. "Okay, let's leave it for now."

"Forever."

Her mother just smiled at her, and MJ knew that wouldn't be the end of the sofa talk.

"How's dad?"

"Oh, you know him, caught up in the latest school drama. He wanted to come but . . ." She shrugged and gave MJ sidewise glance.

MJ understood all too well. Teachers get to take a lot of holidays and summers off, but getting time off during the school year could be difficult, and next to impossible for an administrator like her dad.

Toni sighed. "Only a year to go, then he's a free man."

MJ's father planned to retire at the end of the next school year. MJ would believe it when she saw it. He became a high school principal in Las Vegas the same year MJ started her first teaching job at Orcas High. He loved his high school and would find it difficult to leave.

"So where shall I set my things?" Toni asked, looking around.

"You can have my room. I'll take the pull-out in my office." MJ stood up and grabbed her mother's suitcase. Toni followed, with Edgar close on her heels.

"I just changed the sheets. You remember where everything is?"

"Yes, I do." She looked at the closet. The door was open, and a box was sitting on the floor with half the contents on the floor. "Unpacking? Packing?"

"Oh, sorry." MJ rushed over, threw the stuff back in the box, and then hauled it out to the living room, doing her best to hide the pain radiating down her side.

"I'm just going to freshen up a bit," her mother called after her. "Or take a nap."

"Take a nap," MJ called back. "I'll make something to eat after you've rested."

The bedroom door closed, and MJ felt guilty for being grateful when her mother chose the nap. But she was itching to get to her yearbooks.

She made herself another cup of tulsi mint tea and sat down at the table with the stack of yearbooks and a stack of sticky notes. She took a deep breath to prepare herself. There would be no way to avoid memories of Troy as she searched these pages. She closed her eyes and let the sadness, anger, and guilt pour over her. This toxic emotional mix gave her a strange sense of urgent energy.

She picked up the first yearbook with its hard navy cover. The police may not want her help, but they were going to get it.

***

When the detectives were leaving MJ's house, Rory insisted on driving. He pointed out that Jefferson had just returned from his dad's funeral and drove all night to get back because an explosion shattered most of the city government he works for.

"Take a nap," Rory demanded as he negotiated Cecil Bay Highway back into the city.

He knew Rory was right, but he doubted his ability to sleep. He turned to stare out the window at the water, so deep and unconcerned with what happened on its shores. "I should go home and change."

"Nah, just turn on the seat warmer."

Jefferson chuckled. Leave it to Rory to lighten the mood.

The closer they got to West Sound, the more the houses that dotted the shoreline crowded each other, with barely a breath between them. The sun continued to beat back the clouds. As they reached the bottom of Stanton Inlet, they passed West Sound Marina, where fishing boats, sailboats, and houseboats rested together in a shimmering nest of waves.

He closed his eyes and willed his mind to be quiet. Then his phone buzzed. He pulled it out and looked at the screen. "It's Wells."

He answered the call and hit the speaker button. "Hey Amber, Rory and I are both here. You're on speaker."

"Great. How'd it go with the teacher?"

Jefferson rubbed his eyes and Rory snickered, but neither of them answered right away.

"Are you still there?"

"It was fine," Rory said, still smiling. "Uh, she said she thinks the beanie boy went to her school—a few years ago, of course. She didn't know his name, but we're going to follow up at the school. She also gave us the names of a couple of retired teachers we could check with."

"That sounds promising. I'll send a couple of officers around to the school, the high school too." They heard another voice talking to her in the background. "No, no, have them keep looking," she said, obviously replying to whomever had approached her. "Hey guys," she said, her voice loud again. "Forsberg is back. Before you head over there, Julia and Ron have put together a list of topics you should ask her about, things they've pulled from the agendas and minutes of at least the past year of council meetings. Julia will send it to your email and text Forsberg's address. Look the info over so you're familiar with it before you talk to her. Then head back here for a briefing at 2 p.m. sharp."

"Will do," said Rory.

"See you then." She hung up abruptly. Jefferson guessed the station was a madhouse.

"Ah, good," said Rory. "Just enough time to grab lunch."

"I am not hungry yet, but I'd take a Red Bull."

"No, no, my friend. I'm going to drive over to Seadog's Burgers, and you will stay in the car and take a nap. Then, maybe, just maybe, you can have some caffeine. And don't even think about opening that file from Julia until I am done eating."

"Yes, mother."

"That's the second time I've been told that today. I guess my nurturing instincts are just too strong to deny."

Chapter Thirteen

She found him. It took a lot of digging and forcing herself to avoid memory bird walks, but it paid off.

Dylan Warren stared at MJ from his eighth-grade picture. Even then he looked ready to flip someone the bird, refusing to smile for the camera. His black hair was short and perfectly matched his black hoodie. He had the skinny face of a boy only vaguely acquainted with puberty. He'd changed, for sure, but she knew it was him.

She looked him up in the school's records system.

Sometimes, even if a student graduated, a sibling might still be in the system. If that was the case for Dylan, the system would list him as a graduated brother with all the family's available information.

Unfortunately, that turned up zero leads. There was nothing for Dylan or any siblings.

It crossed her mind to call the school and ask for the phone numbers of the teachers who taught Dylan. She decided against asking the office staff to do anything extra right now. She wouldn't put stress on an already stressful situation.

Now what? Should she call the detectives?

She held Detective Hughes' card in her hand, mulling it over. He would say she needed to call them. In her opinion, he'd been arrogant. He probably wouldn't listen to her, anyway.

No, she wanted to make sure she had solid information about Dylan Warren before involving anyone else.

On the night of the blast, she'd thought the kid looked like one of the homeless people that live in the right of ways and other forested areas around the city. Maybe she was making a misguided assumption. Or perhaps her gut instinct would serve her well. If she didn't try something, he could slip away with no one ever knowing.

Either way, the best place to start her search was in downtown West Sound. The quirky cafes and thrift shops drew regular crowds of young people who were homeless or living a vagabond lifestyle. It was hard to tell the difference between the thrift clothes diehards and those wearing the Salvation Army donations because they had nothing else.

She put the detective's card in her pocket and put her coat on. Edgar glanced up from his dog bed, hopeful.

"Sorry bud, not right now."

He put his head back down and stared up at her with forlorn, sweet-as-caramel eyes.

That's when she remembered. She didn't have a car.

Her mother was still napping, and the keys to the rental were oh-so available. She snatched them up, grabbed the yearbook, and quietly left the house.

***

MJ navigated downtown with the purpose of avoiding city hall. She feared seeing the burned-out remains of the building. Horrific thoughts of the explosion threatened her sanity. It was a minute-by-minute battle. Just the thought of going near there put a painful rock in her chest.

She had to keep moving, keep her thoughts elsewhere.

Luckily, the place she wanted to go was on the other side of downtown.

As she looked for a place to park, MJ noticed the clouds were blessedly scuttling away. They left behind a sky beaming with a show-off hue of the brightest blue, like a tropical beach overhead. Seeing the sun always gave MJ a burst of energy. She was grateful for the sun and something to do.

She pulled in front of The Tea Spot, a local shop she visited often to replenish her supply of herbal teas. It was one of the many unique boutiques that brought local and out-of-town shoppers downtown. On a different day, when her life was normal, she'd head for the shop's burgundy awning and hanging baskets of cascading bougainvillea. It saddened her to see the flowers were on their last legs. The cold had taken its toll.

Much of downtown had the charm of a city center from another era, with its old theaters, classic dark-wood restaurants, and gift shops full of local arts and crafts. But it wasn't all that way. This side of West Sound had become a hub of tattoo parlors, pot shops, and vegan cafes, places that appealed to the young people who seemed to always be hanging out on the streets.

The Docks, a grungy cafe down the street from The Tea Spot, offered vegan food along with ethically sourced coffee. On previous trips downtown, she'd noticed a consistent group of young people clustered around outside. She was pretty sure most of them were not actually homeless, though they seemed to want to appear that way. They wore random, mismatched clothing. Most had painful-looking piercings and ragged hair, like an outgrowth of the 1990s grunge era but without the accompanying music. MJ didn't get it. To her, they seemed engaged in an anti-establishment rebellion against clean clothes and showers. Perhaps if she were younger, it would make sense.

They sat on the sidewalk and chatted at passersby, hoping for some change in their cups. MJ had seen them insult people who walked by without giving them anything. They were obnoxious, but not dangerous.

That didn't mean they were completely harmless. These kids, along with the growing homeless population, had become a cloud over the economy of the downtown area in the past couple of years. Despite its charm, shoppers appeared unwilling to walk the gauntlet of annoying kids or the sometimes more aggressive homeless. Many of the homeless were unwell, either with mental illness or drug addiction, or both. It was a problem the city seemed unwilling or unable to address. The result was more empty shops, as owners called it quits.

The kids outside The Docks could be intimidating. MJ prepared herself for the potential insults they would throw at her as she approached.

She zipped her jacket. The heat of the sun was being spent in some other part of the world, apparently. It was beautiful outside, but cold. She held the MMS yearbook in her hand as she walked to the corner. There, she waited for the light to change so she could cross. Her eyes fell on a bright yellow sign hanging in the window of an empty shop on the opposite corner. "Beth's Bakery! We've moved!" it boasted. "Come see us on Gull Street and 7th!"

MJ remembered the little bakery. She'd had a scrumptious chocolate muffin there with Claire after hiking the Skyline Trail on Mt. Rainier. Claire belonged to a hiking club. She often convinced MJ to tag along during her summer break. Gull Street and 7th wasn't so far away. It was out of the downtown area, though. She wondered if the group across the street prompted the move. She guessed that was the case.

The light changed. MJ walked across the street. Suspicious eyes were already on her. No turning back now, she thought.

She smiled warmly as she stepped onto the sidewalk. Today there were only three of them hanging out, a smaller group than she remembered. Two guys and a girl—they were sitting on a grubby black bedspread, the puffy kind. This one had little of the puff left in it.

"Hey," said MJ in a friendly tone. "I'm sorry to bother you all, but I was wondering if you could help me out."

The girl stared at her without speaking. She was one of the thinnest people MJ had ever seen. Her twig-like legs were bent so that she could almost rest her chin on them. She wore purple leggings with fishnet stockings over them. The stockings had huge, gaping holes in them. MJ wondered if that was a fashion statement. The girl's eyes were hostile beneath choppy bleach-blond hair that looked like she'd cut it herself. She had piercings on her nose, lips, and up her ears. The nose piercing looked angry. Probably infected, MJ thought.

One guy, sitting to the right of the angry girl, picked up his cup and rattled it. Far from angry, he seemed to sense an opportunity—not smiling, but not scowling, either. He was all begging business. He wore a light blue sweater with large roses embroidered on the front and a beanie that said "GBR" with a scorpion symbol, which meant nothing to MJ.

She reached into her pocket, pulled out a dollar bill, and stuck it in the cup.

He rattled it again with an expectant look, which was intensified by his black eyeliner.

MJ stared at it. "You don't even know what I want yet."

"Doesn't matter." He shook it again.

MJ glanced at the young man sitting on the other side of the girl. He had his head down, intensely studying his fingernails. He wore a sweatshirt and jeans that didn't quite match the scene. She wrinkled her brow curiously, but then turned back to the other two.

"Fine." She reached into her pocket and pulled out a five-dollar bill. She stuffed it in the cup, making eye contact with the guy holding it. "That's all I've got."

He looked at her skeptically.

The girl snorted. "You look rich enough."

MJ shrugged. "Not really. And I also don't carry a bunch of cash around."

"She's a teacher."

All three of them turned to look at the previously silent young man.

"You know her," sneered the girl.

The young man finally looked up. MJ did not recognize him at all. He had a face full of acne scars. Puberty had not been kind to him.

"Yep," he said. "I had you for language arts."

MJ looked at him closely. She still couldn't place him.

"I didn't think you'd recognize me," he said. "I was only there for half a year. My parents made me go live with my grandma in Shelton."

If possible, the girl's face became angrier. "Better than living with those jerks."

He gave a half-hearted shrug.

"Whatever," said the girl. She scowled at MJ. "What do you want?"

MJ opened the yearbook where she'd marked it with a sticky note.

"Do any of you know this kid? His name is Dylan Warren. He looks different now, but not too much."

The angry girl and cup guy looked at each other.

"Sorry, don't know him," said the cup guy. His eyes told another story. He knew something, but wouldn't tell her.

MJ looked at the girl. "You?"

"Nope."

Her former student sat up and looked at the picture. Then he looked at his two companions.

"Don't you dare," threatened the girl.

"Why? She's not going to do anything to him."

"No, definitely not," agreed MJ. "I just need to ask him some questions about a thing I'm working on. No big deal." She tried to sound casual, but her heart was thumping inside. He might just tell her.

He sat up straighter. "I don't know where he is or anything, but I've seen him down at the city services building a few times. There are showers and stuff there, sometimes food." He sat back again. "Someone there might know where he is."

"You little snitch," said the girl with venom.

"Shut up, Max," he said wearily.

Max glared at him, but she stopped talking.

The first guy suddenly stood up, cup in hand. "Let's go get some food."

MJ reached into her pocket and pulled out a ten-dollar bill. She smiled as she shoved it into his cup.

He cracked a smile for the first time.

"This is because of your friend here." She motioned toward her informant. Her face softened as she looked down at him. "You take care of yourself."

He nodded without speaking. He probably thought he was taking care of himself.

"Well, thanks again." She turned and hurried back to her car. The cold had seeped into her bones, into her mood. She wished she could have at least recognized that kid.

Chapter Fourteen

West Sound Services operated out of what used to be a Circle K convenience store. The short, flat-roofed building sat on the edge of downtown. It still had the red stripe around the top of the building. The ghostly outline of the Circle K logo could be seen beneath the utilitarian black and white West Sound Services sign. It wasn't pretty, but it met its purpose.

A couple of picnic tables occupied a grassy area in front. Three men sat at one and an older woman sat by herself at the other. They all glanced her way as she pulled into the parking lot. She fully realized the conspicuousness of her mother's rented Range Rover. She really missed her Bronco.

She parked and got out. The onlookers had already lost interest in her. One guy stared straight ahead. He seemed to look at her, but he wasn't. The other two guys faced away from her, but she could tell they were young as she glanced at their loaded-down backpacks. They were eating something and talking to each other.

MJ was fine with being ignored as she hustled to the door, the yearbook under her arm.

Pushing the door open was like peering inside a beehive. People were everywhere. One side of the room held a group of desks. They all had computers and what she assumed must be social workers or volunteers helping people.

The other side of the room had a line of washing machines and dryers. A young man in a polo and jeans was monitoring and helping people use the machines. A few tables were scattered in the middle. Some people were eating and judging by the two older ladies cleaning up a counter, they must have served lunch.

A short hallway was directly in front of MJ. A sign above said "Showers: DO NOT ENTER UNLESS YOU HAVE A TICKET. FIRST COME, FIRST SERVED."

It was very loud. People seemed to talk at an unusually loud volume. One man, sitting at a table, was shouting in intermittent bursts at no one in particular. MJ thought he seemed quite old, but she couldn't be sure.

As she took it all in, wondering where to go, she felt a hand on her shoulder. She just about jumped out of her skin.

"Oh, I'm sorry dear," said a woman in a short brown and gray bob. "I didn't mean to scare you."

MJ quickly regained her composure. "Oh, I'm fine." She ignored her racing heart. "But I have a question." She held out her hand. "I'm MJ."

The woman took her hand. "Nice to meet you, MJ. I'm Jenny Dunn. I'm the director here. What can I do for you?"

MJ pulled up the yearbook and turned to the page with Dylan's picture.

"I'm looking for this, well, man. He doesn't look like one here, but this is an old picture. Someone told me he might come here sometimes."

The woman barely glanced at the picture. She pasted a civil-servant smile on her face. "I'm so sorry, but I can't give out any information about our clients."

MJ faltered for a minute. She should have expected this. As a teacher, she knew all too well the rules of confidentiality. She tried again anyway.

"I am concerned about him," she said. "I'm a teacher, and he was a student at our school. I have good reason for believing he could be in some serious trouble, maybe even in danger."

Jenny Dunn's smile stayed etched on her face like a loyal guardian. It would not allow her to spill any secrets.

"I'm sorry, the answer is the same. I'm sure you understand."

MJ tried to hide the disappointment. She'd made such excellent progress until now.

Jenny sighed. "If you are really concerned, I would suggest going to the police. If they need to get information, they have the tools to do that."

MJ nodded. Of course, the police. Detective Hughes' face flashed in her mind. Not yet, she thought.

"You're probably right. Thank you anyway."

MJ couldn't accept that this was the end of the road. Someone knew something. She looked around the room, but Jenny Dunn never left her side, obviously expecting MJ to leave.

Frustrating as it was, MJ knew there was nothing more she could do as long as the Dunn woman eagle-eyed her every move. She said thank you again and turned to go. Jenny Dunn looked very pleased.

As she walked back out the door, she set her eyes on the two young guys who were still sitting at the picnic table with their backs to her. They could be about Dylan's age.

She walked up to them and cleared her throat. "Excuse me, I could use your help."

The two men turned at the same time to look at her. They were young, and not as haggard-looking as she'd expected. If they weren't sitting outside West Sound Services, she might expect to see them hiking the Pacific Crest Trail.

They both squinted up at her as the sun shone behind her back. One had a Seahawks baseball cap and brown hair that just brushed his shoulders. The other wore an olive-green beanie and had a long reddish beard.

"Sure," said the bearded one with a crooked grin.

MJ took a deep breath. "I'm looking for this guy—"

"You're looking for a guy? It's our lucky day, Benj," he said, slapping the arm of his friend.

Benj closed his eyes and shook his head. "You're an idiot." He gave MJ a very serious look. "I'm sorry about this idiot. You were saying?"

MJ ignored the idiot, focusing her attention on Benj.

"Thanks." She opened the yearbook and pointed to Dylan's picture. "I'm looking for this guy. His name is Dylan. He's older now, about 20. Do you recognize him? Have you seen him around?"

Benj looked up at her. "Why? You related?"

She hesitated. "No," she said truthfully. "I just think he needs some help. I saw him recently, and I'm worried about him. He was a student at our school."

"School, ew." The bearded guy hacked up a loogie and spat on the ground.

MJ continued to ignore him, keeping her eyes on Benj. "Please, I'm not trying to get him in trouble." She felt dishonest. If he had something to do with the bomb, he would be in a world of trouble.

"Uh oh," said Benj, looking past her.

She turned to see Jenny Dunn marching out of the West Sound Services door.

MJ turned back to Benj. "Please."

"Okay, because you have really pretty blue eyes. Meet me at the McDonalds across the way.

Before he could finish, Jenny Dunn stood between them. Her eyes were on fire as she stood face-to-face with MJ.

"You need to leave. Now. My next step will be to call the authorities."

MJ nodded. "Okay, I'm leaving. I'm sorry to have upset you." She backed away. Before she turned to go, she glanced at Benj. He nodded once.

***

MJ stood in the McDonald's parking lot, leaning against the Range Rover, waiting.

It didn't take long for Benj and his idiot friend to come walking around the corner.

They were talking as they approached. The idiot was making arm movements, gesturing toward her and then back to themselves. They're arguing, MJ thought.

When they reached her, Benj glanced at his friend. He looked slightly embarrassed for some reason.

This worried MJ. Maybe he didn't really know anything. Maybe they lured her here for ... she didn't know what. She was losing patience.

"What's going on?"

"The idiot here," said Benj, "says I need to trade my info for some food. I told him we just ate, but he really wants a McChicken."

MJ gave Benj a skeptical look. "How do I know you really know anything? How do I know you won't just skip out with your McChickens?"

"McChicken," Benj corrected. "I don't want one."

She pushed away from the car. "Fine. I get the food; you tell me what you know. But I'm holding the bag until you speak."

"Deal," interjected the bearded guy.

MJ ignored him and just looked at Benj.

"Deal," he said.

She walked toward the restaurant. The two guys stayed put.

"You two coming?"

Benj and the idiot looked at each other.

"They don't like us coming in." Benj pointed his elbow at his buddy. "Cole here may have gone in for a few too many refills," he said with air quotes.

So Cole was the idiot.

"Well, anything else while I'm in there?"

"Fries," piped up Cole.

"Maybe an ice cream cone?" said Benj hopefully.

"Got it." She left them behind to go order the food.

***

When she came back out, Cole tried to grab the food bag. She whisked it away.

"Tsk, tsk, tsk. Remember our deal." She had the ice cream cone in her other hand. She really wanted to hand it off. The liquid was already dripping.

"But the ice cream is going to melt," pointed out Benj.

MJ held it up and looked at it. "Yep, so you better talk fast."

Benj nodded. "Okay, okay. You are demanding." He smiled like a teenager. MJ wondered why these two were living such a nomadic life. They seemed educated and didn't appear to be on drugs. She didn't get it at all. Well, for Benj she didn't get it. Cole seemed to have some antisocial behavior. There must be something keeping Benj on the streets.

"So, here's what I know. The guy, Dylan, I've seen him around at a lot of different camps. He was at the parking lot the city set up a while ago, but then they closed it. Most people headed further north, but Dylan stayed around."

"Stayed around where?"

"The last place I saw him was at the camp by the freeway, Cherry St. I don't think he's gone anywhere else."

"You're sure?"

"No. But that's the best I can do."

MJ looked up at the sky. A clump of clouds at that moment cut in front of the sun. She shivered.

She handed the bag of food to Cole and the cone to Benj. "Thanks for your help."

"I hope you find him," Benj said as he took a lick of ice cream.

"Me too."

Cole was too deep in his McChicken and fries to make any comment.

She prayed Benj's information was good. She felt the detective's card in her pocket. Now was the time to call.

Chapter Fifteen

Despite his misgivings, Jefferson drifted off to sleep while Rory sat in the restaurant enjoying a Bulldog Burger, his favorite at Seadogs. The restaurant was little more than a shack near the marina. It'd been there since the dawn of time; its weathered siding had been every color of the rainbow at one point or another. Now it was a shocking lime green with royal blue awnings. They had the best hand-cut French fries, served in a "world-famous" fry boat with an unbeatable secret fry sauce.

When returning to the car, Rory carried an order of fries for Jefferson. Awake and refreshed, Jefferson surprised himself by eating through them at a hungry pace as they read over Julia's report.

"This is interesting," said Rory, scrolling on his phone as he sipped the remnants of his chocolate shake. "You know, I remember when this happened. It didn't seem like a big deal at the time, but now, after the kid in the video . . ." His voice trailed off.

Jefferson cocked his head at him. "What are we talking about?"

"Look on the page for the June tenth minutes. Julia made some notes about the public speakers seen on video from that meeting. You remember it was a big hullabaloo. At the previous meeting, the city passed the no-public camping ordinance. So, at this meeting, the council heard about it in the form of an angry crowd."

Jefferson nodded. "I remember. People started fighting in the audience."

"Yeah, the ordinance essentially meant the city could kick all the homeless out of all the public property, right of ways, parks, etc." Rory shrugged. "Doesn't seem unreasonable, but the homeless advocates were screaming mad."

"Some at the station weren't too happy either."

Rory nodded. "Nothing like extra work for the police department with no new funds. Those clean-ups are expensive and quite nasty. I heard some stories . . ."

Jefferson put his hand up. "No, thank you. I'm not interested in hearing those."

Rory chuckled. "Your loss."

Jefferson continued reading. "One woman made a public threat at that meeting."

Jefferson realized he recognized the name in the report. He looked up at Rory, who seemed to realize it simultaneously.

"Aspen Klein," Rory said, knowingly.

Aspen Klein owned and operated the "Room at the Inn" homeless shelter. Despite its name, there was no religious affiliation. In fact, Aspen had probably picked that name to offend West Sound's religious community. Aspen professed to be not only an atheist but an activist atheist who made it a point to stick her finger in the eye of religion. The detectives knew of Aspen's political ideas because their cases sometimes took them to the shelter searching for suspects or witnesses. She never seemed to appreciate their presence.

"Let's see . . . She said that the council members would soon see people dying in the streets without shelter, and maybe they should join them because that would be 'the only justice.'" Jefferson put his phone down. "I don't remember anyone following that up?"

Rory shook his head. "Nah, she says a load of inflammatory stuff; we'd have to hound her all day, every day." He looked out the window. "It seems more sinister now, though."

"Would that be enough for someone to commit mass murder?"

Rory considered the question. "Aspen has always struck me as a bit unhinged, you know, super passionate about her cause, to the point of being caustic, especially to cops, but," he paused, "I just don't know. I don't see her doing something like this. Could she even afford it? Someone paid a lot of money for that C4."

Jefferson wiped his hands on a napkin. "She could have inflamed some other nutcase with more funds."

"True."

"Alright, let's head over to Forsberg's house. Maybe she can shed some light on the situation."

Chapter Sixteen

Lisa Forsberg stared at her computer screen. With shaking hands, she moved the mouse and dragged the email to the trash. She'd almost missed it in her hurry to remove them all. That was the last one; it had to be. But what if it wasn't?

She put her head in her hands and raked her fingers through her short, graying hair, resting her chin on her hands. Her red-rimmed eyes darted without focus, which most people would attribute to the expected grief and stress of the situation. Two of her city colleagues were gone. She represented the only uninjured and functioning city official.

In reality, she was in a panic. Her heart hadn't been at a normal pace since the explosion.

She should never have started this. And now she didn't have the knowledge to get herself out of it. She hated technology, but she'd give anything now to wipe her computer clean. She knew enough to know that she didn't know enough. They would find her emails eventually.

She heard her husband Ray's voice coming toward her home office. "Yes, she's been a wreck from the moment I picked her up at the airport. Really, we're both in shock. Hasn't really sunk in yet." He stopped in her doorway. "Here she is, gentlemen."

Lisa smiled weakly. She went to stand up, but the taller of the two men put his hand out.

"Please, don't get up."

She smiled gratefully. She gave her husband a brief nod.

"Well, I will leave you to it," he said. "Can I get anyone a drink? Water, coffee, Mountain Dew?"

"I'll take one of those," said Jefferson.

Rory shook his head. "No, thank you."

"One Mountain Dew coming up."

Ray left. The two detectives sat in stiff navy armchairs across the desk from Lisa. She had quite the home office, full of serious dark wood and bookcases. The house itself was one of the stately old homes in West Sound's hilltop neighborhood.

Jefferson knew the councilwoman by sight, but he'd never said more than a few words to her at city functions. She wore her salt and pepper hair in a chin-length bob and wore no makeup. That was normal for her, though today she had some color. Red cheeks and a peeling nose revealed she'd vacationed somewhere far from the typically gray October of the Pacific Northwest.

"I'm Detective Hughes and this is Detective Jackson."

She nodded. "I have seen you both from time to time for city functions." Her voice wavered. She cleared her throat.

Rory tipped his head at her. "First, we are sorry for the losses you have suffered. The entire city is mourning right now."

She nodded and wiped at the corner of her eye.

Jefferson continued. "Thank you for agreeing to answer a few questions. I'm sure now that you are back in town there will be many demands on your time." He smiled as he pulled out his pen. "So, we will try to not keep you too long."

Ray entered the office again and plopped a frosty cold Mountain Dew next to Jefferson with a tall glass of ice.

"Thank you." He glanced up at Ray, who smiled warmly. His face had a kindness to it that reminded Jefferson of his father. The pain punched him in the gut so unexpectantly, he quickly took an intense interest in opening his soda, giving himself time to control the tremor in his hands.

Ray left the room and quietly closed the door behind him.

Jefferson poured his soda over the ice until he was sure his voice wouldn't betray him.

"So, what took you out of town, Councilwoman Forsberg?" he asked casually, taking a big sip.

She looked out the window and smiled wistfully. "My sister's birthday. Every year we pick a fun location to meet for our birthdays. She lives in Albuquerque, so I don't see her much. This year, we went to Cabo. And I got a little too much sun, as you can see." She motioned toward her face.

Jefferson nodded. "So, you have had this trip booked for a while? Can you tell me when you bought your tickets?'

Confusion flashed across her face. "Why would you need to know that?"

"It's a common procedure-type question," answered Rory. "It helps us confirm your whereabouts."

She considered this. "So, I need an alibi?"

It surprised Jefferson how quickly she became defensive. This interview might be of more interest than he'd imagined.

Rory shrugged. "You could call it that, but at this point, we're just ruling people out so we can focus our efforts."

"I see." She sat back in her chair and looked at the ceiling with a sigh. "I bought my plane ticket about a month ago. My sister made all our other arrangements—hotel, rentals, and restaurants. I can give you her phone number so you can check it with her. She is still in Mexico. I left a little early."

"That would be helpful, thank you."

She wrote a number on a sticky note and handed it to Rory. She sat back with her hands clasped on the desk in front of her.

Jefferson's smile was gentle, but he held a steady gaze on her. "I apologize ahead of time. These next questions may feel somewhat insensitive."

She furrowed her brow but nodded warily. "Go ahead, detective."

"The attack on city hall has left you as the only acting elected official for West Sound, with two deaths and the rest injured, including the mayor. That leaves you with a tremendous amount of control, doesn't it?"

She stared at him; her face expressionless until even more color began to creep into her sunburned cheeks. "I can't believe," she sputtered, "you would even suggest I . . ."

She stood from her chair and laid her hands on the desktop, looking down and breathing deeply. She was a petite woman, and the massive desk made her appear even smaller. For a moment, it seemed she might kick them out.

Jefferson wondered at this dramatic reaction. Was this genuine anger? He studied her posture and listened to her breathing as she stared down at her desktop. Her fingers curled into fists. Something had agitated her, and he didn't think it was just indignation. "Would you like us to get Ray?"

She looked up, eyes blazing, "No!"

They locked eyes for a moment, her angry glare meeting Jefferson's cool, dispassionate face. He needed to tread lightly here. She could cut the interview short. Still, the questions needed to be asked.

"How is your relationship with the rest of the council? Or the mayor?" As soon as he spoke the words, Jefferson noticed a definite tensing of her jawline. She glanced toward the doorway, perhaps looking for Ray or showing a subconscious desire to leave.

Slowly, she turned back to face him briefly before looking down at her hands on the desk again. "We get along just fine. We don't always agree, but the suggestion that I had something to do with this . . ." She shook her gray head violently.

She said the right words, but Jefferson sensed her lack of eye contact meant she wasn't being completely honest.

"Is there anything else we need to know regarding your interactions with your city colleagues?"

She threw her head back, the anger flashing again. "No, detective. I've already told you that."

"Council member Forsberg," Jefferson said calmly, "we are not accusing you of anything, but I hope you of all people would understand that we need to ask uncomfortable questions of everyone who is in any way associated with the city council, that meeting in particular."

She slowly lowered back into her chair. "I will have you know," she said angrily, "as far as control, the county commissioners will select interim city council members for the two we lost. I've had a phone call from our city attorney, as well as Governor Harrison. They've informed me of the procedure according to Washington State code, especially should our mayor or any other council members succumb to their injuries." Her words trailed off as she seemed to lose steam. "It's not something I ever thought I would need to know, but there you have it."

Jefferson vaguely knew the three Rainier County commissioners. He tried to stay out of politics and away from politicians, but he couldn't completely ignore it. Politicians decide budgets and make laws that affect the ability of police to do their job.

Rory cocked his head to the side. "Any idea who they might consider?"

She stared back at him. "Some of the commissioners' pets, I'm sure."

"Pets?" repeated Jefferson.

She scowled. "You know what I mean, detective. Our city council has been a thorn in the side of the commissioners' developer friends for a decade or more. If they had their way, West Sound would look like Peak View Point."

"Peak View Point? Isn't that area thriving?" asked Rory. Peak View Point was a bustling city on one of the inlets to the east of West Sound. Population growth boomed when their city council decided to welcome more commercial development in the area.

She sat up. "They've ruined their shoreline, and we all pay the price." She glared at Rory.

He simply nodded. Jefferson could tell he was holding back a grin. Rory loved to poke a nest. He probably agreed with her feelings on the subject as a naturalist in his own way. Rory spent his days off in search of the perfect hiking, fishing, or other outdoor adventure. His wife and kids were all just as enthusiastic about the outdoors as Rory. With Forsberg, he used her love for the environment as a tool to get her to say more than she might otherwise.

"It wouldn't surprise me to see Jon Atherton back in the picture. He's got friends on the county commission," Forsberg added.

"Atherton? He lost a race for council a few years ago. He's the Atherton in Atherton Development if I remember right?" Jefferson asked as he made notes.

"Yes, the idiot who wants to ruin our shoreline by stacking condominiums all the way up Stanton Inlet," she said with an angry flourish of her arm. "His plans are criminal if you ask me."

Jefferson and Rory glanced at each other.

"It's a figure of speech," she said testily. "Trying to destroy the Sound just to line your own pockets. That's criminal in my book, even if what people like Atherton do is technically legal. We have been able to hold them off. I don't know what will happen now." She sat back again and studied them. "If I were you, I might spend some time looking into that man. If anyone hated the majority of the West Sound Council, it was Jon Atherton. He'd gain mightily from a less environmentally concerned council."

Jefferson wondered if the man was as bad as she made him out to be. If so, did he have it in him to kill innocent people just to develop land? He couldn't imagine that kind of greed. He worked on many cases in which people shocked him with their unhinged violence, but this was beyond even those.

"That's helpful information," said Rory. "We do have a couple of questions concerning a different topic. Are you familiar with Aspen Klein?"

"Of course. Aspen and I have worked closely together on several initiatives for the unhoused people in our area. She works hard for our community."

"In a recent meeting, she made some threats to the council. Do you recall that?" Rory pressed.

She waved her hand in the air dismissively. "She was showing her understandable anger at the council's move to clear the homeless encampments. They essentially called it public camping. Then the majority of the council voted to make public camping illegal. Silva, Mayor Sully, and I were the only ones to vote against it. Aspen knows those people have nowhere to go, and all their belongings will be scattered. She can only house so many of them; so, she was angry." She shrugged. "As I said, I voted against the measure, but the business lobby won out."

"Was Aspen angry enough to want revenge?" Jefferson watched her carefully. She was eager to throw a developer under the bus, yet she seemed equally eager to absolve Aspen Klein.

She smiled. "Detectives, go see Aspen. She has a heart much bigger than her temper. Hurting people is not her thing."

Her words appeared genuine. Still, Jefferson felt there had to be some connection between Aspen and the apparently homeless bag deliverer. He pulled out his phone and swiped to get to the picture.

"Do you recognize this man?"

She put her glasses on and took his phone. After a few seconds, she shook her head. "Can't say that I do."

"This man delivered a duffle bag to Council Member Silva. We believe this bag held the explosives that killed and injured your colleagues and citizens at the meeting."

Her eyes widened and she sat back. Tears sprang to her eyes. She grabbed a tissue from a box behind her. "I'm sorry." She dabbed at the corners of her eyes.

"Please, don't apologize," said Rory. "This is a tough time for everyone."

She nodded. "I'm sure this is hard for you as well. Who would expect such a thing to happen in our beautiful community."

Jefferson did not want an emotional birdwalk. He'd had other cases where interviewees used their "feelings" to sidetrack the detectives' questions. He plowed ahead.

"You said earlier that Aspen was angry about the homeless camps being cleaned up—"

"You mean raided," she interjected.

Jefferson continued, ignoring the correction, "Can you think of anyone else who might have made threats against the council, regarding this resolution or anything else?

There it was again, that flex in her jaw. What is she hiding?

She rubbed her eyes with her fingertips. "Am I to understand that you think a homeless man blew up city hall?" She asked, avoiding Jefferson's question.

Despite her wet eyes, she looked at them incredulously. "We are talking about people who may not even own a toothbrush, but somehow this guy can purchase explosives?" She sat back, shaking her head. "I don't buy it."

"What theory would you buy?" asked Rory.

She looked between them intently, "I've said who you should check out. I don't put anything past Atherton and his cronies."

Jefferson realized they weren't going to get much more out of her than this one line of attack. But it was clear that she was holding something back. They'd have to do more digging on Lisa Forsberg.

"Thank you, Councilwoman. We appreciate your time. We have a briefing to get to." He stood and reached out with a card. "If you think of anything we should know, please call."

"Of course. And if you need anything, don't hesitate to reach out."

Jefferson wasn't sure she meant that.

Chapter Seventeen

"Well, that was interesting," said Rory, as he drove them back to the station.

"Politicians always are."

"You have to be dead inside to be good at it."

Jefferson's face tightened. "That is true."

"Sorry man." He hit the steering wheel. "I am such an idiot sometimes. Well, most of the time."

Jefferson shook his head. "Don't worry. It's water under the bridge. And you aren't wrong."

Even though it was almost fifteen years ago, Jefferson still blamed politics, and a few politicians, for ruining his father's health.

His dad, Clinton Hughes, was an idealist who thought he could fix everyone. That's why he became a family doctor and served on a local government board in Jefferson's hometown of Redding, advocating for affordable health care. A few powerful people convinced him to run for a county seat. Then the press ripped him to shreds.

The opponent's campaign dredged up a former patient who made unsubstantiated claims of medical negligence. His father was not prepared for the nasty waters of politics. It literally made him sick. All those powerful supporters suddenly disappeared.

The allegations proved false, but the damage was done. He lost the race, resigned from the board position, and quietly went about his work until he retired ten years later. He must not have been dead enough on the inside. And now he was just dead.

Jefferson's phone buzzed. He was grateful for the interruption of his thoughts.

"Hughes here."

"Detective Hughes. I'm so glad I got you. It's MJ Brooks."

Jefferson looked over at Rory. "Hello, Ms. Brooks. What can I do for you?"

Rory raised an eyebrow at him. Jefferson ignored him and looked out the window. A group of seagulls floated on the breeze over the beach. Three dived toward the sand, picking at something there before flying back into the air.

"First, call me MJ. And second, I know who that kid is, the one in the picture. I looked through my yearbooks until I found him. When I did, I looked him up in Skyward to find his parents' number. That wasn't any help. They must've moved or something. So, I called a few friends who teach at the high school to see if they had any info on him. Sandy Thomlinson said he was a part of her robotics club, and she'd tried to keep in touch. Last she heard, he was definitely living on the streets in —"

"Ms. Brooks."

"Sorry, yes?"

"Do you have a name for him?" Jefferson fumbled with the phone and his notebook. "Wait, are you okay with me putting you on speaker? Detective Jackson is here with me."

"Oh, sure."

Jefferson switched it over.

"Hi, Detective Jackson. My mother thinks you're the sweetest for helping her with her luggage."

"Oh, it was no problem at all," said Rory, winking at Jefferson.

Unamused, Jefferson asked, "The kid's name, please."

"His name is Dylan Warren. He graduated four years ago."

"Dylan Warren," he repeated as he wrote. "Thank you for finding that information. We will follow up with it right away."

"No, you don't understand. I'm here, right now at the last place he was spotted. It's a homeless camp by the Cherry Street exit? Do you know it?"

Jefferson sat speechless. Rory shook his head with a crooked smile creeping up his face.

"Are you there?"

"Yes," Jefferson responded, trying to keep his voice calm. He rubbed his forehead. "Ms. Brooks, interfering in an investigation can be very serious. I suggest you go back home, and we will follow up on the information you provided."

"It's MJ, and I'm not interfering. I'm helping." He could hear the cars flying by her in the background.

"I understand you want to help, and you have, but now you need to leave it to us."

"Look, I only called you because I don't want to scare him off and lose track of him. You will probably want to arrest him or question him or something. So, you can come down here and go into this camp with me, or I'll just do it myself."

Jefferson gritted his teeth. "Just a minute." He muted the phone. All the exhaustion, anger, sadness, or whatever he'd been burying was bubbling to the surface. It was all he could do to keep from screaming at this woman over the phone. "Drive to the station," he told Rory, his voice low with forced steadiness. "You go to the briefing, and I will go deal with Ms. Brooks. And get the team digging up everything they can about Forsberg. Something about her doesn't add up."

Rory nodded, "Roger that. But . . ."

"But what?"

"Don't forget. It's MJ."

He glared at Rory as he unmuted the phone. "Ms. Brooks?"

"I'm here."

"We've got to run by the station, and then I will meet you there, in about fifteen minutes. Don't make a move."

"See you then." She hung up.

Chapter Eighteen

On the way to drop Rory at the station, Jefferson requested a patrol car to meet him at the homeless camp. They should park a couple of blocks away, he said, and wait for a signal that he needed them. If Dylan Warren was in that camp, this could be their big break. He just had to keep MJ Brooks from ruining it.

As Jefferson approached Cherry Street, he saw the black Range Rover from earlier parked on the side of the road. The all too confident Ms. Brooks leaned against the passenger door.

He parked and walked up to meet her. The sun had banished the day's clouds, but she looked like a trained Northwesterner, not fooled by a blue sky in the fall. She was ready for a soggy hike with jeans tucked into hiking boots, her sapphire Columbia raincoat zipped up to her chin. A navy beanie covered her head, and her long, dark curls framed her face.

She watched him with defiant eyes, but her arms folded protectively across her chest told him a different story. She didn't enjoy being here. Her threat to go in on her own had been just that, an overly confident bluff.

Jefferson lamented rushing out here, especially since he was not as outwardly prepared to go trudging through the woods as Ms. Brooks.

He needed to change his shoes. There was no way he could do that now. His shoes were destined for ruin.

"Glad you came," she said. "Ready?"

Jefferson looked toward the patch of suburban forest. Blue tarps and tents choked the trees throughout. Trash lined the road in front as if the camp had a garbage leak. Several shopping carts sat empty and abandoned among the sprawling ferns and other foliage. He dreaded seeing the state of the people in that camp. The filth, the soulless faces of drug addicts who selfishly let their families worry and wonder if they were even alive. He hated it and what it had done to his parents. Shoving the hate down, he looked at MJ with an impassive face.

"I am ready," he said, "and I have a couple of patrol cars on the way. You can go. I cannot risk taking you into that area. It would be unprofessional and break police procedure."

She pushed herself away from the car. "Detective, you need me to soften your look."

"Excuse me?"

"If you go waltzing in there by yourself, dressed like that, those people will scatter like leaves in the wind. I can throw them off a little. You know," she said, lifting a shoulder, "make them wonder." She looked past him to his car. "In fact, do you at least have a parka or some tennis shoes you can put on?"

"Doesn't matter, and this is coming from the person who parked a Range Rover in front of a homeless camp."

She turned and looked at the car. "Yeah, I couldn't avoid that. It's my mom's rental, but she's napping, so what she doesn't know... you know how it goes. Besides, they still have my Bronco tied up behind crime scene tape."

It surprised Jefferson to hear she has a Bronco.

"What makes you so sure the kid is in there?"

"I'm not one hundred percent sure."

"How did you get the information, then?"

"It was easy. I took my yearbook downtown and stopped to talk to the first group of kids I saw hanging out there. One guy recognized Dylan and sent me to the West Sound Services building. I talked to a couple of guys there, and someone finally gave me a location," she smiled and then added, "In return for a McChicken."

Jefferson looked toward the camp again. "You still can't come."

If she heard him, she pretended not to. She was looking over his shoulder. "Looks like your cavalry has arrived."

He turned and saw two patrol cars as they parked a couple of blocks down. When he turned back around, he was watching MJ's back as she headed toward the woods.

***

MJ didn't know if the detective would follow her. She was flying by the seat of her pants, hoping she didn't end up in jail.

"Ms. Brooks," he called after her.

She turned around, put her finger to her lips, and motioned for him to follow. Then she kept walking, holding her breath. She really did not want to go into this camp on her own. She would, if she had to, but she wasn't a fool and knew it could be dangerous.

Then there were footsteps behind her. MJ breathed out and closed her eyes in gratitude. He may not like her—he may even arrest her—but he was coming.

Without looking back, she slowed a bit to let him catch up. He was behind her with unexpected suddenness, surprising MJ by grabbing her arm so that she faced him. She winced involuntarily.

A brief flicker of concern wrinkled his brow. "I'm sorry," he said stiffly. "But you really cannot be here."

She looked him directly in the eyes, anger flaring in her own. She intended on really letting him have it. Then she noticed that even though his words came out rough and his face looked hard, his eyes were soft and sad, the chameleon blue that never holds a constant shade. She looked away.

"I have to." She pulled her arm away and started walking again.

She reached the trees, the detective begrudgingly trailing behind her. She ducked underneath a low group of evergreen branches and headed toward the first tent in her path. As she approached, a man suddenly popped out of nowhere and rushed toward her.

She stopped in her tracks. He stopped too, looking at her curiously from a grimy face with a thousand wrinkles. Before she could make a move or say a word, the detective was in front of her, putting himself between them.

The man scanned Jefferson's clothes.

"Cops," he sneered.

MJ pushed past Jefferson. "No, no. I am not a cop."

"Do you got sandwiches then? I thought you might be the lady from the church. They bring food sometimes." He licked his thin lips.

"No, I'm sorry," she said. "I'm a teacher, and I'm looking for a student of mine. I . . . I mean we," she said, motioning toward Jefferson, "have something important to talk to him about."

He shook his head. "Nope, not interested."

"Not interested . . . ?" MJ repeated, but the man just continued shaking his head as he retreated to his tent.

She looked at Jefferson. He raised his eyebrows. "I'm not sure what you expected."

She continued walking. They had attracted attention. Several faces peered out, watching them suspiciously from makeshift living quarters. Suddenly, an unwholesome smell hit MJ. She resisted the urge to cover her mouth and nose, quite certain the stench related to the lack of bathrooms. It completely overwhelmed the normal commingled pine-and-dirt scent of the northwest forest. Doubt started creeping into her mind. Maybe this was a bad idea. A terrible idea.

As MJ picked her way over tree branches and rubbish, she looked back to see the detective continuing to follow her. He had a look of disgust on his face that she hadn't expected. She didn't want to be there either, but she thought he might be at least somewhat used to it. Didn't cops come in the homeless camps? Maybe cops do but detectives don't?

After moving a little further into the camp, MJ noticed an older woman sitting in a white plastic lawn chair. A blue tarp tied between them connected four trees. The woman sat underneath with a gray, dome-shaped tent behind her. She had a flowery quilt draped around her shoulders. A knit hat the color of a Granny Smith apple covered her gray hair. She was reading a book, completely ignoring the intruders.

MJ walked over to her and took a chance.

"What are you reading?"

The woman looked up at her with stern eyes.

"I'm sorry," said MJ. "I know how much serious readers hate being interrupted. It must be good, though. You seem engrossed."

"I was." She looked past her to the detective. With an annoyed shake of her head, she put the book back up to read. "You can tell my daughter to quit sending social workers out here to check on me."

"We're not social workers," MJ said. "Nothing like that. We're trying to find someone." She looked back at the detective. "Can you show her the picture?"

His face had the same look as the woman whose reading they'd interrupted, but he took out his phone and pulled up the picture.

The woman ignored it, continuing to appear very interested in her novel.

"Let's keep moving," said the detective.

MJ heard new tension in his voice. She looked up and saw a group of men had congregated on the side. They were whispering and glaring in their direction. She knew the detective would drag her out of there if they didn't get something soon. She turned back to her reader.

"*The Mayor of Casterbridge*. Few people read Hardy these days. Pretty dense stuff."

The woman looked over the top of her book. "You're a fan?"

"Yes, but *Far from the Madding Crowd* is my favorite. Gabriel Oak's dedication to Bathsheba is breathtaking."

"What's a young woman like you doing reading Thomas Hardy's books?"

"English teacher," she said. "And an avid reader, like you."

"Hmmm," said the woman, considering her. Then she leaned forward and put a long finger to her lips. "Shhh. Librarian." She pointed to herself. "Once upon a time."

"Oh, I bet you were a great one." MJ smiled at her. She suddenly felt overwhelmed with sadness.

"Ah no," she swiped away the memory. "I love the books, but not the people."

"Hey, cops!" yelled a skinny man from the group. "I got something for you."

MJ made the mistake of looking as he pulled down his pants and stuck his skinny white butt in the air. She looked away, but way too late.

"Alright, that's enough," said Jefferson, grabbing her arm again. "We're out."

The woman suddenly stood up. "Hey Glen," she shouted. "You guys pipe down. They're just teachers and they're here to see me. Put your hackles down and keep your dang pants up."

The men were laughing, but the woman seemed to have some authority over them. They started drifting apart, still glancing their way, but with less intense loathing.

"Whatever, Maggie," said Glen the mooner. He flipped her off. She returned the sign as he ducked inside his waterlogged tent.

"Thanks," said MJ. "So, you're Maggie?"

She threw her hands up. "Well, I guess that cat's out of the bag."

"My name is MJ, and this is," she stopped, realizing she didn't know the detective's first name.

"Jefferson," he said in a wooden tone.

"That's an interesting name," said Maggie as she slowly lowered herself back in her chair, tightly gripping the handles to support herself.

It was an interesting name, MJ agreed. She chanced a glance at him. His face, still tight with angry wariness, had thawed just enough to show his interest in what happened next.

He shifted uncomfortably when MJ's eyes were on him, moving his gaze to scan the woods. MJ smiled inside. He was letting her take the lead right now, but he didn't like it. She found his discomfort amusing.

She turned back to Maggie, who was adjusting her blanket around her shoulders.

"Alright," the older woman said with a sigh, "show me your picture. I won't promise anything."

Jefferson took a step forward and held out the phone. Maggie glanced at it and then up at MJ.

"He was here."

"Was?" asked Jefferson.

"Yeah, was. He left."

MJ let out a frustrated sigh. "Well, how long ago? Do you know where he went?"

Maggie glared up at her, clearly tired of their company. "Why would I know that?"

Jefferson started walking away. "Come on, Ms. Brooks, we have our answer."

MJ wasn't ready to go, though she could see Maggie was done with them. "Can you think of anything that might help us find him, anything at all?"

Maggie put her book back up.

MJ stood rooted to the spot, unwilling to accept that there wasn't more Maggie could tell them.

"Time to go," said Jefferson.

She sighed in disappointment and turned to follow him.

"His girl is still here."

They stopped.

"Maroon tent, just up the way. Name's Rachel," came from behind the book.

Chapter Nineteen

They passed trash pile after trash pile on their way to the maroon tent. MJ couldn't help but think of the phrase "One man's trash is another man's treasure." There was no treasure here, just random clothes strewn among paper and plastic debris that used to be something useful. She even saw a microwave missing a door sitting on the back of a baby blue toilet. It all had the eerily familiar feeling of going camping but with an apocalyptic twist.

A few wary faces peered out at them from the surrounding tents. The smell of marijuana hung in the air like a pungent fog. MJ placed the back of her hand over her nostrils, but breathing through her mouth wasn't any better. She knew the drug was now legal, but she didn't understand the allure. The smell reminded her of a cross between a skunk and body odor. Still, it wasn't just popular among the homeless crowd.

It didn't take long to see the tent. They approached quietly. MJ led the way, with Jefferson walking cautiously behind her. His head moved on a constant pivot, an alertness she secretly appreciated.

The tent's zipper was closed. MJ put her hands on her hips to assess the situation. How do you knock on a tent? Her phone buzzed in her pocket. She knew it was her mother. She'd been ignoring her calls since she first parked outside the camp.

She glanced over at Jefferson. He had a look of pure disgust on his face. He was eyeing a small table holding a syringe, a crusty spoon, a lighter, and a brown apple core. It was a strange combination of a healthy food choice and drug paraphernalia. Didn't he see that kind of thing all the time? For someone who kept a constantly impassive expression, his visceral reaction to a homeless person using drugs confused her. She'd fully expected to see more people wandering around the encampment in a drug-induced haze.

Jefferson pulled out his phone and started texting. She knew he was calling in the calvary parked down the road. Her chance to talk to the girlfriend would evaporate as soon as those dark blues entered the camp.

She moved toward the tent.

Jefferson's hand shot up like a stop sign. In a firm whisper, he said, "Don't."

This time, his steely eyes stopped her.

"If she is on something, this situation is too unpredictable. Stay clear." He pointed to a spot off to the side where she would be out of the way.

Suddenly, the zipper opened. A girl with stringy blond hair peered out. She looked at MJ curiously with half-open eyes. Her mouth curved into a goofy smile. She was clearly out of her mind.

"Hey, don't I know you?" she slurred.

"Um, I don't know. Are you Rachel?"

She didn't answer as she struggled to pull the rest of her body out of the tent while watching MJ. When she finally had both feet on the ground, her eyes landed on Jefferson, a smile still floating on her youthful face. She tilted her head as if thinking. The fog in her brain seemed to lift briefly. Her eyes became wide and fearful. Then, without a word, she bolted in the opposite direction.

Jefferson darted after her, his overcoat flying behind him like Batman. MJ knew his long legs would make easy work of catching the small girl. Sure enough, within a few steps, he had her by the back of her shirt.

"Let go of me, you pig," she shouted while trying to twist away from his grip.

Just then, four uniformed officers walked up the path. As soon as they saw Jefferson, they rushed over to assist.

Rachel ended up facedown on the ground with one officer putting a zip tie around her wrists. He patted her down before reaching into the pocket of her sweats and pulling out a plastic bag.

The officer held it up for Jefferson to see. "Heroin, I'd guess."

Jefferson nodded. "Bring her back over here."

MJ cringed. It felt like they'd ambushed the girl. How much information would she be willing to share with them after this episode?

The officer walked Rachel back toward the tent. The northwest carpet of dirt and dead pine needles covered the front of her. Her head hung low as she'd lost the spurt of energy that propelled her attempted escape. She struggled to hold herself up, so the officer sat her next to a log.

"Let's give her a minute to get her breath back, then take her in. I'll talk to her at the station when she's sobered up." Jefferson wiped dirt from his suit front.

With some effort, the girl rolled her head up. "What'd I do?" she asked, dragging her words out through a carefree grin.

No one answered her. She turned her gaze to MJ again.

MJ smiled. "I'm sorry. I didn't mean for it to turn out this way. Do you need me to grab anything for you?"

The girl shook her head, but it was more like a head wobble. Her glassy eyes stayed on MJ's face.

"Ms. Brooks?"

Shock grabbed MJ's heart. She bent down and examined the girl's face. Something about her hooked a memory. MJ closed her eyes and imagined this face in her classroom. With some effort, she found her. Rachel Downing, front row, a stripe of blue hair. She liked to draw anime cats.

"I had you for history," the girl was saying.

MJ opened her eyes. As she saw the girl's face, still so young but so destitute of her eighth-grade innocence, her eyes stung.

"I remember," she said, smiling warmly. "You had blue hair. You did NaNoWriMo too, right?"

She nodded sluggishly. "I wrote the stupidest stuff."

"I remember it was quite creative."

Despite sitting on the ground in handcuffs and under the influence of illicit drugs, the girl smiled proudly. This pierced MJ's heart even more. How did life go so wrong for Rachel?

MJ glanced up at Jefferson. His face held a strange inquisitive impatience, as if her conversation with Rachel pained him but also interested him. That look didn't last.

"Alright," Jefferson interrupted. "It's been long enough. Let's go."

MJ stood up. "Do we have to take her in? Couldn't we talk to her here?"

"*We* aren't doing anything. I appreciate your help up to this point, sort of, but we are taking her down to the station for questioning and booking for drug possession. I suggest you go home and get some rest. I believe those were your doctor's orders."

MJ glared at him.

He nodded toward the officer standing Rachel up. "Hey Morgan, you and Johnson get her in your patrol car. I'll follow." Then, addressing the other two policemen, "Howard and Shepp, make sure Ms. Brooks here gets to her car safely."

With that, he ducked beneath the limbs of a low-hanging fir tree toward the trail.

Chapter Twenty

Dylan spent most of the day too afraid to spend any of the money. He finally broke down and bought a Big Mac meal and a bus ticket to Wenatchee. From there, he knew he could make it into Canada through the backcountry.

His friend Marcus had done it. He regularly snaked his way back and forth across the border without so much as a driver's license. He'd shown him on a map one night when they were joking about being bank robbers for a living. Except for Marcus, it wasn't a joke. He'd already used the trails to run drugs and stolen goods down from Canada. Marcus was crazy.

Dylan didn't really want to go to Canada. Mexico would be warmer, easier, and cheaper. But it was too far. He needed to disappear fast.

The bus didn't leave until 10:30 p.m., so he waited, sitting behind a dumpster in the Safeway parking lot. It smelled like a rotting corpse. That was fitting; he might as well be one. He'd never felt so alone. Even being homeless, he had places he could go. The Salvation Army for a good meal, the Westin for a shower, do some laundry, and if things got bad, like freezing or unusually hot, he and Rachel would head over to Aspen's shelter. She always got them in.

Sometimes he went home when he knew his dad wouldn't be around. Not because he didn't want to see him, but because the disappointment in his eyes never went away. At least his mom switched it up to looking sad sometimes. He could handle sad. And sad was more likely to help him out with a few bucks.

He put his hands over his face. How could he have been so stupid, following Rachel around like a sick puppy? Unfortunately, he didn't realize the extent of her addiction until he'd burned every bridge in his life. His parents warned him, telling him to stay away from her, but that just made him mad. He knew he was an idiot. Yet he still cared about Rachel, and he just couldn't leave her alone. Until now.

He pulled out his phone. The battery was low, but he might chance to call his mom, or maybe Rachel. He only had a phone because his mom was worried about him. His dad would cut him off, and he'd deserve it.

He tapped the screen. He stared at it, indecision keeping his fingers from moving. Finally, he clicked on "mom" and let the phone dial her number.

She answered on the first ring.

"Dylan?" she sounded out of breath.

"Yeah, mom. How's it going?"

"Oh, I'm just out walking Dotty. You know what a bundle of energy she is if I don't get a couple of miles under her belt."

"True." He sniffed and sat back against the cool metal of the dumpster. He missed walking that stupid dog.

"What's up, sweetie?" He could hear the concern in her voice. She'd stopped walking. He knew his mom.

He closed his eyes. "I'm just sorry for everything, Mom. I want you and Dad to know that."

"Dylan," she said slowly, her voice low and deliberate. "Are you okay? Where are you? I can get in the car right now and pick you up. No questions asked."

He shook his head and pressed his finger and thumb into his eyes. He had to hold it together. It was stupid to call.

"No, Mom," he said, finally. "I'm fine. I just might be gone for a while, but it's okay. You were right about so many things. I'm sorry. I love you. Tell Dad too."

He hung up.

As he sat staring at the phone in his hand, regret filled every fiber of his body.

He didn't hear the man approach. He didn't feel the shadow that crept over him until the man stood close enough to touch. Dylan turned just in time to glimpse the man's face before the silencer claimed his field of vision.

Chapter Twenty-One

Jefferson returned to the station just as the afternoon briefing was ending. People were slowly filing out of the briefing room, some deep in conversation. Ron stopped next to him.

"How was the field trip?" he asked, dropping one of his enormous paws on Jefferson's shoulder.

Jefferson glanced sideways at Rory, who followed behind.

Rory shrugged. "They all wanted to know where you were."

Jefferson looked at the big man's amused face. "Surprisingly productive, and supremely annoying."

Ron laughed. "Sounds like you have yourself a detective groupie. It happens. Especially to handsome fellas like you."

Jefferson imagined MJ hearing herself called a detective groupie. He almost laughed out loud.

Just then, Julia joined the group. "I hear you were following up on a 'hot' tip."

"Alright," said Jefferson, shaking his head and walking away as they all snickered. "You've had your fun. But I need to update Wells."

He found Amber standing in front of the evidence board inside the briefing room with Jared sitting at the table. She glanced at Jefferson as he approached, continuing to listen intently to something the young techy was saying.

"They aimed the threats mostly at Council Members Cochran, Knight, and Olsen. I have seen none for Forsberg, Silva, Weinberg, or Mayor Sully."

"Hmm," said Amber. "Strange, given that Silva received the bomb. I guess it's possible the deliverer didn't know it was a bomb?" She mulled the thought over. "How far have you gotten in tracing the sender?"

"Still working on it. The easy methods have failed, but they're not too sophisticated. I should be able to get to the source by the end of the day, tomorrow morning at the latest."

Amber smiled. "You say that like there will be an end to today for any of us." She looked at the board again. "Thanks, Jared. Keep working on it."

The young man said he would. Then he picked up his computer and left the room while still typing and staring at the screen. Jefferson smiled. He appreciated Jared's use of every single minute to keep working.

She turned her attention to Jefferson. "What about you, Jeff? Rory shared the excellent news. We now know the name of our prime suspect. So, this guy is Dylan Warren," she said, tapping the picture of Dylan from the security footage. "This is key. Nice work."

Jefferson inwardly thanked the universe that, unlike his other colleagues, SSA Wells was purely professional. She made no awkward jokes about MJ Brooks. Still, he didn't enjoy taking credit when he was only there because MJ couldn't leave well enough alone.

"That is correct. Ms. Brooks discovered he was in a homeless encampment near Donald Street. She went there on her own, so I felt it was necessary to meet her there, both to ensure she didn't get herself into a dangerous situation and to check out the information. After questioning some people, we found he had recently left the camp. I did, however, apprehend his girlfriend."

Her eyebrows shot up, "Apprehend?"

"She was in possession of what we suspect is heroin, and she'd been using. Morgan and Johnson brought her in. I plan to give her time to sober up while sitting in lock-up, then we'll interview her. I'm sure you want in on that."

She nodded. "Why don't you and I take it? I have a few things for Rory to follow up on; namely, getting more information on Forsberg. I don't like how that interview went, according to Rory's summary. What did you think?"

"I sensed she was not being completely honest about something. I don't think it was all sunshine and roses on the city council."

She nodded thoughtfully before glancing at the board again. "You missed a few other important developments at the briefing, but good work. This information on Dylan Warren could be the break we need." She looked back at him with a gentle squint in her eyes. "I know how you dislike this kind of . . .," she looked off to the side, searching for the right word, "unconventional police work. I'm glad you didn't ignore it."

"She didn't give me much choice." He reached back with his hand and rubbed the back of his neck, wishing for once that Amber couldn't read him so well. What would she think if she could see how his mind kept flashing back to MJ talking to Rachel in the woods? Seeing a former student in such a condition had to have been shocking for the teacher, but her compassion for Rachel was obvious. Her ability to communicate with the girl, putting her own feelings aside, almost made him feel guilty for his own disdain. Almost.

Wait till she burns you 20 times, he thought bitterly.

Amber was looking at him questioningly. "Everything okay?"

He rubbed his face. "Yeah, I'm fine. I think the Mountain Dew is wearing off. So, what threats did Jared find?" he asked quickly to avoid any further conversation about his well-being.

She tilted her head and gazed at him as if considering how, or if, she should explain the threats and allow this change in subject. After a drawn-out pause, she seemed to decide against probing his mental state any further.

"They're strange," she said. "Almost like rants that have some threatening elements. Mostly around the theme of how those council members were aiding in the earth's destruction. In a couple of them, the person threatens to get them off the council in whatever way possible."

Jefferson raked a hand through his hair. He could almost feel the stubble on his face growing by the second. How he longed for a shower and a fresh change of clothes.

Amber eyed him. "Have you been home yet? Never mind," she said, shaking her head. "That was a stupid question. Of course, you haven't." Her face softened. "Look Jeff, I know we are all going full pedal to the metal, but your situation is different. Take some time to go home. Get what you need and be back here to talk to the girlfriend. Got it?"

Without waiting for an answer, she looked at her watch. "I've got to go meet with the Chief. We are preparing for another public briefing this evening. I think it's time we share the info about Dylan Warren." She stared at the young man's picture. Then she turned abruptly toward Jefferson. "Alright, have the team fill you in on anything else you missed, set a time for interviewing the girlfriend, then get home for a few."

Jefferson reluctantly nodded. He hated the idea that he would get any special respite from the investigation. He knew, however, that Wells would not appreciate him putting up an argument.

He left the briefing room and found Rory and Mendez in conversation at Rory's desk.

Jefferson removed his coat and pulled an empty chair over to join them.

"So, what'd I miss besides the email rants?"

Mendez sat back in his chair. "Well, we know why Silva got the duffle bag, or at least what he thought he was getting."

"Really?"

"Yeah, Larson and I interviewed his wife. Apparently, he had a campaign going with the homeless community called," he looked at his notes, "'Understanding Our Unhoused Neighbors.' He'd put out a call for homeless folks to bring in bags containing the whole of their possessions."

Jefferson wrinkled his brow. "What was the point of that?"

Mendez sighed. "She said he planned to do a 'show and tell' kind of thing at the meeting that night. Go through the bags, essentially showing how little the homeless people have, that they need help, not fear, something like that."

"I'm sure a bomb is not what he was expecting," added Rory, flipping a pen between his fingers.

"So why would that kid want to blow up the city council? It sounds like Silva was trying to help?" asked Jefferson.

Mendez shrugged. "That's what we don't know. If connected to the emails, he could be a rabid environmentalist. Who knows? Maybe the girlfriend will spill some info."

Jefferson nodded. "Anything else?"

Rory looked at Mendez knowingly. "No one can find anything on the pumpkin tie guy that the teacher saw right after the blast."

They both wore grins of conspiracy.

Jefferson shook his head. "No."

Rory chuckled. "Boss wants a composite. We need to bring her in."

Jefferson put his head in his hands. Not again. All MJ needs is another excuse to inject herself into the investigation.

He looked up at Rory. "Fine. But you are calling her."

Rory chuckled. "Alright. I guess that's fair."

"Before we do that," Jefferson said, "let's find her ex. I want to know more about him before we talk to her again. I can see her having the ability to drive a man to madness."

"I am already checking on that." Julia, sitting at the desk opposite, was apparently not as engrossed in her computer as she appeared. "Rory shared the information about your little peach's ex at the briefing. I'm on it."

"Please never call her that again."

Julia just laughed and turned back around.

Just then Ron walked up carrying a foil-wrapped something that made their mouths water.

"Better get yours while they're hot."

Mendez sat up, his copper eyes suddenly wide and eager. "Is that an Agua Azul burrito?"

"Sure is. There's an entire table full, compliments of Atherton Development."

Jefferson stood up and grabbed his coat. He also loved Agua Azul, a food truck that parked outside the station on most weekdays. "Atherton, huh?"

"Yeah," said Ron. "And some ladies from the Methodist church brought some cookies and cupcakes. I already ate mine." He grinned at them.

Mendez shot up like he was starving. Rory rose a little more slowly, probably still digesting his Seadog burger. "Want me to grab you one, Jeffy," Rory asked, stretching his back. "Before Ron eats them all."

Ron looked up, about to bite his burrito. "You know it." He winked at Jefferson before taking the most gigantic bite Jefferson had ever seen.

"No. I'm going to head out for a bit. You guys enjoy."

Jefferson didn't want to tell them he suspected Atherton's offering of free food might be something other than pure altruism. If Forsberg was right, Atherton stood to gain from this tragedy as a potential appointee to the city council. Not because city council members make any kind of money, but because the power they hold often decides who wins and who loses.

He believed Atherton only wanted the seat to ensure he was always a winner. The idea of eating his offerings left a foul taste in Jefferson's mouth. He didn't see any reason to ruin it for the others, so he said nothing. But if Atherton had anything to do with the explosion, he would bury him.

Chapter Twenty-Two

When MJ got home, her mother was awake. In fact, she and Shannon were deep in conversation in MJ's living room.

"MJ!" said her mother. "Where have you been? I've been calling."

Shannon smiled. "You might have had both of us worried."

"Sorry," said MJ, dropping her mother's keys on the table. "I had an errand to run. Sorry, I took the car, Mom, but I didn't want to wake you," she lied. Her mother would have tried to stop her if she knew even part of the truth.

She sat down across from them. "How are things at school?"

Shannon smiled gently. "Tough, as you'd expect. Most of the staff were at the building today. We're healing together." She took a deep breath. "Kevin came by."

MJ felt a pit open in her stomach. "How is he?" she whispered.

"He's a rock. He came to comfort all of *us*, even bringing Troy's favorite donuts from the Maple Barn." Shannon glanced at Toni, hesitating before she continued. "I was just telling your mom that Kevin really wants to see you."

Her mom nodded. "I think it would be a good idea, MJ."

MJ sat back against her chair and stared at them. How could they not understand that she could never face Kevin? "No." She shook her head emphatically. "I can't." She felt the all too familiar stinging in her eyes. She stood up and walked to the kitchen. "Anyone want tea?"

"Melissa Jo Brooks," said her mother firmly, "you need to deal with this." She pulled out MJ's full name, something she did when MJ was being stubborn.

"I am dealing with it, Mother." MJ retorted, emphasizing the last word. Two could play that game. "I am dealing with it in my way. I just need time." She pulled some mugs out of the cupboard. "So, does anyone want tea or coffee?"

She caught the look Shannon gave her mother and knew the issue would not come up again tonight.

"I'll have coffee. But let me help you." Shannon came to join her in the kitchen. "How about you Toni?"

"Coffee, thank you, dear."

With her back to Toni, Shannon mouthed "Sorry" to MJ.

MJ shrugged. "Don't worry."

"Oh," said Shannon as she put coffee in the machine. "Dolores sent a pot of her famous beef stew and some rolls with me." She pointed to a paper bag on the counter. "Stew is in the fridge."

"Dolores is an angel," said MJ. She really was. Dolores worked in the front office as the attendance secretary, and she never forgot an important date or event. She sent cards for everyone's birthday and organized a monthly birthday cake for the staff. She knew everything happening everywhere, and she made sure the staff knew when someone needed help or sympathy.

"Should I heat it up?" Shannon asked, looking over at Toni, still sitting on the sofa.

MJ felt slightly guilty for being short with her mother. She was only trying to help.

"Hey Mom," she said in a softer tone. "Are you hungry?"

"Oh, don't go to any trouble for me," she said with a wave of her hand. "I can just grab a sandwich."

MJ turned to Shannon. "Yeah, let's heat it up."

***

When the food was ready, they all sat down at MJ's little table.

MJ took a couple of bites, but she found herself lost in thought about Dylan Warren and Rachel Downing. She remembered more about Rachel than Dylan. Rachel had been an intelligent girl, kind of shy, but observant. She wrote with an intensity of emotion that was unexpected in someone so introverted, the epitome of the idea that quiet rivers run deep. Maybe those closeted emotions got the better of her.

"MJ, what do you think?"

"What?"

Shannon narrowed her eyes. "Were you listening?"

"No," she said, putting her spoon in her bowl. "I'm sorry. I guess my mind wandered."

"Well, I think it sounds like a wonderful idea," said Toni. "A few of your high school art students want to paint a mural to honor the principal on the side of the building. What a tribute that would be."

Shannon nodded. "Mr. Wilkes has several community artists who want to help. The only problem is Jay Butler. He keeps insisting that it wouldn't be appropriate to immortalize, to use his word, a principal when other staff members have died too. I asked him what he meant, and he reminded me that Shirley Green died just a year ago. Then I reminded him that Shirley Green was 94." She gripped her napkin with a sudden force. "I can't stand that man."

"He is a bit of a parasite," MJ agreed.

"A bit?" asked Shannon incredulously. "You know, I think he actually believes the superintendent and board will hire him as principal. If that happened, it would be my last day of work."

MJ nodded. "You and the rest of the staff." She disliked Butler too, but she wasn't sure the mural was the best idea. MJ knew Troy would hate it. He did not like being the center of attention. It would be a wonderful way to help students heal, and that's where Butler was wrong. It was for them, not Troy.

She stirred her stew. "Hey Shannon," she said, shifting subjects. "Do you remember Rachel Downing? She was at MMS about six years ago."

"Sure," said Shannon without thinking. "She lived with her grandmother. Her mother took off and her dad was in prison. Last I heard anyway. Great kid for all the trauma she endured."

"Geez," said Toni. "How does a kid deal with all that?"

"Not very well most of the time." Shannon took a drink of her water. "What made you think of Rachel?"

"Oh, I just ran into her today," said MJ. She tried to avoid any eye contact with the other two women. "She's homeless."

Shannon sat hard against the back of her chair. "No!"

MJ nodded. "On drugs, too."

Shannon dabbed at her mouth with a napkin. "That just breaks my heart. I really thought she'd make it. You know, get a decent job and be able to support herself. Maybe even college. Such a smart kid."

MJ poked at her stew. How did smart kids leave school and end up living on the streets? What was she doing with her life if she couldn't prevent that from happening? She thought being a teacher meant she could help kids understand their potential. Many students came to her covered in layers of self-loathing so deep it would take more than a school year to break through it all.

She took a sip of her water and tried to break out of the sadness spreading through her. This wasn't the first time she'd felt bleak about her role as a teacher. It was Troy who always reminded her of the good that came from her efforts. He did that for all of them. The loss was devastating.

"Oh honey," said her mom, squeezing her hand.

MJ looked up. Only then did she realize her lips were trembling. She stood up abruptly. No more crying. She was done crying.

"I'm going to go change my clothes, maybe kayak with Edgar for a bit. I need to clear my head."

"That sounds like a great idea," Shannon agreed.

Her mother nodded. "You go ahead, honey. We will get everything cleared up."

"Are you sure?" MJ felt guilty for deserting the two of them.

"We insist," said Shannon. "You've got a bit of clear sky, no rain right now, so take advantage and get some fresh air."

"Just be careful," said Toni. "You still have bruised ribs to take care of."

MJ nodded. "I will. Thank you, both of you."

***

Down at the beach, MJ unlocked one of Claire's kayaks and dragged it to the water. She had her dry suit on and both she and Edgar had life vests. Edgar knew the drill, and he knew what a life vest meant. He was almost too excited to get in the kayak without tipping it.

"Hold on, buddy. You know the rules." MJ rubbed her hands together. It was cold, but she knew as soon as she started paddling, she'd be plenty warm.

Edgar sat down and looked at her eagerly, his ears at full point. He whined slightly, which meant waiting was killing him.

"Okay, walk."

Edgar walked calmly into the kayak.

"Sit."

He sat down and stared out at the water. He sneaked a look back at MJ as if to say, "Come on already."

She laughed to herself as she set the paddle inside and gave the kayak a push, jumping in as soon as they'd cleared the shallowest part of the beach. She pulled the paddle to rest horizontally across the kayak allowing it to float while she gave Edgar a pet.

"Good job, buddy."

She didn't know what she'd do without Edgar. To have company without having to explain, make conversation, or endure opinions was a beautiful thing. Everyone should have an Edgar.

She started the back-and-forth motion, dipping each side of the paddle into the opaque, rippling ocean surface. Soon, she lost her thoughts between the rhythm of her breathing and the seesaw of the paddle.

MJ let her muscles take on the tension, releasing her mind from any obligation to think. She pulled and pulled through the water's resistance. The shadowy shores passed by on each side, evergreen trees tangled and rigid like a dark army. The brief respite of blue sky was already gone, but still MJ pulled. Up ahead, the bank rose higher, and it looked like a giant had dug fistfuls of land out from under the trees. Roots dangled down to the beach of warped sand and scattered driftwood.

She paddled without thinking about time or distance. Her mind was blessedly as blank as the ocean ahead, just her and Edgar gliding through space on this watery ship.

Edgar looked back at her, and she saw the wind ruffling his face. That's when she realized how hard and fast she'd been paddling. Water sloshed in the kayak's bottom from the back-and-forth movement of the paddle. She was sweating, despite the cold.

She stopped paddling, letting the kayak naturally slow. She rested the paddle across her lap and closed her eyes.

There was nothing. All she could hear was Edgar panting, her own breathing, and the gentle slapping of the water against the kayak. A few birds twittered, but it seemed even most of them were somewhere else.

MJ took a deep breath, the cold, salty air filling her lungs. She put her head back and opened her eyes, looking deep into the ghostly drift of clouds above. She wondered if anyone was really up there. Her parents weren't religious, so MJ only ever heard about God from her grandma. If MJ knew anything, she knew her grandma believed. She seemed to believe with certainty that she would be with Grandpa again someday.

MJ envied that, and she hoped it was true. Her grandma deserved such a reunion.

Lots of people believed, and lots of people didn't. But did anybody really know? She thought about Troy and the other people so suddenly gone. They had to be somewhere, didn't they?

A breeze blew and gently moved her curls away from her face. She closed her eyes and let it caress her. Without warning, Jefferson Hughes' face jumped into her mind. His hard face and perfect blond hair were at complete odds with the depth of his blue eyes. What pain was he hiding?

It was with her face up, contemplating heaven and Hughes, that she felt the first raindrops. The cold drip brought her back to the present. She shuddered at having let Detective Hughes invade her solitude.

She looked at Edgar. The dog stared at her, looking so wise. Maybe Edgar knew the secrets to life.

She petted his neck and then picked up the paddle. They better get back or they would both be soggy dogs.

***

When they finally got their wet selves back to the house, Shannon and her mother had cleaned up all the dinner dishes. They insisted she go take a shower to get warm and relax. Feeling tired, emotionally and physically, she obeyed. Her side hurt; she overdid the paddling.

Once out of the shower, she laid her head back on the couch with her feet on an Ottoman in fresh clothes, hair up, and slippers on. Her favorite Eagles album played from her Bluetooth speaker. The mellow tunes fit her mood, and she found her eyes growing heavy to the lyrics of "Desperado." For a minute, she relaxed enough to doze off. Then her phone rang. It rang really loudly because it was attached to her speaker.

"Oh, my goodness," said her mother, covering her ears.

"Sorry." MJ reached for her phone on the coffee table.

"Hello?"

"Ms. Brooks?" said a man's voice.

"Yes, can I help you?" She fumbled with her phone, trying desperately to turn off the Bluetooth. Finally, she got it.

"Hi, this is Detective Jackson."

"Hello again, detective. How can I help you?"

"Would it be possible for you to come down to the station? I know it's late, and it's a lot to ask, but we have a bit of a situation."

"I don't understand. What does your situation have to do with me?"

He hesitated. She thought she could hear someone talking to him in the background.

"It's Rachel Downing. She won't talk to us unless you are here."

MJ couldn't help smiling to herself. Detective Hughes couldn't wait to be rid of her, and now it was coming back to bite him.

"Um, sure, detective. Anything I can do to help. I can be there in about half an hour."

"Great. Just tell the officer at the front desk your name. He'll be expecting you."

When she hung up, both her mother and Shannon were looking at her with curious wrinkles on their brows.

"What?"

"Who was that?" asked her mother.

"One of the detectives. They need me to come down to the station."

The two looked at each other. Shannon shook her head with an indulgent smile. "MJ, you are always on the move."

"Always has been," added her mom. "Well, you are not taking my rental this time. I will drive you."

MJ protested.

"No argument," she insisted. "I've had more sleep than you."

"Sounds like it's settled," said Shannon. "I'm going to head home. You ladies, be sure to let me know if you need anything."

MJ walked with her to the door. She gave her a big hug. "Thank you for everything, Shannon. I know how hard you are trying to make me feel better, even though you are hurting, too."

Shannon squeezed her hard. Then she stood back and looked at her. "Sometimes life really sucks."

"Like really bad," MJ agreed.

"But MJ, be careful that you don't internalize too much. Don't run yourself ragged trying to make everything better. Okay? Let people help you. We need each other right now."

MJ knew Shannon was right. But she also knew that she couldn't be normal again, and she couldn't rest until she knew who had killed Troy. Someone had a world of hate in them. Only horrific hate could cause the misery inflicted on the people of West Sound. That person hadn't been caught. That person could cause more pain. MJ feared that the most.

Chapter Twenty-Three

The police station lobby pulsed with activity as MJ and Toni entered. A man was filling out a form while a toddler boy knelt beside him playing with a toy car on the seat of his chair. A female officer talked quietly to an elderly man. He nodded, but he looked distraught as he folded and refolded an empty dog leash on his lap. A few others were sitting and waiting while scrolling on their phones.

MJ and her mother walked to the counter. A young male officer sat behind a glass partition, all of his attention focused on whatever he was typing into his computer.

"Hi," said MJ. "I'm Melissa Brooks. I am meeting Detective Jackson."

The officer checked a paper sitting next to him and nodded. "Yes, they are expecting you," he said without looking. "If I can just have you sign in here." He picked up a clipboard and finally glanced their way. His eyes narrowed as he realized there were two of them. "I'm sorry, but only Ms. Brooks has clearance to go back." He directed this to Toni. "You are welcome to wait out here in the lobby." He said welcome, but his facial expression said he couldn't care less where she waited.

"Hey, Ms. Brooks." It was Detective Jackson. He moved beside the desk officer. "Why don't you two come on back? It's okay Brody," he said to the young man. "I'll take care of it."

"To my rescue again," Toni murmured under her breath to MJ.

"Mother," MJ hissed.

They signed the clipboard and followed the detective into the backrooms of the station.

"Thank you for coming so quickly," he was saying as they walked.

"It's no problem," said MJ.

The room they entered opened into a spacious area with a high ceiling and bright lights. A few desks filled the middle of the room, while gray doors and a few windows lined either side. MJ guessed those were offices. Every desk was full, some with more than one person. Some were in police uniform, and others, like the detective, were not. It smelled of coffee and faintly of sweat despite the airy quality of the room.

A few heads turned as they walked by. MJ felt her breath catch as she saw Jefferson Hughes watching her from his perch on the corner of a desk occupied by a woman with dark hair in a baseball cap. The woman followed Jefferson's gaze. As her eyes landed on MJ, she glanced back at the detective with a knowing grin. MJ felt her face redden. She looked away.

"Ms. Brooks, we will be in one of the interview rooms shortly," Detective Jackson was saying. "Until then, there is a small waiting area I will take you to, and," he stopped and turned to look at Toni, "it's Ms. or Mrs. Devey if I remember correctly?"

"What a fine memory you have. Yes, it is Mrs. Devey. But please just call me Toni." She flashed a radiant smile at him. MJ's mother had always been a first-class flirt. It was just a part of her personality, her charm. MJ knew, however, that she would never seriously flirt with anyone. Her parents were high school sweethearts. They had a bond that MJ found annoying in her teen years. She could never pit them against each other in the way her friends did to their parents. Her parents talked about everything.

"Then you should call me Rory," said the detective, continuing to lead them down a corridor.

"And here we are." Rory pointed to the doorless opening of a cozy room with a sofa and two armchairs. "There is coffee, some chips, and cookies. I think the fridge has some soda and water. So, if you hang out here, Ms. Brooks, we'll come and get you as soon as we're ready, and Toni, if you don't mind waiting here while we do the interview?"

"That's just fine, thank you," said Toni.

MJ furrowed her brow. "I thought Rachel was already here."

"She is," he confirmed. "But she needed more time to cool off and out from under the influence, so we took her back down to the holding area. It will only be a few minutes, I'm sure."

"I see," said MJ.

"I won't be in the interview," said Rory. "So, I'll leave you two here, and Detective Hughes will be by any minute now."

The two women sat on the couch. MJ suddenly felt very tired. She leaned her head back and closed her eyes. Her mother reached over and put her arm around her. MJ sighed and let her head fall to her mother's shoulder. She closed her eyes.

***

Rachel sat on a chair with black leather-like material on the back and seat. There were five chairs in the tiny interview room, all around an off-white, rectangular table. A two-way window made up part of the wall opposite Rachel. No one was looking on today. The other detectives all had their plates full of other tasks. One uniformed officer stood just outside the door for emergencies. Amber and Jefferson were conducting the interview.

The detective observed Rachel. Her eyes darted from person to person, but this was an improvement over her wild, frenzied behavior from earlier that day. The public defender, Jess Miller, sat next to Rachel. Jess was a regular, and Jefferson worked with her often. He liked her. She had a no-nonsense way about her. She was probably in her late sixties by now, but she hadn't slowed a beat.

Amber sat across from Rachel and the attorney. Jefferson pulled a chair up to the end of the table nearest Rachel and motioned for MJ to take it before he sat next to Amber. Rachel reached out and latched onto the woman.

"Ms. Brooks, I'm so glad you're here." Big tears welled up in her eyes and started falling down her face in rapid succession. "They just don't listen to me. They just hate me." She glared at Jefferson through water-logged eyes. Then she turned back to MJ. "I'm so sorry."

MJ touched her arm gently. "What are you sorry about?"

"I'm sorry I didn't listen to you," she sobbed. "I should've . . . I should've done better . . . in school. I'm so stupid." She folded her arms on the table and buried her head in them.

"Rachel," MJ spoke softly. "Look at me."

The girl wiped her eyes and nose unsuccessfully with her sleeves.

"Could we get a tissue here?" she asked, looking at Jefferson.

Jefferson stood and opened the door, whispering to the guard.

"Rachel," said MJ. "I will never say school doesn't matter, because it does, but messing up doesn't mean you can't make a good life. There are many people who want to help you."

The uniformed officer opened the door and handed Jefferson a box of tissues. Jefferson set the box on the table and pushed it toward Rachel. He wondered how long this little drama would take. They needed answers now.

"I can help you," MJ was saying. "We can figure all of that out. But right now, we need your help. Can you help us?"

As Jefferson studied the way MJ spoke to Rachel, he experienced a curious sense of admiration mixed with a fool's errand. It didn't seem to matter to her that this girl would rob her blind to get her next hit, and he could tell Rachel knew her former teacher really cared about her. Whether she'd remember that tomorrow was another story.

He could see this teacher setting herself up to be Rachel's next victim. She'd spend time and money, maybe even give her a place to stay, only to discover that these leopards hardly ever change their spots.

Rachel looked at the tissue in her hand and then at MJ.

"Before we go any further," interjected Jess Miller, "my client would like to know the status of the drug charges."

Jefferson and Amber looked at each other. They had discussed this, knowing Jess would most likely push for a deal. Jefferson hated the idea of dropping drug charges. Making deals with drug addicts or dealers usually meant they'd be picking up the same addict or dealer within a few days' time. The merry-go-round of drug busts would just keep going and going, and addicts would continue to kill themselves or hurt the people around them, like his own brother. But even he had to concede that this time was different. Finding Dylan could be the key to this entire case.

"We are prepared to ask the prosecutor to drop the possession charge," Jefferson answered. "And for using, we will recommend her for treatment in a State-funded facility."

Jess cast a questioning glance at Rachel.

"What do you think, Ms. Brooks?" Rachel asked.

Jefferson looked over at Jess and noticed her giving MJ an almost imperceptible nod of the head.

"I think it sounds like a pretty good deal. You want to get better, don't you? Get off the drugs? This could be the chance for you." MJ squeezed her arm. "I think you should take it, but you have to do what you and your attorney think is best."

Rachel turned to face Jess. The woman nodded her approval of the deal.

"Okay," said Rachel. "But that doesn't mean I have to do whatever they say, right?"

"No, no," said Amber, who had been watching this whole exchange quietly. "We have some questions that we think you might answer, that's all."

"Like what?"

"Like," repeated Amber, "where is Dylan Warren?"

Rachel wrinkled up her nose. "Why do you need to find Dylan? Is he in trouble?"

Amber smiled. "We hope not. That's why we really need to talk to him."

"I don't know where he is," she said matter-of-factly.

Jefferson sat up. "When was the last time you saw him?"

She stared up at the ceiling. "Last night, I think. He didn't feel good, so he wouldn't go shower with us, which he needed, for real. When I came back, he was gone. Packed up all his stuff and split, without even saying a word to me."

"Has he done that before? Just left?"

She sat up tall and looked askance at Jefferson. "If he had, I wouldn't be hanging around for him to do it again."

"Can you think of where Dylan might go? Do you have his parents' information?"

Rachel sighed and shook her head. "I have no idea where he went. I mean, he could have gone to any of the hundreds of encampments in the state. Even just around West Sound there are a bunch." She paused as if considering whether to offer the next bit of information, picking at the frayed tissue in her hand. She looked at MJ, who nodded.

"His parents live in Leafland Estates."

Jefferson's head shot up. Leafland Estates held some of the most expensive homes in the county.

Rachel laughed at his reaction. "Yep, rich boy gave it all up to live in a tent by a freeway exit. I thought it was because he loved me." She blew her nose.

No one said anything for a minute.

"I know it's hard, but this information is helpful. Just a few more things," assured Amber. "What had Dylan been doing the last day you saw him?"

"I didn't see him much. I think he was doing some things in town. He said something about going up to the shelter. I think to talk to Aspen."

Jefferson's jaw tensed. That name kept coming up. "Do you know why?"

"I'm sure it was about the campaign. Dylan was really into that political stuff. He was mad about the city clearing out homeless camps. Aspen too."

"How do you know he was mad about that? What did he say?"

Rachel seemed to think, then her face suddenly became grave. She stared at Jefferson without answering. Then she looked at Amber and at MJ. Jefferson could see her brain making connections. She understood why they were asking.

"Wait," she said, getting much more animated. "You don't think Dylan had anything to do with that bomb?" She shook her head back and forth with determined force. "No way. You don't know him."

"We are just trying to understand some information we have about Dylan," assured Amber. "That's why we are here, talking to you. You can help us 'know' Dylan."

"I will not help you do anything that will hurt him," she said between clenched teeth.

Jess put a hand on Rachel's arm. "I'd like a moment with my client."

Amber nodded. "That's probably a good idea." She stood up. "Will 15 minutes be enough time?"

Jess nodded. "I think so."

Jefferson stood with Amber. Looking at MJ, he motioned with his head toward the door.

"Oh," said MJ, surprised. She stated to get up.

"Ms. Brooks can stay," said Rachel, placing a protective hand on MJ's.

"No, no, she can't," said Jefferson. "But she'll come back when we do." He would not risk losing evidence because of an irregularity, even if he didn't know what the irregularity would be, technically. An attorney would find it, though. With any luck, Jess was planning to remind Rachel of her deal.

"It's okay, Rachel. I'm not going anywhere. I'll be right next door." MJ said as she pulled her hand away. She joined Jefferson and Amber as they left the room.

As soon as the door closed behind them, Amber excused herself to go check for updates.

Jefferson turned to MJ. "You know, you really should be careful with that girl."

"What do you mean?" She stared up at him, her eyes wide and curious but tired. Jefferson noticed for the first time that she had a small birthmark near her right eye. It was just slightly darker than her skin.

"I mean, drug addicts create misery for the people who care about them. I can tell you're getting attached, and she could take advantage of you." Jefferson knew his tone was a little too fatherly. He couldn't help himself. He'd seen it too much, been a sucker too many times himself. A picture of his brother rummaging through his father's drawers flashed through his mind. He willed it away.

MJ searched his face. He couldn't tell if she was going to flip out or thank him. She had a caustically independent side, and he'd probably stepped too close to it.

"Your concern is noted," she said, looking directly into his eyes.

Jefferson nodded, not sure how to take that.

She was still looking at him. She seemed to study him and he didn't like it.

"Hughes," Wells called. "You're needed in the briefing room."

"On my way," he said, turning to go, grateful for the interruption.

"Detective," MJ said, lightly grabbing his arm before he could leave.

He turned back, looking down at her hand holding his arm, and then back at her.

She released it quickly, and he surprised himself by wishing she hadn't.

"You seem . . ." she bit her lip, searching for the right words. "You seem really bothered by Rachel and her addiction. I mean, I'm bothered, too, but you . . ." she hesitated. "You almost seem angry at her, and I just wondered why."

"Aren't you?"

"What? Angry at her?"

"Yeah, I mean, she's wasted her life. She's probably stolen from people, from her family, her friends. Who knows what else she's done to get a fix?"

She looked down at her hands. "You're probably right, but I'm not angry. I'm incredibly sad."

When she met his eyes again, they were indeed wells of deep blue sadness. He knew what it was like to feel that way. He still felt that way. But he also felt angry and disillusioned. All his family's love and attempts at intervention for his brother would change nothing.

She continued. "It just seems like you've taken it personally."

He clenched his jaw. What did she know about it? What did she know about watching someone you love choose drugs over and over again?

"I assure you I will do my job professionally."

She looked at him, then closed her eyes briefly. "No, that's not what I mean." She shook her head. "I'm sorry, this is coming out wrong. I just wanted to say that if you have lost someone, I'm sorry. That's all."

This sympathy surprised him and left him speechless. How had she read him so well?

He cleared his throat, realizing a small lump had formed there. A picture of Alex, alone on the bus platform, floated into his mind. He closed his eyes.

"I have to get to the briefing room," he said without looking at her.

He turned and left without another word.

Chapter Twenty-Four

MJ wondered what was up in the all-important briefing room. She turned around to see her mother sitting in the waiting room, coffee in hand, staring at her.

"What?" MJ asked too harshly.

"Nothing." She took a sip of her coffee with a smile on her lips.

"Oh, my goodness, Mother." MJ rolled her eyes. "I'm going to go find the restroom."

"It's down the hall to the left," her mother called after her. But MJ wasn't going in that direction.

She crept back toward the main office area. As she suspected, it was empty. Everyone must be in the same meeting as Detective Hughes, she thought. A man's voice came from the door nearest her. She moved toward it, trying her best to tread softly. She always had the "I'm looking for the restroom" excuse in her back pocket if someone found her there.

She crept toward the door, surprised to find that it was open. She got close enough to hear the conversation but stayed back enough to avoid being seen.

"One shot to the head. No one heard anything, but that's a busy spot, or the shooter could have used a silencer. Forensics are on the scene with the officers who answered the call."

"Da — I mean daaamp towels," said a voice she recognized as Rory's.

A few people snickered. MJ wrinkled her nose. What the heck did that mean?

"This changes things. We should consider this a sign of continuing threat," Amber said.

"Unless he offed himself," another man said.

It was quiet while they seemed to consider this.

"It's also possible he was an unsuspecting murderer and didn't know what he was delivering to the councilman," she heard Jefferson say. "Whoever sent him to deliver the bomb could just be covering his tracks."

"Or some other scenario we just aren't seeing yet," Amber said thoughtfully.

"I guess Rachel's deal isn't necessary anymore." Jefferson sounded relieved.

That annoyed MJ. Why was he so determined to throw Rachel to the wolves?

"I know it bugs you, Jeff," Amber said. "But she's fulfilled her part. We got his parents' information. Unfortunately, we are going to have to make a very unpleasant visit there."

MJ covered her mouth and stood against the wall. Dylan was dead. She took a deep breath to calm her heart.

"I know it's late, but Hughes and Jackson, I want you to get over to the scene and touch base with the medical examiner. See if she can draw any conclusions ruling out suicide. Then head to that shelter and find Aspen Klein. I don't like how often she's coming up in this investigation."

"Got it," responded Rory.

"Larson and Mendez, I'm sorry, but please go see Dylan's parents. Break the news to them. If it's possible, and if they are up to it, see what they know about their son's whereabouts in the past two days, his affiliation with Aspen, or anything else that can explain why he dropped that bag at city hall."

MJ closed her eyes. She saw Dylan again, crossing the street and flipping her off. It sickened her to think that just minutes before, he'd dropped off a bomb that would destroy city hall and ruin so many lives. Why? Her mind raced. And why would someone kill Dylan?

She heard movement and random chatter. The meeting was over. She turned and started rushing back toward the interview rooms.

"Ms. Brooks," she heard behind her. It was Amber.

She turned back. "Yes," she said as innocently as possible. "I was a little lost looking for the restroom."

"Very lost," said Jefferson.

She ignored him and looked directly at Amber.

"We were hoping to steal a bit more of your time." Amber's tone was alert and businesslike, but she removed her glasses and rubbed her eyes with the back of her hand. "I know I am imposing on you, but we haven't been able to locate the man who helped you after the blast, the one in the suit. I was hoping you might sit down with Jared here." She pointed at a young man busy working at his computer. He looked up and waved with a serious face.

Amber continued. "He can work with you to create a digital sketch."

MJ nodded. "Sure. I only remember a little, but I can try." She paused. "Are we going to finish the interview with Rachel first?"

"Ah, I think we are finished for tonight. We've had some other developments."

"Well, whatever you need," said MJ, a little too brightly.

Amber considered her. Then her eyes narrowed shrewdly. "How much did you hear?"

MJ cleared her throat and looked at Amber, avoiding Jefferson's eyes. "Um, I think most of it. I know Dylan is dead." She almost whispered the last part. Too many people were dead.

Amber sighed and glanced at Jefferson.

He was shaking his head. "Now you understand," he said.

MJ's face grew hot. He didn't have to be so condescending right in front of her.

Amber turned back to MJ. "You know, I could probably find a reason to arrest you. Interfering in an investigation or something similar." Her eyes bored into MJ's like she was trying to discern the nature of her very soul. "But that would be counterproductive. I need to know that you will share nothing you may have 'accidentally' overheard with anyone."

"You can be sure of that," MJ felt an angry resolve flow through her spine. She stood up taller. "Finding whoever did this is very important to me."

MJ glanced around and realized other people were watching.

Amber didn't seem to care. Her face softened, and she smiled gently. "Let's get that digital sketch done. Then, Ms. Brooks, go home and get some rest. But I want you to know we appreciate your help." She glanced up at Jefferson. "Don't we Hughes."

A crooked smile cracked his face as he met MJ's eyes. "Absolutely."

MJ knew he didn't mean it. She also knew that was the first time she'd seen him smile. Unfortunately, it looked good on him.

"Alright, everyone, you have your next steps," Amber said to the room. "Once completed, do what you need to do to get some rest. You can leave instructions for the night crew if something needs immediate follow-up. We've made some good progress today. Let's keep it up."

With that, the group dispersed to their various tasks. MJ went to check on her mother and let her know she'd be a few more minutes.

***

MJ looked across the desk at Jared.

He had a laptop open, with two additional large screens on each side. He was looking rapidly between the three screens, but he hadn't yet looked at her.

She cleared her throat.

He glanced at her briefly before his dark eyes darted away and back to the screens.

"Is there something I should do?" She asked.

"I'm opening the program. It takes some time." He still did not look at her.

She studied him closely since he wasn't paying her much attention.

He had a mass of silky milk chocolate curls that hung just above his eyes. His features were taut with the intensity of his task. His skin still held a youthful fullness, and she could tell he was much younger than all the other agents.

"Hair color?"

MJ jumped, startled. She'd been so deep in thought that his voice shocked her.

"You mean the man's hair color?"

He looked up at her, not annoyed so much as focused.

She nodded. "Um, it was a dark brown, maybe even a little gray in it."

"Where was the gray located?"

She shrugged. "I don't really know, I guess all over, but just like sprinkled, not a lot."

"Length?"

"Mm," she said, thinking. "It was a standard professional-looking haircut. Pretty short."

Jared turned one of his computer screens toward her.

"The program will offer a variety of eye shapes. Please stop me when you see one that looks correct or close."

MJ watched the blank face on the screen with nothing but hair and eyes of all different shapes and sizes flashing through it.

She replayed the moment after the explosion in her mind, trying to focus on the eyes of the man as he reached out his hand to her. The more she tried to see him, the further away from her memory he seemed to be.

Despite her efforts to concentrate on the screen, Detective Hughes' changeable blue eyes kept crossing her mind. They'd seemed so deep and thoughtful outside the homeless camp. But then he acted so arrogant. What was his deal?

She looked up, almost afraid someone would read her mind.

She shook her head to clear it and turned her attention back to the screen. It didn't matter. He didn't matter. Finding the killer was all that mattered.

All the eyes were looking the same, so she decided to just pick one so they could move on to other features. Maybe that would help her memory.

"Stop, I think that's a pretty good match," she told the young man.

As Jared did his thing, she sneaked a look around the room. Was he still here?

He was. She saw him sitting at a desk typing. It looked like paperwork.

Jared was staring at her. He turned to look back at Jefferson and then back at her.

She smiled, "Next?"

He turned back to his computer quietly, but she sensed he wanted to say something.

"Noses," he said.

The next thing she knew, all kinds of noses were there for her inspection.

"He's one of the best," Jared said, as the noses flashed.

MJ looked at him, an eyebrow raised. Jared glanced away from his screen just long enough to meet her eye. His look said she shouldn't pretend she didn't know who he was talking about.

"I only know him a little, but he's a good person."

"I'm sure he is." She pointed at the screen. "That one, I think. Can you make it a little skinnier on the bridge?"

Jared moved his mouse and hit a few keys.

"I just thought you should know," he said stiffly.

"I'm not sure how that relates to me, but thank you."

Jared nodded once.

They finished the rest of the composite, talking as little as possible.

Chapter Twenty-Five

He hadn't wanted to kill the kid, but it was part of the plan. If he knew anything, he knew he had to stick to his plan.

Dylan did his part masterfully; unwittingly but masterfully. Still, he couldn't risk what the kid might do once he realized he had delivered a bomb to city hall. A bomb that killed a few seemingly innocent people. Luckily, money cured the kid's curiosity. He never asked, never looked in the bag. Maybe some sixth sense told him the truth. Whatever. He did it, and the first stage was complete. Almost.

He followed Dylan long enough to know that the police were clueless about where to find him. It was obvious the stupid kid thought he could leave town. He sneered. Like the feds and the police weren't watching every bus station, airport, rental car company, you name it. Nope, he couldn't risk it. Dylan served the purpose; he'd made those people pay. He was a hero in his eyes.

Unfortunately, he still had a problem to take care of. He thought about her as he packed his backpack. She thought she'd done her part, but her fight was weak and half-hearted, and in the end, she caved. He knew she didn't really care, so she would pay like the rest of them. Besides, he found this work profoundly therapeutic, cleansing even.

So tonight, he'd tie up that loose end. He smiled and his teeth were bright against the black he'd smeared over his face. It was fitting. She'd be asleep as the flames came for her. The flames would make her pay.

Chapter Twenty-Six

Jefferson and Rory found the crime scene easily with all the blue lights creating a beacon in the Safeway parking lot. The forensics team also set up a few mobile white lights that created a patch of temporary daylight.

The detectives flashed their badges and signed in with the officer at the entrance. She instructed them to use the paper the shoe covers provided.

They did as she requested and then headed toward the dumpster, where most of the lights were concentrated.

"You going to be able to handle this?" Rory said, without looking at Jefferson.

"Why wouldn't I?"

"You know, you two . . . " his voice trailed off.

"It was nothing, Rory, just a couple of dates. Nothing came of it. We're fine."

"Okay, if you say so."

Jefferson stared ahead. This was not a topic he wanted to discuss.

It didn't take long to see Dylan's body sitting on the ground, slumped over unnaturally at the waist.

Dr. Stacey Underhill, Rainier County medical examiner, knelt in front of the body with a clipboard. She looked up at them as they approached.

She was new in the position since Dorlin Hunter retired a year ago. Dorlin had insisted that he only agreed to leave because Stacey, though young, had unprecedented skills and a spine of steel.

She was also extremely good-looking.

"Gentlemen," she said, looking back at her work.

Okay, Jefferson thought, so there was an edge to her voice.

"Dr. Underhill," Jefferson said in greeting.

Her eyes flashed up to him. "That's rather formal."

Jefferson shrugged. "What would you prefer?"

She stood up. A smile spread across her face. "I'm just giving you a hard time, Jefferson."

He'd forgotten how disarming she could be with her quick wit and charming smile. Her paper hood hid her honey-colored hair, but a few strands were still visible around her face.

"Sorry, it's been a long day."

"I'm sure," she said, nodding sympathetically. She glanced at Rory. "How are Marissa and the kids?"

"Growing by the day," he said affectionately. "Wait—I mean the kids, not Marissa. Do not tell her I said that."

Stacey rolled her eyes. "No worries. Still the joker, I see."

"Always," said Rory.

"Well, I'm sure you're not here to chit-chat, or ask me out again." She glanced at Jefferson.

He didn't know what to say or do. Was she still kidding? He was so confused.

She laughed out loud, "Oh my goodness, you are too easy to rattle." She shook her head while referring to her clipboard.

"So, what do you know so far?" asked Rory, saving Jefferson from responding.

"I know I'm freezing my tail off out here." She put her head back and glanced up at the sky. "At least no rain. That's something. But that's not what you want to know." She pointed toward the body. "It looks pretty cut and dried. One gunshot to the head, poor kid. Without getting him on the table, I can only give you an educated guess about the caliber." She looked down at her clipboard again. "Judging by the measurements of the entry wound, I would say 9mm."

"Any possibility he did it himself?" Jefferson asked.

"Only if he had twenty-foot arms that would bend very unnaturally. No, the angle appears to be consistent with a shooting at close range but not suicide. And there is no gun here." She put her hand up. "Of course, this is not official. Until we examine him back at the lab, we won't be sure about anything."

"Well, we all know your initial findings are usually pretty close to the truth," Jefferson said.

She considered him through narrowed eyes. "Truth. What I do is scientific. I think the truth, what really goes on between people, that part is up to you all."

"True," chipped in Rory.

Stacey rolled her eyes and groaned. "I have to finish up here. I'll let you know as soon as I have an official report. But you should check with Bud over there. He has all the evidence bags, and I know they have some interesting stuff," she said, raising her eyebrows like this should be really tempting.

"Thanks, Stacey," Jefferson said. "We'll be in touch."

She laughed as they walked away. "Don't call me, I'll call you."

Jefferson certainly hoped she didn't call him. There was a reason they'd only gone out twice.

"Dang, aggressive," Rory said as they headed over to the forensics van.

"Yep," agreed Jefferson.

"But that can't be all bad, I mean . . ."

"Shut up, Rory."

Rory smiled, but he did shut up.

Bud Lochlann waved as they approached.

"Hey boys, I wondered if we'd see you. You've got to be running ragged about now."

"We'd never miss a chance to come visit you, Bud," Jefferson said.

Bud had been the lead forensics officer for as long as Jefferson could remember. He was a tall man, bald but not dealing with it very well. What hair he had was pulled back in a thin ponytail at the base of his neck, thin wisps of white doing a poor job of covering his dome.

But what was under his dome was the amazing part. The man managed an immense mental library of forensics knowledge. They were lucky to have him.

"As much as I want to believe you two handsome fellows are here to see me, I know it's our unlucky victim you want to know about."

"I am afraid that is why we are here," Rory admitted, smiling. "And Stacey seems to think you found a few things of interest."

He reached down and grabbed an evidence bag out of a crate sitting in the back of the van. He reached inside and pulled out a wallet.

"You're lucky I haven't sealed this yet."

He flipped it open so they could see inside.

"If you want to put gloves on, you can check it out yourself, but I can tell you right now there wasn't much in it. A driver's license," he said pointing. "This says our young man is one Dylan Warren, which I think you already know."

They nodded.

"What is really interesting is what we found in his shoes."

He returned the wallet and grabbed another bag. As he pulled it out, the two detectives looked at each other in shock.

"Blimey," said Rory. "He had all of that in his shoes."

Bud nodded. "We counted it. Just under $5,000."

Jefferson wondered if this had been payment for dropping the bag at city hall. Where else would a kid like Dylan Warren get that kind of money?

"Someone killed him and left the money?" he asked.

"Sure looks that way." Bud put the money back in the crate. "And I'll tell you another thing. Whoever shot him didn't take any time to search for that cash or for anything else. His wallet was intact, his pockets weren't turned out, and his shoes were still on his feet. He was left sitting up, and most of the time, if it's a robbery, they lay the victim down and take everything." He shook his head. "Not this time."

"So, the killer either didn't know about the money or didn't care," surmised Rory.

"Something like that." Bud shrugged. "We'll get all this stuff logged. If anything else stands out before you get a report, I'll let you know."

"We'd appreciate that. We know how stretched everybody is right now."

"Yes, it's a sorry business. But the feds are picking up some of the slack, which is helpful. Our itty-bitty team couldn't do the work at city hall alone." He picked up another crate and heaved it into the back of the van.

"We'll take off and let you get back to it. Thanks again."

"No problem. Be careful out there."

They both said that they would. As they walked back to the car, Jefferson tried to imagine what Aspen might say about Dylan hiding that much money in his shoe. Her reaction to that piece of information would be very interesting.

Chapter Twenty-Seven

Seeing Aspen meant driving to an industrial area of West Sound known as the Shopside Docks. Less than a quarter mile from the water, the shelter was an old warehouse purchased and transformed by Aspen's charitable group. It had "Room at the Inn" painted in broad white letters on its side. The words stood out in the darkness, highlighted by the low moon. A salty mist from the Sound constantly enveloped this area, sticking to the skin. The empty street echoed the distant creak and squeak of moorings and the gentle lapping of water against the docks.

Jefferson buttoned his coat as they stepped out of the car. He never enjoyed visiting this area, and the temperature had dropped about ten degrees. It was quickly approaching 11 p.m. It should be peaceful, but there was always an edginess in the air around here. Now it just reminded him how long it had been since he'd gotten any proper sleep.

In the shelter, one bearded young man sat at the front desk with only a tiny lamp emitting a low light. He looked up as Jefferson and Rory entered.

"Can I help you?" he whispered. The light glinted off his metal ear gages.

Jefferson pulled out his badge. "I'm Detective Hughes and this is Detective Jackson. We are looking for Aspen Klein."

The young man put his finger to his lips. "If you don't mind keeping it down. We have strict lights out at 10 p.m., and noise is not a good thing for our guests."

"Sure," Jefferson nodded. "And Aspen?" he whispered.

"She's," he looked behind him like he was afraid of being overheard, "she's across the street at the Captain's Closet."

Jefferson raised an eyebrow. "Okay, we'll head over there then."

They thanked the young man and left.

The Captain's Closet was a bar that catered to a distinctly local crowd. It was too out of the way for random visitors. The clientele varied little. It surprised Jefferson to hear that Aspen was there. He wondered if she was a regular.

They walked across the street and down a block. It was the only building with its sign on. As they entered, the bar's atmosphere was the opposite of the shelter. A couple of enormous TVs were showing a repeat hockey game, country music blared from somewhere, and a full contingent of drinkers filled the stools at the bar.

Rory tapped Jefferson on the arm and motioned toward a booth in the back.

Aspen was hard to miss. She had bright red hair with bangs cut about an inch above her eyebrows. Not any kind of natural red, but the kind only found in a bottle, somewhere between blood red and cheap pizza sauce. She pulled it off, though.

She noticed them walking toward her and looked instantly annoyed.

It always surprised Jefferson how young Aspen looked. Their paths didn't cross often, so it was the kind of thing he forgot until the next time he saw her. He realized it again as they reached her table. She wore heavy makeup, but in the way young girls do, with heavy eyeliner and thick lashes. She stared up at them, waiting for one of them to speak.

"Hello, Aspen," said Rory.

"Hello detectives," she said with forced pleasantry. Then she glanced at the man sitting across from her. "Do you two know Mr. Atherton?"

Jefferson tried to keep his shock from showing. What was Atherton doing in this joint, and with Aspen Klein?

"Atherton of Atherton Development?" asked Jefferson as if he didn't know.

Atherton stood up and reached out a hand. "One and the same."

He wore a blue oxford, no tie. His hair had just the right amount of salt and pepper. He fit in at the Captain's Closet about as well as Aspen would fit in at his country club.

Jefferson shook his hand but kept his eyes directly on the man's face, watching every facial expression.

"It is an honor to meet you gentlemen," Atherton said. "I am in awe of everything our law enforcement and other first responders are doing right now. It's such a difficult time. I hope you grabbed some food from Agua Azul today?"

"Yes, we," Rory glanced at Jefferson, "I mean, I did. Generous of you." Rory said, shaking his hand.

"Ah, it was the least we could do. I'm sure you guys are burning the candle at both ends."

"Something like that," said Rory. Then he turned to the woman. "Aspen, can we have a word?"

Jefferson noticed that even though Atherton's words were full of confidence, his demeanor was all nerves. He did not like being caught in this situation. Atherton jumped on the chance to leave. He took out his wallet and threw some bills on the table.

"Ms. Klein, can we continue our discussion at another time?"

"Sure," she said with an air of non-committal.

"Gentlemen," said Atherton with a nod. And then, without a backward glance, he left.

"Sorry to ruin your date," said Rory, as he slid into the booth across from Aspen. Jefferson took off his coat and did the same.

She snorted. "Date. That's funny. No, that dude just wants to buy my support."

Rory cocked his head. "Buy? Support for what?"

She looked at Rory like he was stupid. "Come on," she said incredulously. "For city council. He is one of the guys applying with the county to be appointed. Didn't give much time for the dust to settle, eh?"

"So why is he talking to you?" Jefferson asked.

She shrugged and sipped her drink. "I guess they have to have character witnesses or something. I don't know why he's asking me. Most of those county jerks hate me. Feeling's mutual."

A waitress walked toward the table, ready to take their order. Jefferson waved her off before she got there. She looked annoyed, but then just shrugged, put her pen and pad back in her apron, and walked away.

Aspen took another sip of whatever was sitting in front of her. "I have a theory."

She leaned forward and whispered. "I think he and his buddies at the county think it will be too obvious that they plan to develop the hell out of this town. They want some support from the fringe. And I," she said, sitting back and making a flourish with her arm, "am the fringe." She smirked. "He promised a bunch of money for the shelter, though."

"Well, I guess you have quite the dilemma," Jefferson said.

"Um no," she said. "But he at least paid for my drinks."

Jefferson smiled despite himself. "This is all very interesting, but we need to talk to you about something else."

"Okay . . . I think. What?"

"You know Dylan Warren?"

"Yeah, great kid. He's been helping me with the 'Understanding the Unhoused' campaign." Her expression became somber. "Well, he was. I don't know what will become of it now. Council Member Silva was leading it for the city. I'm hoping Forsberg will take it on. Thank the universe she survived."

Jefferson remembered how much Forsberg had praised Aspen. They must be tight allies.

"Did you see Dylan yesterday at all?" Rory asked.

She traced the rim of her glass with her finger as she tried to remember, or decide, whether to tell them. Jefferson guessed she was feeling pretty good after her drinks, because she seemed less caustic than usual.

"Yeah, he came by around lunchtime. I remember because he loves grilled cheese, and that was on the menu."

Rory continued. "Did he say anything or seem to act differently than normal?"

"He seemed a little hyped up, but you know the people I work with don't really have a normal." She caught Jefferson's eye and then looked at her hands.

He sensed she had more on her mind.

"Aspen," Jefferson said. "This is really important. We have evidence that Dylan delivered the bomb that killed Silva and the others."

Her head snapped up. "What makes you say that?"

Jefferson and Rory exchanged glances.

"Just before the explosion," Rory began. "Dylan delivered a duffle bag to Council Member Silva. We have it on security footage. That bag is the source of the explosion."

She stared at them. Then she covered her face with her hands.

"No," she said. "You don't understand. Silva asked for unhoused people to bring him bags with their most important earthly possessions. He was going to show them at the meeting. That's what Dylan was bringing." She sat back. "Not a bomb. You're just wrong." She folded her arms and glared at them.

"We have heard something about Silva's request. Maybe Dylan thought that's what he was doing," Rory suggested. "Can you think of any reason he might take a bag that didn't belong to him?"

"Have you asked him about this?" She asked. "I mean, I'm not even sure I should talk to you about it without his permission." Her face crinkled into a sneer. "Just like the police to pin this on a homeless person."

There's the Aspen we know and love, thought Jefferson. He lowered his voice as he broke the news. "Aspen, Dylan is dead."

She looked back and forth between them, like she expected one of them to let her in on the joke. When no punchline came, her arms dropped to her side. She looked up at the ceiling and blew out a long breath.

When she looked back at them, her glassy eyes reflected the lights. "How?" she asked.

"We can't share the details," Jefferson lowered his voice almost to a whisper, "but we consider it a homicide."

"Murdered?" She plopped her elbows on the table and put her fists against her eyes. "No, no, no!"

She sat that way for some time. An upbeat country tune bounced through the air, at odds with the moment. Jefferson knew Dylan's death would hit her hard. With the amount of addiction, crime, and death that plagued the homeless community, she must suffer a lot, he thought.

When she pulled her hands away, her perfect eyeliner had smeared around her eyes. She groaned and sat back again. "He was just a kid."

"He was a kid that, for some reason, had $5,000 in his shoes." Jefferson watched Aspen with cat-like intensity.

"What?" she asked incredulously. "That's not possible. Dylan literally had nothing. I mean, the kid didn't even do drugs, but any money he scraped up doing odd jobs or panhandling, he spent on Rachel. If he had $5,000, I guarantee she would have spent it on drugs."

"Maybe she didn't know," Jefferson said. "He appeared to be hiding it."

Aspen shook her head and then held her hands up. "I don't have any idea if or why he had that much money. I can't explain it. But it sounds like whatever he was involved in cost him his life." She stomped the floor with her feet. "I am so angry! He deserved a chance!"

She put her head in her arms. Jefferson sensed she did not much like getting emotional in front of them. They'd be lucky if she didn't bolt.

Rory nodded. "We are trying hard to understand how this young man got mixed up in all of this. Can you think of any time when Dylan behaved differently, hanging out with new people, that kind of thing?"

Aspen sat up, but she covered her face with her hands and set her elbows on the table. Then she grabbed a napkin and blew her nose. Jefferson sensed a delay tactic and that she knew something, but didn't want to share it.

"Look, Aspen," he said. "I know how protective you are of the people in your program. And you should be. But I feel you know more than you are saying, and keeping quiet will not help Dylan or the people who died at city hall, including Silva, who was trying to help."

She balled the napkin into her fist. "Don't lecture me, detective. And excuse me if I don't automatically trust the police. You all do a lot of damage every time you destroy an encampment. And I get to pick up the pieces."

Jefferson sighed in frustration. He was too tired to do this soft sell for long.

"Alright," he said, looking over at Rory. "I guess we need to take her back to the station."

Rory nodded. "Sounds good. I bet there are a few donuts left, too."

Aspen rolled her eyes. "Oh okay, that's how you're going to play? Look, I don't believe for a second that you have any legal ability to 'take me to the station.'" She put her hands up in air quotes. "But I will tell you what I know, but only because of Dylan, not because of your empty threats." She stared at them with angry eyes.

Jefferson didn't care why she told them, just as long as she did. He waited. For too long, she still said nothing.

"And?" prompted Jefferson.

She took a drink. As she set down the now empty glass, the anger seemed to drain out of her. "There was a new guy." She didn't look at them but at the table as if a memory played out there.

"I'd never seen him before. He just showed up around a month ago," she said thoughtfully. "He and Dylan would hang out when they showed up for meals at the same time, even though he seemed to be quite a bit older than Dylan."

She looked up. "I tried to get some of his information once, and he was really cagey." She shifted in her seat. "That's not all that unusual with the unhoused, but I just got a weird vibe. He said his name was Job, which I thought was weird." She glanced up at them. "I doubt that was his real name. I mean, who names their kid that?" She folded her arms.

"Job was the man in the Bible who lost everything because God and the devil made a deal to see how much suffering he could stand, and still be faithful to God," Rory informed them.

"Yes, I know," Aspen snapped. "That's why people don't use that name. I may hate religion, but it's only after growing up stewed in it."

She pressed her arms tighter together. "Anyway," she continued, "this Job guy got really into the campaign. He volunteered to hand out flyers to the people at camps in the area, letting them know about it." She put her finger to her lips. "But the part that I think might be important is that I remember hearing him tell Dylan not to worry about getting a bag together for Silva."

"Why?" asked Jefferson.

"I only heard him say they had enough. There were many unhoused people who wanted to help but didn't want to appear before the council, so I figured Dylan would deliver someone else's bag. I was only halfway listening. We were handing out gloves and hats." She unwound her arms and put her palms on the table. "I thought nothing of it—until now."

She stared ahead. Jefferson wondered what she was thinking. Her eyes shifted back to them and away from whatever she'd seen in her mind.

"That's it," she said. "I haven't seen that guy in a while. I was glad he moved on. He gave me the creeps."

"What did he look like?" asked Rory.

"Ha," she said, "a bit like a Job, I think. White guy, long graying hair and a long beard that needed a serious trim. I'd guess he was forty-something."

Both the detectives were writing. "Do you have security cameras?" Jefferson asked.

She pointed at him with a long, skinny finger. "For that, you will need a warrant. They are only on the outside, but I have too many vulnerable people to allow that."

"You mean criminals," Jefferson said.

"Some may have warrants out." She said with a slow nod, as if that was the most normal thing in the world.

"You should expect to see our warrant quickly. No judge is going to get in the way of a lead on this case." Jefferson put his notebook away, and Rory did the same.

"Thanks, Aspen," Rory said, scooting out of the booth. "We'll be in touch."

Jefferson stood and pulled his coat back on. "I would suggest having that footage ready to go," he said. "The easier you make it, the faster it will go."

"We'll see," she said, motioning to the waitress.

Jefferson shook his head and walked away. That had gone better than he expected.

Chapter Twenty-Eight

As soon as they were back in the car, Jefferson called the station to update Amber and have her start the warrant process. She didn't think it would happen until the morning, so she instructed them to go home and get a few hours of rest. They were to be at a briefing at 7 a.m.

When Jefferson finally made it home, he stepped in the door and slipped off his shoes. They were in sad shape, but he was too tired to care. It smelled fresh inside, and he realized his cleaning lady must have been by since his nap and shower earlier. He was immediately grateful. Oh, how he loved cleaning day, especially on an extremely stressful day—no, week—like the one he'd just endured.

He knew there would be no sleep for him if he didn't shower again, and he had an awesome shower. The water pressure coming out of its monsoon shower head would wash away the dregs of the day. His bathroom, with its cavernous shower, was the place in his house where he'd spent a lot of money. The rest was what he'd call well-appointed functional. He bought nothing cheap, but he bought little. The place was functional, neat, and didn't require a ton of upkeep.

After showering, he slipped into a t-shirt and sweatpants. The shower did its work, but he still had too much running through his mind.

He walked over to the fridge and poured himself a glass of lemon sparkling water. His stomach wanted food, but the thought of starting something, even just microwaving, felt like too much to attempt right now.

He grabbed the remote to his sound system and turned on some music. "Do I Wanna Know" by the Arctic Monkeys started thumping out of the speakers. This was the last thing he listened to before leaving for his dad's funeral. He ran a hand through his hair. There were so many things he wanted to know, but wished he didn't need to know.

Standing at the patio doors, he stared out at the blackness, interrupted here and there by streetlights. He didn't live on the water, but in the daylight, he had a view of Mt. Rainier when the clouds permitted it. He found himself thinking about the view out of MJ Brooks' window. Then he was thinking about MJ Brooks. What a headache she'd turned into. He hoped the interview with Rachel would be the last time he'd have to deal with her. He'd already had too much of her type of help.

They needed to find this killer soon, for a lot of reasons, one of them being no more interactions with MJ Brooks. She had provided them with some important information, but he had a nagging sense that she would keep butting in until something disastrous happened. He didn't need another thing to worry about.

Something Aspen said had really bothered him. It wasn't just the bit about the guy hanging around Dylan. It was how she'd been grateful that Forsberg had survived the blast. Jefferson wondered if that was a mistake on the bomber's part, or if Forsberg was involved.

Dylan probably wasn't the culprit, not on his own anyway, and maybe not at all. He'd been murdered to hide the actual killer's identity; Jefferson was almost sure of that. Was Forsberg alive because she was in on the plan? Or, if the council members were the target, did the murderer not know she would be gone? What if he tried to finish the job? What if she knew who bombed city hall? Would the killer take her out too?

He should call it in. Maybe just have a patrol car swing around and check on the house. They wouldn't even have to wake her.

He picked up his phone. One call, and then he would go climb into his bed with its crisp clean sheets.

It was Brody, the officer in reception, who picked up.

"West Sound Police Department."

"Hey Brody, It's Jefferson Hughes. Any patrol officers in the building?"

"Um, I think Anderson and Romero are in the back. Want me to put you through?"

"Yes, please."

"Here you go."

It was only seconds before the absurdly perky voice of Shauna Anderson came on the line. "Officer Anderson here. What can we do for you?" Jefferson had to remind himself she was just starting her shift.

"Detective Hughes here."

"Hello Detective Hughes, what's up?"

"I am concerned about Council Member Forsberg, that she might be in some danger. Could you or another patrol swing by her house, check things out, and make sure everything is okay? No need to wake her or anything."

"Check Council Member Forsberg's house," she repeated. "Anything else?"

"No, that's it—"

"Jefferson?" It was Amber on the line.

"SSA Wells, you're still there?"

"Yeah. Look, I wasn't going to tell you this until the briefing tomorrow morning, but Jared has traced the threatening emails. And you will not believe this." He could hear her letting out a very controlled breath. "They came from two private email addresses belonging to Lisa Forsberg."

"What?"

"Yeah, I'm sure she didn't mention that bit when you interviewed her," she said with angry sarcasm. "While that doesn't make her a terrorist, it puts her squarely in the frame. We will be questioning her again. I gather from what I overheard that you want a patrol to go by her house?"

"That's right. I have nothing concrete, but I thought she might be in danger. I would feel better if they just did a drive-by. At least that was my idea a few minutes ago."

"Hmm," she said, thinking. "I will send them, but I'm not in a generous mood. She needs to come to the station. Tonight."

With the phone on speaker, Jefferson made his way to the bedroom. "I can be ready in five minutes. I'm close."

"Jeff, they can handle it. Go to bed. She can sit in a cell tonight. Let her sweat it out. We'll talk to her in the morning."

Jefferson could feel the exhaustion deep in his bones. Amber was right, but he did not want to miss Forsberg's reaction to being taken in for questioning. She could very well know more about this explosion than anyone wanted to believe, including him. He hadn't doubted her earlier protestations and emotional response to losing colleagues. Now, all he had were more questions.

"If it's all the same, I would like to be there when they put her in the car."

Amber chuckled softly. "I don't blame you, but this is not on me. You understand that, right? I need you to get some rest, so if you go, then it's right back home and to bed. Got it?"

"Got it."

"I'm headed home for a bit of sleep myself. Let me know if anything happens that can't wait until six hours from now."

"Will do."

They hung up. Jefferson looked down at his t-shirt and sweatpants. He cringed, but that couldn't be helped right now. He did not want to miss this.

***

Jefferson arrived before the uniformed officers. He parked across the street from Forsberg's house to wait. Clouds had scuttled across the moon, and no other light shone on or near the looming old house. It sat on a corner lot with the house facing the street where Jefferson parked and the garage facing the other street.

Jefferson thought it strange they didn't have any landscape lighting. The shadowy yard swallowed the walkway to the front door. Maybe they had motion sensors on their lights.

He might as well close his eyes for the few minutes it would take the patrol car to get there. As he leaned back, a movement on the side of the house caught his attention. He sat up, straining to make out what he was seeing. He could swear he saw movement at the garage window.

With his eyes fixed on the spot, Jefferson slowly opened the car door and crept toward the house.

When he was within a few feet of the garage, a black-clad figure of a man dropped from the window to the ground. The figure turned to stare in Jefferson's direction, as if sensing someone was there. At first, Jefferson wasn't sure the man had seen him. Then, the figure suddenly turned and darted into the dark.

"Stop!" Jefferson yelled. "Police!"

The darkness enveloped the man. Though he couldn't see him, Jefferson had a good idea of the direction he had gone. He followed, running past the garage and across the lawn toward the neighboring house. Looking down the road, Jefferson could just decipher the outline of the mysterious figure running away.

Before he could continue after him, an ear-splitting eruption came from behind him. He felt a rush of heat blow over him, and he instinctively covered his head. He turned to see a room of flames where the Forsberg's garage once stood, flames that were quickly traveling to the rest of the house.

He glanced back down the road, wanting to chase down that man with every fiber of his being. But he knew his first job was to get the Forsbergs out of that house before they had two more dead bodies on their hands.

He ran back to the front of the house while calling 911. Shouting the address into his phone, he ran up the porch to the door. He tried the handle, but it was locked. Please let them be awake, Jefferson thought. He pulled his sweatshirt sleeve down over his hand and punched through a pane of glass near the door handle. As he was reaching through to find the lock, he heard the sirens and saw the blue lights of the patrol cars rounding the street corner. The fire department wasn't more than a few blocks away, but Jefferson knew he couldn't wait.

He found the deadbolt, twisted his hand around, and turned it. He flung the door open, and smoke rushed at him. Covering his nose with the neck of his sweatshirt, he moved toward the area where he remembered seeing the stairs. To his left, he saw flames beginning to eat into the wall of the kitchen. He only had seconds before the smoke would become too much to manage.

He found the stairs and started up them, blinded by the dark and the smoke filling the room. Then he heard coughing above him. "Lisa! Ray! Come toward me!" he shouted as he bolted up the stairs.

As he came to the second floor, he saw Ray hunched over, coughing, trying to pick up the lifeless-looking body of Lisa.

Jefferson went to them and put his hand on the man's shoulder. "Ray! I've got her. Get out!"

Ray looked around, disoriented. "She won't wake up," he said, looking down at Lisa on the floor. "She won't wake up, and I can't—" He bent over in a coughing fit.

Jefferson grabbed his arm.

"Let me get Lisa. Then you follow me. Got it?"

The man nodded his head, but Jefferson wasn't sure he understood. The smoke was growing by the second.

Jefferson reached down and lifted Lisa so that she was lying over his shoulder, thankful she was a small woman. He started down the stairs slowly to make sure Ray followed. Thankfully, the old man stayed on Jefferson's heels.

Once down the stairs, Jefferson hurried toward the door just as the firefighters in all their gear were running up the walk. One of them grabbed Lisa, and another grabbed Jefferson's arm and ran with him away from the door. He looked behind him and did not see Ray. He yanked his arm free from the firefighter.

"Ray is still in there!" he shouted. "He was right behind me!"

"I'll get him, sir," said the firefighter. "You get out. Now."

Other firefighters were on the porch, and a group of them went back to find Ray.

Jefferson staggered down the porch, sucking in as much air as his lungs would allow. He turned around and stood with his hands on his knees, watching the front door intently. It was a chaotic scene. Water spewed from a ladder truck onto the house, an ambulance went tearing off into the night, probably with Lisa. Men and women in uniform were scrambling across the yard doing their various jobs. So much of the house had burned. He knew how lucky he was to be out of it alive.

He felt himself being pulled away. "Sir," someone was saying, "we need to check you over."

He pulled his arm away. "Wait. I need to . . ." his voice trailed off as he sucked in a breath. What is taking so long?

He wanted to run back in. He knew where Ray was and could help them.

He moved toward the house, but a paramedic grabbed his arm. "Sir, you need to come now."

Jefferson ripped his arm free just as a shout went up from someone nearby. "They got him!"

Relief rushed through him. He sank to a squat, his face in his hands.

***

When Jefferson finally convinced the emergency medical personnel that he didn't need a trip to the hospital, he went back to his car to call Amber. He figured this qualified as important enough to wake her.

He relayed everything that happened, adding that he'd put out an all-points bulletin for the man seen leaving the garage. Jefferson didn't think for a second they'd find him. This guy knew what he was doing and would be long gone or well hidden by now.

"I'm not sure of Lisa Forsberg's condition," he said. "The paramedics said she was alive, but that was about all they could tell me. I think I'll go check in at St. John's before I head home."

"Nope." The sternness in her voice surprised him. "No, you will not. Bed, Jefferson. They will not tell you anything tonight, won't let you talk to her tonight, so have the officers on duty call her family. Then they can go to the hospital and set up a watch outside her room. You are done tonight. I need you at 7 am. Go home."

He didn't even try to argue. He knew she was right, and as the adrenaline left his body, fatigue was taking its place. So, he went home, took another shower, and as soon as his head hit the pillow, the overwhelming exhaustion gave way to a deep, dreamless sleep.

Chapter Twenty-Nine

When MJ and Toni arrived home from the station, they said very little. The drive had been quiet. They were both exhausted, and MJ couldn't get the composite sketch out of her head. Despite her fuzzy memory, Jared had created a face that looked vaguely familiar, like she knew it from the past. Her brain was so fried that she could not access the parts of her memory that might hold the secret. She found it very frustrating.

The two women unceremoniously, and a bit zombie-like, did their nightly routines. When MJ climbed into her guest bed, she knew sleep would come.

She'd dozed off easily, and it wasn't long before deep sleep overtook her.

Edgar's barking didn't immediately wake MJ. She'd been hearing it for a few minutes, but her sleeping brain refused to let her acknowledge it.

Then a knock on the door. This broke through, and it startled her awake. Staring at the ceiling, MJ listened to Edgar barking and her heart thumping in her ears.

She got up and threw on a sweatshirt and shorts. It was probably Claire checking on her, though it was late for her to be up. Or was it morning? She did not know how long she'd been asleep. She checked her phone by the bed as the knocking came again. It was one in the morning.

Her mom was standing in the doorway of her room.

"I've got it, Mom. You can go to bed."

"No, I am not, and you should be careful. Don't open that door unless you know who it is."

She walked toward the door, turning her back to her mom. "I'm sure it's fine."

MJ wasn't really sure it was fine, but she wasn't about to cower behind her mother. I am an adult, thought MJ, and I am going to answer my door, with Edgar close by, of course.

She looked through the peephole. What she saw there put ice in her veins. Or was it a white, hot, angry fire? She stood there, deciding whether to open it.

"Who is it, MJ?" said her panicking mother.

MJ groaned and opened the door.

"Hello, MJ."

Justin, her ex-husband, stood on the porch holding a desert camo duffle bag. He flashed his prize-winning grin.

Edgar rushed forward and jumped up like a crazy dog.

"Hey boy," said Justin, rubbing the dog's head. "I missed you, too."

"What are you doing here, Justin?"

"What kind of greeting is that?" He laughed. "Come on, let me in and I'll explain."

She reluctantly stood back and held the door open.

He stepped by her and set his bag down on the floor with Edgar on his heels. It annoyed MJ that the dog still liked him.

"Toni! I didn't know you were here."

They walked toward each other and hugged.

"It's good to see you," Toni said, smiling. She always loved Justin. From the outside, there was a lot to love.

"Okay," said MJ, shutting the door. "Explain."

Justin sat down on the couch, still petting Edgar. "

"Come on, sit down, MJ."

There he goes, she thought, already telling me what to do.

"I'm fine standing," she said, folding her arms.

Her mother sat next to Justin and yawned. "So, where are you these days?"

He glanced up at MJ, clearly uncomfortable that she wouldn't just sit down.

"Georgia, and now, JBLM," he said.

MJ stared at him, not believing what she just heard. Joint Base Lewis-McChord was practically in the backyard of West Sound. "What?" she whispered.

"Yeah, I finished my last overseas tour. Now I'm training guys here."

"But when? I mean, how long have you been here?" MJ finally sat down. This was too shocking to handle standing up.

"I think it's been about a week now, but I've been back and forth between here and Georgia a few times. I had a few things to sell out there, some other stuff to take care of."

He clasped his hands together and sat forward with his elbows on his knees. "But let's talk about why I'm here, here. At your house."

"Yes, why is that? And in the middle of the night." MJ asked, regaining her annoyance.

"Um, sorry about that. My flight from Georgia was late." He cleared his throat. "Anyway, I heard about the explosion at the city hall.

Well, everyone's heard about it." He looked between MJ and Toni. "But imagine my surprise when I got a call from a Special Agent Julia somebody wanting to ask me a few questions."

MJ hung her head. She had really hoped the detectives would leave Justin out of this. She knew what was coming next, and it made her cringe inside.

"I'm sorry," said MJ. "I told them they shouldn't bother you."

"Shouldn't bother me," he repeated incredulously. "MJ, you should have told me what happened. I can't believe I had to hear that from the FBI. You could have been killed!" His eyes were wide with concern.

"But I wasn't, Justin. I'm okay, really."

"Well, it doesn't matter. I have a few days before all my stuff arrives, so unless you are going to kick me out, I'm going to stay here just to make sure you are okay. I can sleep on the couch, whatever, but with some maniac out there blowing people up, I just need to know you're safe."

"Well, I think that sounds like a fine idea," Toni said enthusiastically. "And I am looking forward to catching up with you tomorrow. But for now, this old bird needs to get back to bed. It's been a long, long day."

"Of course." He kissed Toni on the cheek as she got up to go.

"Goodnight," Toni said as she headed back to bed.

MJ was too tired to argue with Justin. She decided she would deal with this development in the morning.

"I'm exhausted, too," she said. "But we will talk about this tomorrow. I will get you some blankets and then I'm going to bed."

"Sounds good." He stood up and took his shirt off.

She turned away. This was not the night she was expecting.

Chapter Thirty

School was about to start. It was still dark out, but lights blazed from inside the building. MJ stood at the doors, trying to unlock them, but her key wouldn't fit.

She put a hand up to the window and looked inside. Some students were walking down the hall while others were standing at their lockers. They were laughing and chatting like normal.

She knocked on the door, but no one came. They didn't even look at her.

They hate me, she thought. All of them hate me.

A sense of deep loss enveloped her in a suffocating fog. She knew she had to get away.

Just as she turned to go, someone pushed the door open.

"MJ!" said Troy with a big smile. "You're late."

Relief flooded through her. He was still here. It wasn't real, she thought with joy.

She smiled and rushed to hug him.

A gust of wind blew her backward.

She watched in horror as first Troy, and then the school, erupted in flames.

Her own anguished cry woke her.

EXPLOSION ON THE SOUND

Her eyes flew open. Her breath came fast as the truth rushed back at her.

She was in her own room, and Troy was dead.

Pulling the covers up to her chin, she rolled over and closed her eyes, her heart still beating with the reality of her dream. She wiped away a couple of unwelcome tears. Why did it have to be real?

She tried to think about something else, anything else, but as hard as she tried, the dream clung to her like moss on rocks. Pieces of it replayed over and over.

Controlling her breath took all her energy and focus. Slowly, the vivid images faded into a mirage of loss and regret.

Rain hit her window in bursts. It must be windy, she thought. Poor Edgar, no walk in this weather. Then she sniffed the air. Bacon. She sat up, sniffing again. Was her mother cooking?'

A man's voice punctuated the air. Suddenly, she remembered who had shown up on her doorstep last night.

She groaned and laid back down. Was there somewhere else she could stay and just let her mother and Justin have the place?

Then she heard another woman.

She listened again. That voice belonged to Claire. It was a downright party out there. That was Justin, throwing his charm around like confetti.

After throwing on some sweats and one of her school hoodies, she wandered sleepily into the kitchen.

"Well, hello, Sunshine," said her mother, already dressed and not only presentable but stunning.

MJ grunted and headed for the teakettle. "Morning, Mom, Claire," she said with a yawn.

"Morning, MJ. I hope you don't mind that Justin invited me in. I came down to check on you and imagine my surprise to find him here." Her tone was not as effusive as Toni's. The charm had not done its magic on her, and that made MJ smile inside. She and Claire had talked quite a bit about MJ's relationship with Justin, something that was hard for her to do with her mother.

Justin was at the stove cooking something that she had to admit smelled delicious. Her mother and Claire sat perched on the barstools watching him work.

"Uh, uh, uh," Justin tutted at MJ. "I already boiled your water and your mug with some tulsi mint is on the table waiting to steep."

MJ stared at him and willed herself not to scream. This was him, pretending to be nice when he just wanted to control her.

"Well," said MJ, "I was thinking of having chamomile this morning."

He laughed. "Are you thinking of going back to bed? You know how that makes you sleepy."

"Then I'll have chai," she said between gritted teeth.

He turned to glance at her briefly. His brow furrowed, but he turned back to his pan.

"Well, the egg and bacon hash are ready, so let me dish up the plates and then we can dig in." He looked at her again, but this time with his broad, perfect smile that was all confidence. His eyes, however, didn't quite match the bravado of his mouth. She wondered when he would quit playing this part. Quit trying to be her life commander. He clearly knew it wasn't working any better now than it did when they were married.

"I need to feed Edgar and let him out," she said, looking around for the dog.

"Already done," smiled Justin. "I was early enough to beat the rain, so he's fat, happy, and tuckered out, over on his pillow."

MJ saw Edgar was indeed snoozing like a log, which he never did when food was about to be served. She was grudgingly grateful for Edgar's sake.

"Thanks." She grabbed the chai and filled her mug. Then she walked to the table as Claire and her mother followed, carrying their own steaming mugs. Justin set plates down in front of them and then sat down himself.

"This looks wonderful, Justin," beamed Toni.

Claire nodded. "Yeah, I don't think I've eaten bacon since 1990, but I will today."

MJ ate quietly. It was very good, and she had eaten little since coming home from the hospital.

"Well," said Justin in between bites, "the police want me to come down and answer some questions on the record."

MJ put her fork down and stared in disbelief. "Why? Didn't you already talk to the FBI?"

Justin shrugged. "Yeah, but now that they know I'm local, they want to nail down my alibi."

"You're local now?" asked Claire, with just a hint of alarm in her voice. She caught MJ's eye.

"Yeah, stationed at JBLM for the foreseeable future." He shoveled another bite in.

"Alibi?" Toni said, her eyes widening. "Whatever for?"

He set his eyes on each of the women. "Ladiieeees," he said with parent-like patience. "It's not unusual for the police to want to check out the ex when there's a murder. I mean, MJ is fine, but plenty of people try super outlandish schemes to kill their ex." He took a big mouthful of food and chewed like his jaw was a battering ram.

They all stared at him. No one seemed to know what to say. A shiver rolled down MJ's spine at the cavalier way in which he mentioned people plotting to kill their ex.

He shrugged again. "Anyway, it's not a big deal. But MJ," he looked at her and took a sip of his coffee, "they say you can get the Bronco, too. You just have to sign some paperwork." He sat back in his chair. "I figure we can kill two birds with one stone and head to the police station together."

MJ recoiled at the idea, especially since he had taken charge of her plans for the day. But she had to admit, she was eager to get her car. And with a little luck, she might get to talk to the detectives and see if they've made any progress. She also wanted to find out where they'd taken Rachel so she could check on her.

She sipped her tea and nodded at Justin. "Sounds like a plan."

***

Jefferson made it to the briefing by 6:55 a.m. Though he'd only had a few hours' sleep, his mind felt sharp and eager to go. His blood was still boiling from what that maniac had almost done to the Forsbergs. That the scum had just narrowly slipped out of his clutches made his need to catch him even more urgent.

As soon as Jefferson entered the meeting room, he could feel tension pulsing through the air. All the bigwigs were there. The region's FBI Special Agent in Charge Chad Wilson and U.S Attorney Paul Morgan joined Chief Carlson and SSA Wells.

The need to show progress in the case weighed on all the law enforcement officers. The pressure from above fell mostly on SSA Wells and Chief Carlson. Having a cadre of bosses in the room was like putting them all in a pressure cooker inside of a pressure cooker.

"Good morning, everyone," Amber said as the group got settled. "I'm sure most of you have heard about the attempt on the lives of Ray and Lisa Forsberg last night. We have Detective Hughes to thank for saving their lives."

A round of clapping and whistles erupted around the room.

"Way to go, Jeffy," Rory said, clapping and nudging Jefferson with his elbow.

Jefferson bowed his head and briefly put his hand up. He really did not enjoy this attention. It was pure coincidence that he was there to get the Forsbergs out of their burning house. Any of these officers would have done the same, he knew that.

Amber nodded at him, then glanced at her bosses, Morgan and Wilson, who stood against the wall in the back of the room.

"That's good work," Wilson said with no expression on his stony face. "This is probably the most serious case any of you will face, and we recognize the sacrifices you are making. We have the same goal, and that is to find the person or persons responsible for these acts and bring them to justice. Continued progress is what we need now."

No one else spoke. Was that an admonishment or a compliment? Jefferson knew he wasn't the only one who suspected Wilson intended it as both.

SSA Wells looked sideways at Wilson. "Thank you, sir."

Jefferson suppressed a smile. Amber focused on the compliment and ignored the rest.

She continued, "Jefferson witnessed a man climbing out of the Forsberg's garage window just before it exploded. The fire spread quickly to the rest of the house. A man of medium build, dressed all in black, is all we know. Federal and local forensics teams are at the scene now. We hope for some breakthrough there, but don't get your hopes up."

"This complicates another part of our investigation regarding Council Member Forsberg. Julia will share more of that information now."

Julia stood up. "Jared and I have been attempting to trace the email threats received by at least three West Sound council members. We determined these threats were coming from two private email accounts held by Lisa Forsberg, as I think most of you are aware by now, but we wanted to share some details."

She picked up a piece of paper from the table. "The threats were mostly dealing with the environment, with such phrases as 'you'll burn in hell if you vote against the shoreline protection act, what if someone raped you the way you are raping the environment, kill the trees at your own peril, watch your votes because I'm watching you and I know where you live.'"

Julia looked up at the group. "Most of them are over the top, even juvenile sounding, like maybe Forsberg wrote them trying to make them appear to be the work of some crazed greener. They also seem crafted to appear as a direct threat or just a play on words."

"What is the timeframe of the emails, recent or . . . ?" Larson asked.

"They are spread out over two years, actually." Julia shrugged. "No one seems to have taken them seriously. This is the first anyone in the police department is hearing about them." She glanced at Chief Carlson, who nodded once in agreement.

"Thanks, Julia," Amber said. "We will most likely have time to question her later today. She is conscious and in stable condition. Her husband reported that she'd taken a sleeping pill," she said, looking at Jefferson. "That accounts for why she was unconscious when Jefferson removed her from the house. A sleeping pill combined with smoke inhalation could have been a deadly combo for Mrs. Forsberg."

"There is another issue with Forsberg. I've called the number she gave the detectives for her sister. Multiple times. No answer." Julia punctuated the last bit with a stab of her pen in the air. "So far, I can not verify her trip with an actual person. Her itinerary checks out, but until we talk to the sister . . ." She shrugged.

"The councilwoman gets more and more interesting as we go," said Amber, tapping the table with her pen. "It's possible neither of these issues relates to the explosion at city hall. But it's possible they do. Keep calling the sister."

"Will do."

Amber paused before speaking again. She seemed to weigh her words carefully.

"I believe that this separate attack, on a surviving council member, points to the conclusion that the council was indeed the target." She took a deep breath. "Which means these two explosions were likely set by the same person or people."

"And Forsberg is still a target," added Rory.

"Or does she know the killer's identity?" Jefferson looked around the room. "If she is involved, wouldn't the killer want to quiet her like he did Dylan?"

Amber nodded in agreement. "That's what we need to find out. Either way, we will keep her safe. We have federal officers at the hospital now. We will use a combo of federal and local officers to keep her under protection until we have this killer behind bars. Detective Hughes and Jackson, I'd like you to follow up with the councilwoman about these emails."

Jefferson focused on Amber with a satisfied grin. "I was hoping you'd say that."

She smiled. "They'll be glad to see you, I'm sure of that."

He wasn't so sure about that.

"On another front," she said, her face turning serious again, "Jared, how goes the hunt for the pumpkin tie man?"

Jared looked up from his computer as if he'd been in the middle of that hunt when Amber said his name. "I have been applying the sketch we created from Ms. Brooks' description to all our databases," he said, looking back at his computer screen.

Jefferson couldn't help but think how uncomfortable the young man seemed when he looked at real people instead of his computer. The added stress of being watched by the higher-ups made it worse for him. Regardless, Jared's expertise was undeniable.

"I have had no hits yet on full facial recognition." Deep furrows sat between Jared's thick, black brows as he eyed the computer screen like it was to blame for his lack of progress. "I'm going to look for just partial facial features. It's not as exact and could mean many more useless returns," he looked up briefly, "but it might get us something." He hid his face in his screen again.

Amber nodded. "We are not sure of this guy's importance or if he has any, but his being so hard to find is troubling. There is no security footage of him anywhere in the vicinity before or after the explosion."

"Is it possible Brooks made him up?" asked Ron. "I mean, she was probably pretty out of it."

This question rankled Jefferson. Why would she make it up? The idea was ridiculous.

Jefferson realized everyone was looking at him. He gazed incredulously between all the faces. "What? How would I know?"

"You've spent the most time with her," Ron said with a smirk. "What's your feeling about it?"

Jefferson wanted to ignore the question, but knew he should answer honestly. "As annoying as she can be, I don't doubt her story."

"I agree," Amber said. "So Jared will keep at it. Jefferson, Rory, what did you get from your interview with Aspen Klein?"

Rory started flipping through his notebook. "The most significant information is that Dylan Warren had been hanging around a guy new to the homeless scene, at least according to Aspen. Went by the name Job, which she thought was weird. Um, white guy, long hair that was graying, probably about 40s, and a long scraggly beard."

Amber nodded. "Your warrant for the surveillance video should be here any minute." She glanced at Morgan, who nodded in confirmation. "Since you'll be at the hospital, I'd like Larson and Mendez to handle that with Aspen today."

Jefferson nodded. "Fantastic." He tilted his head thoughtfully. "One other thing that was odd. When we arrived to see her, Klein was at the Captain's Closet meeting with Jon Atherton."

The chief's eyes widened. "That is odd."

"Not sure it's related," Jefferson added. "It surprised us to see those two together, and in that spot. He plans to apply for one of the vacant council positions."

Amber pointed her pen at Ron. "Can you do some digging there? See what you can find about Jon Atherton in relation to the city council in the past few years."

"Jon Atherton," Ron repeated, making a note. "Got it."

Amber looked around the room. For a moment, she seemed to droop just a bit under the gaze of the team and her bosses. But as soon as Jefferson noticed it, the droop was gone, and she stood straight. Jefferson knew she could put on a tough face when required, but he also wondered how she was really holding up.

"So far, we have been able to keep any information about Dylan Warren out of the news," she was saying. "The Forsberg attack, however, is already in the news this morning, so the chief and I will address that at a press conference today."

"There will be memorials happening in the next few days, and those are likely to take up most of the news cycle. As unfortunate as that may be, it gives us some time to make progress before the reporters get more demanding."

She gazed at them, meeting each person's eyes individually. "We have many pieces, but we don't even know if they all go into the same puzzle. Now we need to find how some of them fit and get some answers for this community."

She gave out a few more assignments before wrapping it up. "Anything else before we all head in our different directions?"

Julia spoke up. "I will take a formal statement from Justin Brooks today. That's the teacher's ex. Turns out he's been at JBLM since before the explosion. It's more of a formality, really. If he wanted to take her out, he probably wouldn't be staying at her place."

On hearing this, alarm bells sounded in Jefferson's head. He listened closely but sat perfectly still, willing his body to show no sign that this piece of news meant anything to him. It didn't, did it? It irritated him to admit that it did. That woman seemed to gravitate to trouble.

A distinct uneasiness sat in his gut. He had to make sure Justin didn't get discounted too fast. The way MJ tensed when they asked about him . . . There is something there.

He looked up to see Amber watching him. "What are you thinking, Hughes?"

He cleared his throat. "I think he could be completely unrelated, but his military background means he could have the skills to pull off an explosion like this. And him just showing up at the same time as the explosion," he shrugged. "I don't know. It feels like more than a coincidence. Just because MJ might trust him doesn't mean we should."

The room was quiet. Jefferson knew no one wanted to believe a military vet could do something so heinous. Many of their ranks were former military. But at this point, they had to consider everything.

"Agreed," said Amber. "It needs to be followed up. Julia, find out his military assignments. I'd be especially interested in knowing if he has experience handling explosives." She stopped, tapping her lips with her forefinger as if considering the possibilities. "Let me know if anything comes of it. We can overlook nothing when we still know so little."

Julia wrote her instructions.

Amber closed the meeting and sent the team to carry out their assignments. As they left, the door to the meeting room closed with SSA Wells, Chief Carlson, SAC Wilson, and U.S. Attorney Morgan left inside to continue the meeting. The idea of being stuck in that room for another hour made Jefferson's head hurt. Thank goodness there were people like Amber and the chief who stepped up to those roles. He respected them, but he knew that life was not for him.

Chapter Thirty-One

Avoiding the media turned out to be a challenge in the hospital parking lot. Jefferson had never seen so many news vehicles in the same place, and certainly not in West Sound. Several reporters and camera operators milled around, waiting for something new to report. They didn't allow any reporters near city hall, so it was the first time he'd seen them all gathered in one place.

Rory let out a long whistle as he pulled into a parking spot. "You might need a hat and some sunglasses, Jeffy. I'm sure they'd love to get your pretty face on TV."

"Whatever."

"I'm just saying. The city wants some good news right now, and I think you are it, my friend."

"Let's get this Forsberg interview over with," Jefferson said, opening his car door. Lisa Forsberg had some serious explaining to do. She either hid her threatening emails out of embarrassment or because they connected her to the explosion and murder. He was not in the mood to play nice for the cameras.

As they crossed the parking lot to the main doors of the hospital, at least one reporter recognized him. She motioned for her cameraman to follow as she jogged to catch up to Jefferson and Rory.

"Excuse me," she called out. "Aren't you Detective Hughes?"

They kept walking, but she reached them just as they were about to open the door.

"Detective Hughes, please," she said, grabbing his arm. "The community wants to hear from you. This has been such an awful time. They need a hero."

He turned to look at her. She had blond hair styled short and boyish, almost like his own.

"I was just doing my job," he said flatly. "And we have a lot more to do, so if you'll excuse us." He opened the door and he and Rory stepped inside.

A security guard came forward and reminded the reporter that the news crews had to stay outside.

"Well, that's bound to make the news," said Rory. "Do I look okay? Maybe I should've worn the navy suit today."

"Shut it, Rory." Jefferson walked briskly with his eyes straight ahead. He could feel Rory still grinning next to him.

They arrived at Lisa Forsberg's room as the doctor was leaving.

"How is she?" Jefferson asked as the man approached. He held up his badge for the doctor, whose eyes narrowed behind his thick-framed glasses. "Detective Hughes and Detective Jackson, West Sound PD."

The man's face relaxed into a surprised smile. "The man who saved her life." He shook Jefferson's hand. "She's doing better than expected and is eager to leave, but she won't be able to do so anytime soon. We'd like to keep her on oxygen for longer to ensure her lungs are clear before we release her."

Jefferson nodded. "That might be for the best."

The doctor's face became serious again. "I assumed so because of the precautions taken here."

"Is it a good time for us to ask her some questions?" asked Rory.

"Oh absolutely. She's wide awake." He arched his brows as if to say Forsberg was being her feisty self. "I'm sure she'd love the opportunity to thank you as well," he said with a glance toward Jefferson. He gave a busy man's smile before moving off. "I'll leave you to it, gentlemen. Best of luck with everything."

The detectives entered Lisa's room after checking in with the officers outside her door.

She sat up in her bed with a cell phone to her ear, looking up as they entered. A woman resembling Lisa sat in a chair next to the bed. Lisa motioned for Rory and Jefferson to come closer.

"Yes, thank you, sir," she said into the phone. "I am, and I will let you know as soon as I am released. Thank you again. Okay, goodbye."

She put the phone down. "The governor wishing me well," she said, motioning toward the device. Then a smile lit up her face. "But even the governor can't beat a visit from my knight in shining armor, Detective Hughes."

The woman in the chair glanced at Lisa and then Jefferson. "This is him?"

Lisa nodded, still smiling from ear to ear.

The younger woman jumped up and unexpectedly hugged Jefferson. He was so shocked he almost fell over. She was squeezing him tightly around his neck and he was awkwardly unsure what to do with his own arms.

"Thank you so much for saving my mother," the woman sniffled as she squeezed.

Finally, she let go and backed away.

Jefferson didn't dare look at Rory. He knew this would be great for a Jefferson roast.

Forsberg chuckled, "Detectives, this is my daughter, Rosalyn."

Rosalyn shook Rory's hand. "You just don't know how grateful we all are, especially my dad." She turned back to Jefferson. "If you hadn't shown up . . ." She stopped and then grabbed her mother's hand.

"It was a lucky coincidence," said Jefferson. "One with a fortunate outcome."

"It is nice to meet you, Rosalyn," Rory said. "Unfortunately, we need to talk to your mom about the events last night and some other things related to the case. Do you mind giving us a few minutes with her?"

"Oh, of course not." She looked down at her mom. "I'll go see what's keeping Dad with those coffees." She patted her mother's hand before picking up her purse and leaving the room.

As soon as her daughter left, Lisa Forsberg's smile faded, and she fiddled with the phone in front of her.

"Do you know why I was at your house last night, Councilwoman?" Jefferson asked.

She refused to look at them. "Not exactly."

Jefferson glanced at Rory, who looked knowingly back at him. Her demeanor suggested she knew why Jefferson had been at her home prior to rescuing her from the fire.

"Lisa, I think you know," Jefferson continued.

She finally looked up. Embarrassment kept her from being able to hold eye contact.

"I am guessing you found some emails," she admitted quietly, looking down at the phone again.

The detectives both pulled chairs over to sit down.

"Can you explain those emails?" Rory asked.

She said nothing at first. She grabbed a tissue and dabbed at the corners of her eyes.

"They were stupid, and I deeply, deeply regret sending them." When she finally met their eyes, hers were red and tired.

Jefferson narrowed his eyes. "What did you hope to gain by sending them?"

"I don't know," she said, raising her hands and letting them fall back in her lap in exasperation. "I don't know. I guess I hoped they might get sick of it and leave, step down, not run again. Whatever."

Jefferson narrowed his eyes. "So you were trying to intimidate them?"

She shrugged. "I guess you could call it that."

"Yes, that is exactly what we would call it," replied Rory. He sat forward. "We've seen email threats for three council members. Why those three in particular?"

She looked up at the ceiling as if trying to find the right words there.

"Because they were liars," she said finally. "They pretended to care about the best interests of the people and the environment, but then they would vote pro-growth. I couldn't stand what they were doing." She'd regained a small amount of her fiery self.

Jefferson eyed her. Her reactions to their next questions would reveal whether Lisa Forsberg had the icy heart of a murderer. Could she be extreme enough to justify killing?

"Did you hate them enough to want them dead?"

She swallowed as the color drained from her face. Her eyes were wide and fearful. "No," she choked out in a whisper. "Never."

"But you wrote some pretty nasty things," Rory reminded her.

She shook her head vehemently. "If I could take it back, bring them back, even with all their stupid ideas, I would. I didn't agree with them, but you must believe me. I could never hurt anyone like that. I know their families, their spouses, their children . . ." She stifled a sob.

"Your sister," Jefferson pushed. "The number you gave us is not working. Did you concoct that entire story so you could be out of town for the explosion? What else aren't you telling us?"

The sobbing became a torrent. "No, no, no," she bellowed, covering her hands with her face.

"Lisa, talk to us," Jefferson demanded.

After a few shaky breaths, she pulled her hands away from her face. Rory handed her the tissue box. She took a few and crumpled them in her hands without wiping her eyes.

"My sister," she said, her voice unsteady and breathy, "was planning a hiking trip after Cabo — some volcano near Mexico City." She took in a long, jagged breath. "She's probably out of range. Rosalyn tried to call her this morning, to let her know what happened."

Her eyes darted between them. "I know you don't have any reason to trust me now, but I swear that's the truth."

"And those stupid emails," she continued. "It was just me. No one else. There was no grand conspiracy to hurt people. Just me. Just stupid, stupid me." Remembering the tissues in her hand, she finally wiped at her drenched face.

The two detectives looked at each other. Jefferson sighed.

"Please, don't tell Ray or Rosalyn. They don't know, and I'm so ashamed."

"We won't be telling anyone anything while the investigation is ongoing, but we also can't promise this won't eventually become public knowledge," Jefferson warned. "You might find it the best course to tell them yourself."

She wiped her eyes and nodded.

"Does anyone else know about the emails?" Rory asked. "You didn't tell any of the other like-minded colleagues about your plan to intimidate the other council members?"

She shook her head. "It was just me, and honestly, it didn't work. I overheard them laughing about the crazy lady's emails." She smiled weakly.

"We'll have to leave it there for now. If you get ahold of your sister, be sure she calls one of us," Jefferson said. "We have a couple of other questions, and then we will let you get some rest."

"Anything," she said. "Ask me anything."

"There is the possibility that someone has a vendetta against the city council. We believe you are still in danger." Jefferson let that sink in, hoping it might help her focus. "Can you think of anyone who might want revenge on the council? Any disagreement, decisions, or policy that might trigger such a response?"

"We hardly ever voted unanimously on anything, so it's hard to think of anything controversial that would make someone hate all of us." She rubbed her hand across her face. "Can I give it some thought? Go back over old meetings and get back to you. Right now, I'm struggling to think straight."

Jefferson didn't doubt it. She looked unwell. Admitting to the emails couldn't have been easy, and she'd already had a dreadful night.

Jefferson nodded. "That's fine. Just let us know as soon as something comes to mind. Anything, no matter how insignificant it might seem to you."

"Of course." She laid her head back against the pillows. "And Detective Hughes, I may not deserve your good opinion right now, but I am still forever grateful for what you did for Ray and me. Truly."

Jefferson settled his gaze on her. "I'm glad you are both okay."

He and Rory stood up.

As they headed for the door, Jefferson stopped.

"You know, the guy who torched your house is still out there. And none of us," he said, moving his eyes between her and Rory, "will rest easy until we've got him. That's a promise."

Chapter Thirty-Two

MJ realized Justin had a new love. It turned out he didn't really miss the Bronco after all. He was driving them to the police station in his "fully restored 1980 Camaro, with a 1986 5.0L 305ci V8 with 4-speed manual transmission."

He'd repeated the car's specs to her from memory. It was white with a sassy blue stripe and a beautiful blue interior. She had to admit; it was a sexy car.

But she still didn't have to like Justin walking back into her life this way. She leaned against the passenger side door and gazed out the window as they drove around the inlet. The wind continued to blow, and the normally placid sound moved with the constantly shuffling peaks of choppy water. Thick clouds raced across the sky at a stormy pace. The rain had subsided for now, but an occasional thick drop hit the windshield. It was only a matter of time.

She sat up. "Can you stop at the 7-Eleven up ahead? I need some caffeine."

"Come on, babe. You know that's not good for you."

She gave him a death stare. "Don't 'babe' me."

He chuckled. "Fine, I'll stop."

"I'm serious, Justin. Don't call me that."

He shrugged. "Sure."

They pulled into the 7-Eleven parking lot. Justin slow-rolled the car, looking for a spot far away from potential door dingers. When he finally parked, MJ jumped out and slammed the door a little harder than she meant.

She took a deep breath, letting the cool, misty air fill her lungs. She needed to get better control of herself. Why did she let him do this to her?

In reality, he didn't *do* anything that she shouldn't expect. He was just Justin being Justin. She had to remember that he was, in fact, out of her life. As soon as she had her car, she would tell him to go. She didn't need his protection. She needed her sanity.

As she reached for the door to the 7-Eleven, her heart froze. Troy's face stared back at her from the glass. She recognized the picture from one of their Tropical Vacation spirit days at school. Underneath the picture were the words "Candlelight Vigil for Our Beloved Principal at Mariner Middle School."

She knew they were planning this vigil, but she had buried the reality by ignoring it. Coming face-to-face with the poster made it all too true.

Shannon had specifically asked her to come, saying that it would be healing for her, the students, and the staff.

MJ closed her eyes. She didn't know if she was ready to face them.

"Excuse me?" A woman was standing behind her, waiting to get in the store.

"Oh sorry," MJ opened the door and let the woman go in first, then she followed.

She was still deep in thought, walking mechanically toward the back of the store. She didn't notice the hooded man coming down the aisle with his head down until they ran smack into each other.

"Whoa! I'm so sorry," said MJ.

The man looked up quickly, his hood having fallen back.

MJ narrowed her eyes as she realized she'd seen him before. Then she remembered. "Hey! It's yo—!"

Before she could get the words out, the man dropped his purchases and pushed past her, knocking her into the rack of potato chips.

"Wait!" she yelled, chasing after him.

He ran out of the store with MJ on his heels.

"MJ!" she heard Justin yell after her.

"Call the police!" she yelled back.

The man was fast. Too fast. MJ stayed fit, but she was no match for this guy. He ran behind the 7-Eleven and then crossed the street, dodging traffic. Then he sprinted to the right down an alley. MJ followed, but when she reached the alley, he was nowhere in sight. With a brick wall on one side and chain-link fencing on the other, she guessed he climbed the fence. She leaned over with her hands on her knees, sucking air.

She heard steps behind her and turned to see Justin running toward her.

"What the heck was that all about?" he shouted. "You could have been hurt or killed, you know? Why would you go chasing some whacked-out dude?"

She turned and started walking back, still breathing hard. "I knew him."

"Um, so?" he said incredulously.

"Did you call the police?" she asked, irritated.

"No, I came running after you. I wasn't going to sit there on the phone while you got yourself killed."

"You came running after me?" She looked at him through narrowed eyes. Justin is fast, much faster than her. If he'd really run right after her, he'd have passed her easily. "I can't believe you didn't even call the police."

"Well, you are supposed to be resting. And why should I call the police on him? He probably needed whatever he took."

"Justin, he's . . ." She looked at her ex and realized she didn't want to tell him who that guy was. She herself was confused. Why did he run?

"Never mind, let's just go," she said. "But I am going to get that caffeine first."

When she walked back inside the store, the clerk glared at her as he mopped the area where her runner had dropped a bottle of something.

MJ walked over to the clerk.

"I'm really sorry about that," she said. "What did that guy drop? It looks like he made a mess."

"Why do you care? You a cop or something?" The glare didn't go away.

MJ laughed. "Oh, heavens no. I just saw that guy sticking things under his shirt," she lied, "and I guess I spooked him when I ran into him."

The glare softened a bit. "People are always lifting stuff from here," he said, shaking his head. "But that guy had some weird stuff."

"Like what?" MJ asked casually, glancing toward the door. Justin was leaning against the car, talking on his phone.

The clerk leaned over and pointed to the shelf behind MJ.

"I set it all there." He picked up a roll of duct tape as if that were a case in point. There was also a pack of D batteries and a protein bar.

MJ didn't think those things were all that odd. That he ran instead of buying them was really odd.

"I assume you have security cameras in here?"

"Yeah," said the clerk, "but since he didn't actually steal anything, no one will care."

MJ nodded. "You're probably right. Well," she said, pointing to the coolers at the back of the store, "I'm going to get my drink and go."

She paid and walked back to the car.

Justin glanced at her. "Sounds good," he said into the phone. "I'll send the address when I have it. Thanks again, Anjelica."

He put his phone back in his pocket and unlocked the car.

"Who was that?" MJ asked, buckling her seatbelt.

Justin didn't seem to hear her, his face a mask of concentration as he started the car. "What?"

"On the phone," she repeated. "Who is Anjelica?" His mood seemed to have shifted. She hoped his distraction meant that Anjelica was a girlfriend. Justin needed a woman who might appreciate all his caretaking.

"Oh that," he said, his cheerful expression returning. "It was the moving company. My stuff is still about two weeks away."

"Two weeks? That seems awfully long." She really hoped he had an alternate plan besides staying at her house.

"That's the army for you."

He pushed the gas, and the engine roared as they pulled away.

MJ took a long drink of her Mountain Dew and closed her eyes. She wanted to avoid any further conversation. She knew taking this drive with Justin would be a bad idea. Thankfully, he also seemed less inclined to talk.

In reality, she didn't need the caffeine. She was still buzzing from the 7-Eleven chase. Putting her head back, she tried to relax. It was no good. She had to know who that guy was.

The sooner they got to the police station, the sooner she could make sure the detectives got that video footage. Pumpkin tie man may not be the Good Samaritan she'd believed him to be.

Chapter Thirty-Three

A noticeable increase in energy met Rory and Jefferson when they returned to the station. Amber, Julia, and Ron were all gathered around Jared's computer, watching the screen with intensity.

Amber looked back as they approached. "Footage from the homeless shelter. Jared was just getting it ready to show us what he's found, so good timing."

Jefferson felt a surge of energy himself. This could be vital information if this was the guy who convinced Dylan to carry that bag to city hall.

"So here I found Dylan walking into the shelter. This is about lunchtime, the day before the blast. He is alone, but if I fast forward some..." Jared moved the video ahead several frames. "Then he comes out with this guy."

Jefferson moved closer to the screen. He could see people milling around outside "The Room at the Inn." Then Dylan Warren walks out the main entrance with a shorter man fitting Aspen's description—a white guy, with long hair and a scraggly beard. Job.

Jared froze the video on a frame that captured a clear image of the man's face. "I believe this is the guy we are looking for."

Amber let out a long breath. "Wow. Fantastic work, Jared."

"It gets better," Jared said. His words signaled excitement, but he said it with his usual monotone seriousness.

He clicked another video on his desktop.

"This is the next day." He played a segment of the video without stopping it.

They all watched, seeming to hold their breath in unison. They first saw Dylan entering the shelter. Within less than a minute, the bearded man entered the frame carrying a duffle bag. He also went into the shelter.

"Damn, that's the bag!" Ron said for all of them.

Amber glared back at him.

"Sorry, boss," he said sheepishly.

Jared sat silently with his arms folded as the video continued, clearly knowing they would be even more shocked.

After a couple of minutes, Dylan exited the shelter. Now he was carrying the duffle bag.

"Bingo!" Amber patted Jared's shoulder. "Nice work! Now get that photo of the bearded guy printed. We are going to circulate it ASAP to all agencies and the public. This is our guy."

Jefferson agreed. He didn't know the guy's endgame or motivation, but he wasn't just some random homeless guy. That Aspen hadn't seen him since the explosion made that clear.

At that moment, Julia's desk phone rang. "Agent Liufau here."

Her eyes moved to Jefferson as she listened to the person on the other end.

"Okay, thank you. Send them back." She hung up the phone. "Brooks' ex is here, and apparently, she came with him. Something about getting her car."

Jefferson shrugged. "Sounds reasonable."

Julia smiled. "It's your lucky day. She wants to talk to you."

Jefferson looked at the ceiling. "Rory?"

Rory shook his head as he started moving away. "No, no man. I am long overdue for my afternoon snack. She's all yours."

"It could be important, Jefferson. Just see what she wants," Amber said. "I wouldn't mind listening in, so bring her over."

Julia picked up her laptop and a pad of paper. "Well, I have to go interview her ex-hubby, though I don't think it will be relevant at all, given the video we just watched."

"I wouldn't be so quick to eliminate him," Jefferson warned. "We already know there were at least two people involved. Why not three? Or more? Someone had to get the explosives and know how to use them. That could be Brooks."

Amber nodded with a slight squint in her eyes. "It would be a stretch to think more than one person wanted to kill the guy's ex-wife, but I agree he still deserves a closer look."

Julia smiled. "Of course. Gotta dot those i's and cross those t's." She glanced at Jefferson. "Shall we go meet them?"

"Let's go," he said with a sigh.

He could never admit how curious he was to meet Mr. MJ Brooks. What kind of man did MJ Brooks marry? Ex or not, she must have found him attractive at some point. He wondered what split them up. He wondered a lot of things that would never see the light of day.

***

MJ and Mr. Brooks were just coming through the door as Julia and Jefferson arrived at the interview rooms. Before Jefferson could fully take in the couple, MJ rushed up to him.

"Detective Hughes, I have to talk to you. It's very important."

He glanced over at Justin Brooks. The man could have walked out of a magazine ad. Okay, so there was at least one reason a woman might be attracted to Mr. Brooks. He didn't appear to have an ounce of fat anywhere on him. He had a close-cropped military hairstyle and an all-too-perfect jawline.

"Hello, Mr. Brooks. I'm Agent Liufau," Julia said, offering her hand.

Jefferson noticed her smile looked bigger than he'd ever seen it.

Justin took her hand and gave it a firm shake. "Agent Liufau, it is very nice to meet you in person, and you can call me Justin." He smiled.

Jefferson could tell it was a weapon he knew how to use. His good-looking face went into handsome overdrive when he displayed his perfectly straight and glowing teeth.

"Great," said Julia, a little too brightly. Then, as if realizing this, she cleared her throat. "We can go back to interview room number two. I just have a few questions that shouldn't take too long. If you'll just follow me."

His smile faded and his eyes narrowed as he glanced at MJ and Jefferson. He hesitated.

"Just go, Justin. I'll meet you back here," MJ said.

Was that irritation in her voice? Jefferson wondered. Or was she just over-eager to share her news?

What he couldn't mistake was how Justin Brooks scrutinized him. What did he think was going on here? He's a detective, not some want-to-be boyfriend trying to move in on his territory. The man gave off a serious jealous-ex vibe.

Could he be jealous enough to want to hurt MJ? His sudden reappearance didn't sit well with Jefferson. He made a mental note to talk to Julia after the interview.

"Yes, Mr. Brooks, SSA Wells is waiting in her office for MJ," Jefferson said in a neutral, professional tone. "We will meet you back here as soon as Agent Liufau has finished with your interview." He smiled reassuringly.

Justin nodded, "Fine." He looked askance at MJ. "Don't take too long, babe."

MJ stiffened. Anger flashed across her face.

She turned away from Justin. "Let's go," she told Jefferson between clenched teeth.

***

As MJ and Jefferson entered Amber's office, she and Ron were looking over an image on her desk. Jefferson could see that it was the bearded man from the homeless shelter. The two of them were deep in conversation while examining it.

"SSA Wells?" Jefferson said quietly.

"Ah, yes. Thank you, Jefferson. Nice to see you again, Ms. Brooks. I hear you might have some information for us?" She motioned for them to sit across from her.

"I'm going to go check on the media releases for the images," Ron said, heading for the door.

"Thanks, Ron. The sooner they get out there, the better."

"On it."

MJ sat on the edge of her chair, the anger of a moment ago forgotten. Her eyes were now bright as she leaned forward, hands on the desk with anxious energy.

"I saw him again."

Jefferson and Amber glanced at each other.

"And who would that be?" Amber asked.

MJ looked at them with wide eyes. "Pumpkin tie man. I saw him again."

Before they could ask any more questions, the complete story tumbled out of her in a rush of words and gesturing arms. Eventually, she stood and began pacing as she recounted chasing him to the alley.

"But then he was gone." She shook her head. "Sorry, I am not a sprinter, and that guy was fast."

Jefferson shook his head. She had taken a serious risk. If that guy had a weapon, he didn't want to imagine what might have happened. When would MJ leave well enough alone?

"You say they have video footage?" He didn't like her getting involved, but Jefferson understood why she was so excited. If this guy ran from her, he had something to hide. Maybe he's a drug dealer or a thief, but they had to consider his presence the night of the explosion in a new light.

"Yes! That's why I'm sure this could be a big deal. I mean, for you all in your investigation." She stopped, but he could see her mind continuing to churn.

"And?" Jefferson prompted.

"Nothing really," she said, still looking pensive. "I just can't shake the feeling that I know him, and not just from the night of the explosion." She shrugged. "Maybe I'm imagining it."

SSA Wells was nodding. "Well, what you've given us is extremely helpful." She turned to Jefferson. "Let's get on this right away. Check who we have in the area available to stop by and collect the footage. With any luck the store will give it up willingly and save us the time of a warrant."

"Yes, ma'am."

As Jefferson left the room, MJ's gaze landed on the photo on Amber's desk.

"Who is that guy? Is that the picture you're sending out?"

Amber nodded. She picked up the picture and passed it to MJ. "You might as well look. This guy's face will be public knowledge in a matter of minutes."

MJ sat down and studied the picture. "Who is he?" she asked without looking up.

"We believe he may have been the person who passed the duffle bag of explosives to Dylan Warren," she said matter-of-factly.

MJ looked up, her eyes wide. "This is huge!"

Amber agreed. "We just hope he's not already on the run."

Jefferson returned and stood in the doorway. "Larson and Mendez were out that way and are heading to the store now."

"Fantastic," said Amber.

He motioned with his head toward the interview rooms. "Julia will finish interviewing Mr. Brooks soon. You can meet up with him in the waiting room."

MJ thought he looked a bit amused when he said this. Her annoyance at Justin suddenly returned.

"I guess I better go," she said.

"Is there any way you could stay for a bit? I'd really like to have you with us when we go through the footage." Amber said. "I don't expect that it will take long for us to have access. They can send digital files instantly."

Jefferson scowled almost imperceptibly, but MJ caught it. Why was he so perturbed by her help? Hadn't she brought them important information?

Let him sulk. She didn't care. She felt like singing. And she could absolutely stay. Being able to do something, anything, to help find this killer was helping her shattered heart heal one small piece at a time.

"Sure, I just need to get the paperwork for my car figured out and head over to the lot where they are holding it."

Amber waved her hand. "Nonsense. You sign the paperwork, and if you don't mind giving an officer your keys, we'll send a couple of them over to bring your car to the station."

MJ tried to hide her satisfaction, but a smile tugged at her lips. Despite trying not to, she glanced at Jefferson. He was leaning against the doorway with a curious expression on his face. When their eyes met, he glanced back at Wells. MJ bit her tongue to hold back the urge to laugh at his discomfort.

"Okay, that works for me," she said. "I'll tell Justin he can head home without me."

As she moved to the door, Jefferson stepped back to let her pass, keeping his eyes on the floor in front of him.

MJ shook her head slightly as she walked away. What a strange and confusing man.

Chapter Thirty-Four

Jefferson watched MJ go as she headed toward the interview rooms, amazed at how she'd wriggled herself back into the investigation. Well, they likely had their guy, and her pumpkin-tie man most likely just had a shoplifting problem.

More concerning to Jefferson was the unsettling feeling that there was something abnormal about her relationship with her ex. Most women would fall head over heels for a guy like that, but MJ's reaction to Justin hinted at some flaw in his personality. Could it be something dark that she didn't want to admit? Victims of abusive partners often blame themselves. Could she be working so hard to help with this case because she fears Justin could be involved?

Just then, he spotted Julia coming back to her desk, carrying her notepad.

"Hey Julia, how'd the interview with Brooks go?" He sat on the corner of her desk, careful not to smash anything, which was hard. Julia didn't keep her desktop particularly clean.

Julia thought for a minute. "It was like talking to a model in a magazine."

Jefferson smirked. "I get it. He's good-looking, but what's he like? What vibe did you pick up?"

"No, I mean, it literally felt like I was talking to a pretty picture, not a real person." She sat back in her chair and pulled her ball cap down on her head, stuffing her hair away from her face. "I'm sure you've talked to people like this guy. It's like he's wearing a mask of perfection, but underneath there's some kind of something else going on." She gave him a crooked grin. "But the perfection is pretty darn nice."

"Do you think he's dangerous?"

She shrugged. "Not particularly, but he's a soldier. Most of those guys have a game face that only comes out when they are in combat. And maybe that's the mask," she said, furrowing her brow. "I bet he's seen some things he'd like to forget."

Jefferson considered this. He knew it was true for Rory. The joking part of his personality masked a lot of pain from his deployments. Jefferson only knew some details because Rory and he spent countless hours in a car together.

"What about his relationship with MJ?"

"Oh, is it "MJ" now?" Her eyes were wide with amusement.

"She insists."

"OK, whatever you say." She eyed him as she continued grinning. "He seems perplexed as to why they are not still together. He told me he didn't want the divorce, and now he can't stop worrying about her. She likes to get herself into trouble, according to him."

They agreed about something, Jefferson thought.

Julia looked down at her notepad. "Anyway, I have all his travel details and whereabouts, so I'm just about to check to see that everything clears. He says he was in Georgia when the explosion happened."

Jefferson didn't think that absolved him at all. He could have hired someone, an old army buddy, perhaps.

"It'd pay to check his financials, too. Make sure he hasn't been paying out any sizeable sums of money."

"You're thinking a hired hitman? But why kill other people?" She shook her head. "I'll check into it, but there are so many easier ways to kill your ex."

"Criminals don't always do the logical things."

"True."

Jefferson stood up. "Do you think she's safe with him staying at her house?"

She looked at him intensely, studying his face with just the hint of a curious smile. He shifted under her gaze and began regretting that he'd asked that last question.

Finally, she released him by looking toward the door. "Look, Jefferson. She's an adult. And unless we have some solid reason to believe her ex is dangerous, there's not much we can do. But if it makes you feel better," she zeroed in on him again, "I will say something to her, subtly of course, and I won't mention that you asked."

He didn't like the turn this had taken. "She's an important witness, and potentially a target. It wouldn't look very good if we didn't at least question Justin's story if something were to happen."

"Agreed." She nodded, but just a sliver of a smile still played over her face.

A phone buzzed on Julia's desk. She moved aside a few papers to find it.

"It's my nanny. I've got to take this. Little Seth has an earache."

"No problem. All the best to Seth."

She nodded, already picking up the call. "Hi Val, how's my little man doing?"

Jefferson walked back to his desk, mulling over their conversation.

He could take the ribbing if it meant conclusively ruling out Justin Brooks as a suspect. It had nothing to do with MJ. He snickered to himself. Julia clearly thought he had more than a professional interest in the teacher. It was laughable. He and MJ had absolutely nothing in common, except perhaps their distrust of her ex-husband.

After talking with Julia, he felt even more certain that Justin Brooks was not a man to overlook.

Chapter Thirty-Five

Justin resisted leaving the police station without her, but MJ gave him little choice. He sulked away, though his sulking was only visible to the trained ex-wife's eye. To a stranger, he would appear to be the happiest man on earth—a broad smile, walking tall, making small talk as he left, but MJ knew. He was sulking.

It had taken her a long time to realize how much she had shelved her own feelings, her own ideas, her own life really, because Justin took care of everything. The "everything" included thinking for both of them. Anytime she dared to contradict him or suggest another idea, he would smile like an indulgent parent, kiss her, and figuratively pat her on the head for trying.

She didn't blame him as much as she did herself. It wasn't like he'd suddenly changed once they got married. He treated her the same way when they were dating. MJ just buried the warning voice in her head beneath a pile of justification and delusion. She wanted to believe she was happy with Justin.

Recognizing and speaking the truth had been the hardest thing she'd ever done. Justin did not take it well. It had taken his deployment overseas to give her the space she needed to figure out who she was without him deciding for her.

And now he was back, trying to take up the same old role as a master puppeteer. She was more than happy to send him on his way. Maybe he would see that she had changed. She could take care of herself.

MJ got the paperwork arranged and handed her keys off to Officers Fogarty and Stewart, who would deliver her car to the station.

When she walked back to the investigation hub, Amber's door was open, but she was talking to someone on the speakerphone.

MJ stood a bit awkwardly near the area of open desks. All the detectives and officers in the room were eating what smelled like Pad Thai. She suddenly felt the hunger pangs she'd been ignoring.

What was she supposed to do now?

The tall guy, Ron, she thought his name was, came to her rescue.

"Hey, MJ, a local place brought some lunch grub in for all of us. It's set up just around the corner there," he said, pointing to the other end of the room. "The boss is on the phone with the store owner, so we expect the footage any minute. Go grab some food and there's a seat here for you."

Julia rolled her eyes and gave MJ a knowing look. "Never mind him. I've got a seat right here for you."

"What?" Ron said, putting his gigantic hands up with a shrug.

"Thanks, I am kind of famished." She didn't dare look at Jefferson. How irritated he must be right now.

***

Once she had some food, MJ took the seat next to Julia and shared her desk space to eat. She'd been right. It was Pad Thai, and it was delicious. They must have all been hungry because the room had grown silent. Then MJ realized that her presence might be hindering their normal conversation.

She could feel Julia looking at her.

"I'm sorry about what happened to you, and to your boss," Julia said, her voice barely above a whisper. "I've seen all kinds of things in my career, but this one takes the cake."

MJ nodded. She met the other woman's probing dark eyes staring out from under a Mariners baseball hat.

"I really appreciate that. Being able to help find this guy," she looked back at her plate, "well, it's helping me more than you know."

"I get it. Sometimes anger drives us during our grief." She smiled sadly. "I've been there. And I can say from experience that it doesn't ever really take us past our grief. That part still comes around."

MJ didn't really know what she meant. She gave her a questioning look.

Julia seemed to weigh whether to continue. She speared a piece of chicken with her fork. She held it and gestured with the meat toward MJ. "Just make sure you understand that after we catch this guy—and I say *after* because we will bag the piece of trash; but after that happens, your grief might just come and punch you in the gut." Her expression became serious. "Be ready for it. Keep your friends close."

This bit of unsolicited advice took MJ by surprise. She had grieved, and was grieving, wasn't she?

She stared down at her plate for what felt like an eternity, unsure of what to say. She had to consider that Julia could be right. Shannon would probably say Julia was right.

She finally looked back up. "Thanks. I'll keep that in mind." And she meant it.

Julia was still fixing her with an insistent stare that threatened to reach into MJ's brain and take out all her secrets.

"How long have you and Justin been divorced?" she asked.

The steadiness in Julia's voice, and the sudden shift in the conversation, made MJ wary of answering. Was this just a casual conversation?

She finally decided there was no harm in answering. "About a year."

"And you're okay with him staying at your house?"

MJ paused. What was this about? "Why do you ask?" Her shoulders had tensed. She didn't want to talk about Justin.

Julia scrunched up her face. "Sorry, was that too personal? I interview people for a living, so sometimes I just dive right in." She shook her head while grinning.

MJ's shoulder relaxed a bit. "No, it's fine." She looked down at her plate. "It's just hard for me to explain. We are still friends, and I don't hate him. I just don't like him with me, if that makes sense."

"Totally. I dated a guy for a year that my family loved. I mean l-o-v-e-d. If my papa could have married him, he would have. The guy was Samoan and steeped in our culture, but he drove me nuts." She laughed at the memory. "No one understood when I preferred my now husband, a tall, skinny white guy, and a cop."

"Does he work here?"

"No, no," Julia said, wiping her mouth with a napkin. "He's at the Tacoma Police Department." She took a sip of her water. "I didn't mean to pry into your relationship, but you can never be too careful, you know? We are dealing with someone that has a serious screw loose, and I just want to be sure you feel safe."

Julia's point was logical to MJ, but she thought any suspicion of Justin was unfounded. He wouldn't hurt her. He never had.

"I appreciate your concern, but I feel perfectly safe with Justin around. I'm more annoyed than anything. If my mother wasn't visiting, I would have already sent him on his way. She loves him, unfortunately, and this whole thing has her a bit freaked out. Having him there helps keep her calm."

"Well, isn't that interesting," said Ron, breaking up their conversation.

Julia peered over at his desk. "What ya got Ronnie?"

"Our Mr. Atherton has had quite a few dealings with the city council. Now," he said with a cautionary hand up, "he's a developer, so that's not so surprising." He leaned closer to his computer and scrolled. "But about five years ago, he and the city council got sued over a development."

"Which one?" asked Jefferson, getting up to look at Ron's computer.

"It's called Green Hill." He pointed to the screen as Jefferson leaned in.

"Green Hill," Jefferson repeated as if trying to place the name. He looked over at Rory. "Why is that familiar?"

Rory snapped his fingers in the air, and Jefferson's eyes widened as they remembered at the same time.

"The fire," they said in unison.

Ron was nodding. "Yep, a fire in the subdivision spurred a Mr.," he squinted at the screen, "Mr. Joe Garrison to sue."

Joe Garrison, MJ thought, rolling the name around in her brain. A connection was there, but she couldn't quite find it.

Suddenly, she gasped, covering her mouth. "His children all died in the fire."

They all looked at her.

"He had a daughter at the high school, and I think two kids at West Sound Elementary," she said, rubbing her temples as if that would help her remember. "I never met him personally, but it affected many people in the district. It was all over the news." She got up and hurried over to Ron's computer.

"Can you pull up a picture?"

Ron hit a few keys. "This article doesn't have one, but let's see what the internet can show us."

MJ and Jefferson both stared at the screen. MJ had to remind herself to breathe as she waited for Ron to click on one of the search results.

She and Jefferson both stood up sharply and looked at each other.

"That's him!" She pointed at the screen, hardly believing it herself. "That's the pumpkin-tie man."

Just as she said this, Amber's office door opened.

"Good news, everyone. The owner has just agreed to send the video file over to Jared."

They all stared at her. MJ could feel the energy pulsing through the room, and she knew Wells couldn't miss it.

"What have you found?" Amber looked from one to the other. She kept her face emotionless, but her eyes burned with hope. Something was about to give.

Chapter Thirty-Six

Jon Atherton walked back into the kitchen after stepping outside to put the steaks on the grill. His kids and their cousins were playing Marco Polo in the pool. He smiled. He remembered playing that game with his friends at the community pool in Yakima, where he grew up. It only cost a dollar to swim all day, and his frugal parents took advantage of what was essentially free childcare.

Few people in Western Washington had in-ground pools, and even fewer would heat their pool for use all year. Atherton considered it an investment in family happiness. An investment that meant his kids and their cousins could swim comfortably on a cool, slightly misty fall day like today. What was the point of working for his money if it didn't make life better?

"I'm just saying, I think the Seahawks need to invest in the offensive line. You can't expect the quarterback to run for his life every play and still be productive," his brother-in-law Jay Butler was saying from the kitchen table.

"True," said Amy, Atherton's wife, "but they can't afford to upgrade the line because they dedicated too much to his salary. If you want protection, maybe consider that fact in your salary negotiations." She carried on this all-important discussion while setting the table for dinner.

Lana, who was Jay's wife and Atherton's sister, walked into the room carrying their nine-month-old and youngest cousin, Sarah. She plopped the baby on Jay's lap. "That was a big one, so you owe me."

Jay started bouncing the baby on his knee. "I'll get the next one."

"That's what you always say," said Lana as she went to dispose of the stinky diaper.

"I think everything is just about ready," said Amy. "Jon, next time you go out to turn the steaks, tell the kids to get out and dry off."

"Sure, hon." He kissed her on the cheek as she brushed by him to set the table. Then he turned to Jay.

"How are things over at the school, Jay? I'm sure it's got to be rough."

"Is this Jon Atherton my brother-in-law asking, or is it Jon Atherton future city council member?"

Jon chuckled, "Let's not count our chickens."

"Oh, come on, it's a slam dunk. You have a lot of friends at the county."

"Maybe," smiled Atherton. "Anyway, school?"

Jay let out an exasperated sigh. "It's a nightmare. The whole thing is just awful, and you add in the drama of middle schoolers, and the women I work with, if I'm being honest, and I don't know when school will ever open again."

"Jay!" exclaimed Lana. "For goodness's sake, it's only been a few days. Kids and adults need time to process."

The baby squirmed, her face contorting as she prepared to wail. Jay stood up and patted her back.

"I get that," he said, "but people are really making Troy out to be a god or something, and I don't think that's healthy either. We need to get back to work soon."

The baby's face crinkled and turned red as a wail broke out. "I think she's hungry," Jay said, handing her back to Lana.

Lana rolled her eyes but scooped the baby up and snuggled her close.

"Anyway," Jay continued, "Shannon, the counselor, and the Booster Club have planned a candlelight vigil for tomorrow night. After that happens, I'm hoping we can get the school board to set a date for return after the community has had their moment."

Atherton considered his brother-in-law. He was an interesting study of a man who was a weakling and a brutally vacant troll, all rolled into one annoying personality. Still, Jay's parents had left him a nice sum of money, and he didn't mind taking a risk. Some of their joint investments had really paid off.

"I'm sure you plan to go to the vigil?" Atherton asked.

"Pretty sure I can't get out of it. You should come. It'd be a good chance to shake hands and kiss babies."

Atherton smiled patiently, as if dealing with an annoying child. "I got an invitation in my email today. I suppose I should." He gave Jay a sideways glance. "But I will leave the glad-handing for another time."

Jay shrugged. "I'll just be glad to get back to normal and hire a new principal." He grinned with a wink at Atherton.

Atherton raised his eyebrows. "You applied?"

"Of course. I'm the only one keeping the ship afloat right now. I'm sure the board will see that. I can get us back to business."

"I'm sure as soon as you're back in school, there will be something else to complain about," retorted Amy.

"True," said Jay. "I won't deny that. And it will probably have something to do with MJ Brooks. She can't keep her nose out of anything. I heard she's been following the detectives around trying to do their jobs." He snorted a bitter laugh. "Welcome to my world."

"You're just mad that she almost died and not you. We all know how you love the limelight." Amy ruffled his hair as she went by to set another plate on the table.

"I'm not the one milking this thing to take days off work."

Amy just shook her head as she pulled her red hair up into a ponytail. She looked wide-eyed at Atherton. "Jon! The steaks!"

"Oh!" He dashed out to the grill.

***

A man watched this spectacle through binoculars. He didn't feel the mist falling or the chill of the October air as he knelt on the fir-covered hillside with its perfect view of the Atherton property. This scene of family bliss captivated all his senses, and it reminded him of the very thing that Jon Atherton and Jay Butler had taken from him. His gaze followed Atherton as he walked to the pool's edge and spoke to the kids as they splashed around. One of them sent a spray of water at Atherton, who jerked back to avoid getting wet.

The man watching chuckled. He willed the child to splash Atherton harder. Send a tidal wave over his head and drown him. He imagined this happening, Atherton choking and fighting for breath as the water filled his lungs, his hands clutching at his throat, his legs flailing for solid ground as the wave carried him away. While his death in this manner would be some justice, it wouldn't give him quite the same satisfaction as doing it himself.

He sent the picture scurrying from his mind and focused again on the reality. The children were climbing out of the pool, toweling off. They hurried to get out of the cold. It must be time to eat. How lovely.

Sitting back on his heels, he put the binoculars in his bag. He had a decision to make about his next steps. Killing Atherton here would be easy. He knew enough about the property to be in and out.

He stood and swung his backpack over his shoulder. Staring down at the house, he could feel the clock ticking. He couldn't risk killing them separately. The detective who spotted him at Forsberg's may have gotten lucky, but every action he took gave them more information. He felt them getting closer to him. So much so that he may have to settle for "almost" killing Forsberg. The media wasn't reporting her condition, so she may be dead or close to it. Either way, she wasn't his prime target now.

And the teacher. That was unfortunate. She'd recognized him from the day of the bombing, he was sure of it.

He felt disappointed in himself. His plan had gone so smoothly until now.

Regardless, he would finish his mission. It would be best to take out Atherton and Butler in one final awe-inspiring act. He'd kill anyone who got in his way. Then he would bow out and join his family.

A tear rolled down his cheek. He wanted that almost as badly as he wanted to make these people pay. He wiped his face and cursed himself for being weak.

Today, he had formed a new plan, and it would be better than the old one. He'd already sent Atherton a fake invite to the vigil tonight. Both men would be there, he was certain. Atherton wouldn't pass up an opportunity to appear as a grieving member of the community.

The man grinned as he imagined Atherton's face as he took his last breaths.

He turned away and made his way down the hillside.

Chapter Thirty-Seven

The footage provided by the store owner confirmed MJ's assertion that Joe Garrison was, in fact, the pumpkin-tie man.

Agents and officers began scouring the internet and a variety of databases to learn all they could about this man. What did he have to do with the explosion? Why did he sue the city?

Jefferson called Forsberg. If anyone would have the inside baseball, she would.

Lisa answered the phone on the first ring.

"Detective Hughes." She sounded cheerful for a woman who had just lost her home and almost her life. "How is my favorite detective?"

He ignored the question. "I'm glad to hear you sounding so well. Are you up for answering a few questions?"

"After my conduct, I'm surprised you're asking. But yes, I will help with anything you need."

He explained to her what they knew about Joe Garrison and asked what she remembered about the lawsuit.

She took a deep breath. "What happened to that man is one of the worst things our city has ever done. I'll forever regret my part in it."

Her answer was quiet, but a quaver in her voice verified the emotion in her words.

Jefferson thought briefly about ending the call. Forsberg's doctor probably would not approve of upsetting her more, but they were too close to a break. He needed her to talk.

"I know there was a fire at his home, but what does that have to do with the city council?"

The line was quiet for a long time.

"Lisa, are you still there?"

"Yes, I'm sorry, it's just I don't like to remember. You'll understand once I explain."

She took a deep breath to regain her strength. When she spoke, her voice was stronger.

"You know Garrison lived in the Green Hill subdivision. Atherton development built it. They sold many of the lots before they even began construction. It's a beautiful location that overlooks the inlet. They planned it as a very upscale neighborhood."

Atherton again, thought Jefferson. Why did his name keep coming up?

"Anyway, that beautiful location became a problem. They promised people who paid for their lots they could move in at a certain time, but when that time came, the city blocked occupancy. It turned out the developer had failed to install a pump required for fire safety because of the elevation. Without it, there would be no water pressure available to fight a fire in the development."

"But if the city blocked occupancy, how did Garrison's family end up living there?" Jefferson said, not quite seeing the full picture.

"That's the awful part." He could hear her moving around on the other end of the phone as if adjusting herself in the hospital bed.

"Atherton," she continued, "had a huge stake in this development, but he wasn't the only one. Other investors, all shielded by shell companies, also stood to lose out if the development didn't get finished and occupied."

"Why not just build the pump?"

"They were working on it but had run out of time. Lot owners had contractual options to either pull out of the deal or receive a cash payout as a late fee. The developer and investors stood to lose millions." She said the last part with an emphasis on the money. "Our city inspector made the right call, but that would not fly with Atherton. He brought the issue to the city council, asking us to overrule the inspector."

"You're telling me that the city council overruled an inspector and knowingly let people move into homes that had no fire protection?" Jefferson asked incredulously.

"Now hold on there. It wasn't that simple. Atherton brought some families to the meeting. They all pleaded with us to let them move into their new homes. Some of them had already sold their homes and were living out of hotels." She sighed. "That excuses nothing, but my progressive friends and I were moved by their stories. I should have known better than to vote in favor of something Atherton wanted."

Jefferson rubbed his eyes. "Was Garrison one of the people asking to move in?"

"Yes," she breathed. "Yes, he was. He and the other families even signed an agreement that wouldn't hold the city responsible if a fire occurred. He paid a terrible price for that decision."

"What do you know about the fire itself?"

She was quiet again. "I only know what the media reported or was in the court documents. Garrison and his wife went out. Left the kids home with their oldest daughter. They left a stove burner on with a dish towel close by. The kids were all upstairs. The fire department dispatched a water truck, but the fire was out of control by the time they got there."

Jefferson couldn't even imagine how it would feel to lose a child. He only knew he would feel responsible in that situation. It wasn't difficult to see how Joe Garrison might go a little mad.

"Despite the agreement he signed, he tried to sue the city?"

"Yes. He believed that some of the council members were investors in the development, and I'm not sure he was wrong."

This shocked Jefferson. How could such an accusation go uninvestigated, especially when a whole family of children had died? Such investments would be an obvious conflict of interest and possibly even criminal.

"Was any of this proven?"

"No. He had the names of the shell companies, but the investors were well hidden. And everyone saw him as a grieving father, out of his mind." She sniffled and went quiet again.

Jefferson understood now why she didn't enjoy recalling the story.

"Not long after," she added, almost reverently, "his wife committed suicide. He truly lost everything."

Jefferson closed his eyes. She was right. This city had not done the right thing, and they had decimated a family. Joe Garrison should never have signed that agreement, but the city had an obligation to ensure the safety of the development. Now Joe Garrison was on a one-man mission to make them pay. Jefferson wondered who else was on his list.

"But he lost the lawsuit?"

"No, he took a deal. The city paid him off."

Neither of them spoke, lost in their own thoughts.

Finally, Lisa broke the silence. "I'm guessing from all these questions that the payoff didn't work. You think Joe Garrison is responsible for the bombing." She said this as a statement, not needing to ask if it was true. "And he's still after me."

Jefferson didn't confirm or deny her conclusion. He needed to get this information to the team. "We are taking your protection very seriously, councilwoman."

"I know. Thank you."

"Of course. I'll be in touch."

"Detective?"

"Yes."

"Please be careful."

"Always."

Chapter Thirty-Eight

Amber's eyes narrowed with concentration as Jefferson updated the team about his conversation with Lisa Forsberg. Her glasses sat atop her head, and she held her chin with one hand while the other rested around her waist, a position she took automatically when listening. She leaned her slight frame against the briefing room table.

When Jefferson finished, Amber nodded as some pieces were finally fitting.

"We may have a man with a revenge list, with only a partial idea of who is on it," she stated ruefully.

"We know it has to be Atherton and Forsberg, at least," said Jefferson. "There could be others we don't know, or not. But we know he's willing to kill again, and I don't think he'll wait, especially since MJ recognized him."

MJ had been listening, quietly working on the puzzle in her head. At hearing her name, she looked up and their eyes met briefly.

Amber focused on Ron, her eyes still narrowed with thinking. "Find out everything you can about this neighborhood. I don't care who you must harass or favors you need to call in to get information on whatever shell companies are involved. We have to assume Garrison found out, so we need to know." She rubbed her chin, thinking. "How long will that take?"

"Not as long as it used to, and it means I get to rattle some cages at Treasury," Ron said with a devilish grin. "Congress passed a little-known law in the years since they created this shell corporation. People hide all kinds of crap in shell companies: drug trafficking, human trafficking, dirty investments, and . . . real estate." He reached back and locked his hands behind his head as he leaned back in his chair. "The Financial Transparency Act means the feds have the names of everyone receiving any benefit from a Shell corporation. It's not available to the local guys. No offense to the fine detectives here."

"None taken," said Larson.

"I've got a buddy at Treasury. I'll give him a call. If they didn't create a million subsidiaries to throw up a paper trail puzzle, then it should be pretty quick." Ron yawned and stretched his arms out wide before reaching into his pocket to pull out his phone.

"Good," Amber said with relief. "I'm glad you understand this part of it. Let me know as soon as you know something. Jefferson and Rory, you need to get over to the Atherton's house. He needs to know that he and his family are in danger. We'll also send a squad car over to provide some protection."

"Julia and Jared, work with communications to get this picture of Garrison out to the public. The more uncomfortable we make his movements, the more likely he is to slip up. Also, Julia, find out who else on the council voted in favor of letting the Garrisons and other families move in. We'll keep protection on all the injured council members, but we may need extra support for Forsberg and anyone else who voted yes."

"You got it. Having them all in the hospital makes it somewhat easier," said Julia.

Amber glanced over at MJ and seemed to contemplate her next move. Jefferson wondered how she would handle that situation. He suspected MJ was also in danger. Garrison knew she'd recognized him.

MJ, however, was gazing at the board. Jefferson followed her eyes to the photo of the bearded man who'd given the bomb to Dylan Warren. She pointed at the picture and seemed like she was about to speak, but then stopped and stared at it again.

"Ms. Brooks?" Amber said.

MJ turned her head, as if surprised to hear her name. She looked at all of them, but her eyes still held the look of someone deep in thought. Much to his consternation, Jefferson knew he shouldn't ignore that look. MJ had a knack for knowing things.

"What are you thinking?" he said. He felt the eyes of the team on him, surely shocked to see him taking her thoughts seriously. He'd hear about it later, but he didn't care. They were too close to breaking this thing wide open.

MJ looked at him. A look of confusion flickered across her face, and she seemed to decide whether she should trust that his curiosity was genuine. He didn't blame her for that. She wouldn't even be in this room if it'd been up to him.

Turning back to the board, she pointed to the picture. "Would it be possible to remove his beard, like edit the photo, or put a beard on Joe Garrison? I might be mistaken, but I'd swear it's the same man."

This drew everyone's attention to the picture. Amber pushed herself away from the table and walked to the board. She unpinned the picture of Joe Garrison and pinned it next to the picture of the bearded man from the Room at the Inn video footage.

Jefferson stepped closer. The bearded man's picture was grainier than Garrison's, and his beard obscured much of his features, but both men shared dark, round eyes and a slim nose that flared a bit at the nostrils. He couldn't believe they hadn't seen it before. MJ was right. They were the same man.

Amber looked at the floor and shook her head slowly. Then she glanced up at MJ.

"Are you sure you're in the right profession?"

MJ's eyes widened as a faint pink rushed to her cheeks.

Jefferson found her embarrassment surprising. She never seemed at a loss of confidence. Apparently, Wells had made an impression on her. That was Amber's magic. She knew people.

"Thank you," said MJ sheepishly. "Maybe all those years of deciphering student handwriting have paid off."

"Wherever it comes from, you have a knack for making connections. And this is important. Now we know we are looking for just one guy, but one who is skilled at disguising himself." Amber looked over at the group. "This makes our job easier and more difficult."

She blew out a sigh. "Julia and Jared, let's work together to decide how to present this information to the public. I don't want to scare people, but we could use some help in finding this guy. Someone must have seen something."

She looked thoughtfully at MJ, tapping her index finger on her chin. "Ms. Brooks, I am going to have Detectives Hughes and Jackson follow you home. I will make sure we have some officers available to watch your house until we have a better idea of what we are dealing with. I think it would be best if you stayed home where we can keep watch."

MJ shook her head. "I appreciate that, but Justin will be on high alert, I guarantee it. I will be fine."

"That may be true, but it would make me feel better."

MJ gave a gentle shrug. "Okay," she nodded. "I understand."

That was too easy, Jefferson thought suspiciously. He studied her, looking for some sign that she was just saying what Amber wanted to hear. MJ glanced over at him, feeling his inspection of her. When their eyes met, she snapped hers away like a kid caught cheating. Jefferson almost laughed out loud. He was getting to know her better than either of them wanted.

"Alright, everybody. Let's get back to work. We are close, I can feel it. But I also feel the threat that Garrison still poses to this community. He's dangerous, and he clearly doesn't care who gets in the way of his desire for revenge." She stopped to let her words sink in. "I have all the faith in the world in this team." She scanned the faces looking at her. "You know what to do." She gave one last curt nod, and they all scattered to their various assignments.

Jefferson and Rory moved toward MJ just as a young officer entered the room and strode up to her, dangling a set of keys.

"Here you are, Ms. Brooks. Your Bronco is waiting out front for you."

She took them with a broad, unencumbered smile. "Thank you, Officer Fogarty. I have missed her so much."

"I can see why," said the young man. "That's a sweet car."

Rory looked between the two of them. "I can't wait to see this machine. It must be something."

MJ smiled with delight. "Yes, yes, it is."

The young officer nodded emphatically at Rory. "Well, thanks for letting me drive it over here."

"No, thank *you*," said MJ.

Fogarty smiled, "Anytime." Then he turned and headed back toward the office.

"Are you ready, then?" asked Jefferson. He was curious to see the Bronco but wasn't about to let her know that.

"I am," said MJ.

"I mean, are you ready to go home and stay put?"

She looked at him with wide, innocent eyes. "Of course. I can't believe you think I would do otherwise."

Rory sputtered.

She shot him a death glare.

He put his hands up. "Sorry, allergies."

Jefferson shook his head in disbelief. "You know Wells is just trying to look out for you, and it makes all our jobs more difficult if we are worried about you."

"Well, *you*," she emphasized, "don't need to worry about me. I can take care of myself. Besides, I really, probably won't go anywhere."

"Excuse me, but don't you teach English? That makes no sense." Jefferson couldn't keep the half grin from his mouth.

She glared at him. "It makes perfect sense. Shall we go?"

Jefferson met her glare with a steady stare of his own. There wasn't much else to be said. She would do what she pleased, and, whether either of them wanted it, he would worry.

Chapter Thirty-Nine

MJ hesitated before getting into the driver's seat. She stared at herself in the window as she grasped the handle, remembering the last time she'd driven her car. A shudder ran through her. She brushed it aside and opened the door.

It was no good. As soon as her hands gripped the steering wheel, her mind flooded with images from the day she'd parked the Bronco and started her walk up the block to city hall. The sudden eruption of the blast ripped through her mind, and she felt the heat and the confusion all over again. She closed her eyes, trying to clear the smell of smoke as it curled its way through her memory. Then Troy's smiling face crowded out the other images. She felt tears burning her cheeks. These were not the feelings she expected when being reunited with her car.

She let out a frustrated breath and wiped her face. With forced resolve, she started the engine. She had to get going. Detectives Hughes and Jackson, waiting in their car, were probably wondering what was taking her so long. She shook her head as if the motion could empty her mind of the searing memories. With a trembling hand, she turned on the radio to a rowdy Brooks and Dunn song and started the drive home.

Daylight hadn't completely abandoned the Sound, but a ghostly fog cloaked the city and floated above the water. To MJ, it appeared her sudden resurgence of grief was playing out in the darkening mood outside her windshield. The Bronco pushed a path through the fog as she wound around Stanton Inlet. Her mind, likewise, continued wading through all that had happened in the past few days.

When they got to her house, she waved to the detectives as she closed the door to the Bronco and locked it. She knew they would wait until she was in the house before leaving. At least they didn't get out and insist on following her into the house to do a check of every room.

Edgar's muffled bark signaled her arrival. When she opened the door, he almost knocked her over in excitement, his dark, furry body wagging at both ends. Her mother and Justin were engrossed in a jigsaw puzzle at the kitchen table.

"Well, look who made it home," Toni said brightly. She stood up and hurried over to MJ, hugging her tightly as the door closed.

Edgar circled them, whining and nudging MJ with his nose. She released herself from Toni and bent down to take Edgar's face in her hands.

"I have missed you, too, buddy." She ruffled his silky head and rubbed her cheek against his.

"How are you?" Toni asked as MJ stood up.

"I'm fine." She sighed as the emotional intensity of the day finally hit her. Edgar followed as she walked over and sank onto the couch. Without warning, she hung her head and cried. Then her tearful shower became a downpour. Her shoulders shook as all the emotion she'd held in while driving home came out in waves.

"Oh, honey," said Toni. She sat next to her on the couch and wrapped her arms around her shoulders.

"I'll make some tea," said Justin, jumping from his chair.

"I don't even know why I'm crying," MJ wailed in a pitiful crying voice that even she found pathetic. She couldn't stop it. At that moment, she surrendered herself to crying like a baby in her mother's arms. The ride home, alone in her car, opened a wound she hadn't yet treated.

"The last time," she said between sobs, "I drove my car," she said, gulping air. "The last time was the night those people died. Troy died."

For once, her mother didn't explain anything or offer a solution. She just stroked her head, saying, "I know, I know."

They sat that way until Justin came and set a mug of tea on the coffee table. He stood nearby with his hands awkwardly in his pockets. He started to say something, but Toni shook her head.

Edgar, seeing MJ's tears, kept trying to put his head on her lap and lick her face.

"Edgar," Justin said, "Let's go out, boy. Come on."

Edgar looked at MJ reluctantly. "It's okay, Edgar. Go ahead." She mustered a smile of thanks to Justin. He wasn't all bad.

When they'd gone, Toni got up and grabbed a box of tissues. MJ mopped her face and blew her nose. "I hate crying," she said with disdain.

"You always have." Toni gave her a gentle smile. "Do you remember when you were learning to ride your bike?"

MJ blew her nose and nodded. "I was so mad when I fell."

"And," said Toni, "you had two bloody knees, but you wouldn't let me clean them or put bandages on. You insisted on getting right back on your bike. Your eyes might have watered a bit, but not even one tear came out."

MJ smiled at her determined young self.

"I, for one, feel a little better seeing you get it out." Toni looked at her like deciding whether to continue talking. "You probably don't want to hear what I think, but I'm going to tell you anyway." She touched MJ's cheek with her hand. "You need to mourn with your friends, colleagues, and students. Going to the vigil tonight might help you heal."

MJ looked down at the tissue in her hands. She knew her mother was right. The thought of it made her stomach hurt, but she felt a little less fragile now. She knew some of her reluctance to see others was really her fear of falling apart in front of them. She'd never really felt she deserved to grieve like everyone else. Troy died because of her, but now she knew too much to continue blaming herself.

"You're right. I think the vigil is where I need to be."

Just then, Justin and Edgar came back in. "Hey, so there's a cop car hanging out at the end of the driveway. I walked over to chat with them." He stopped and narrowed his eyes at MJ. The scolding look on his face said, "Are you going to make me say it, young lady?"

MJ shrugged, looking between Justin and her mother. "What?"

"Come on, MJ," Justin said as he hung up Edgar's leash. "You can't hide the fact that the cops think you are in danger."

Toni gasped. "What? MJ, what's he talking about?"

MJ held back the urge to throw her mug of tea at Justin. How could he be so thoughtless? Just when she thought he had some tact. All she needed was her mother freaking out about Joe Garrison.

"Justin is overreacting," she said, waving her hand casually. "In fact, the police are overreacting." She ruffled Edgar's head as he came around the couch and put his paws on her legs. "There's just this guy who might be involved with the bombing. I recognized him at the 7-Eleven today." The last few words melted into a mumble as she took a sip of her tea.

Toni jumped up. "What! MJ, the police have every reason to be worried. Didn't you say he went after one of the surviving council members? If you know who he is, he might go after you!" She was breathless with worry already.

MJ glared up at Justin. "Why did you have to go and blurt that out? Look at how crazy she is already."

Justin glanced at Toni. He looked slightly repentant.

"I'm not crazy," Toni said. "But I am worried. You always think you can handle whatever comes at you, but sometimes, MJ, you need to listen to other people." She took a breath. Then she added quietly, "You need to consider other people."

This last bit, the quiet plea she heard in her mother's voice, checked MJ's frustration. She'd just spent the past few minutes being comforted by her mom, but she realized that helping her family and friends come to terms with what happened to her and the others needed to be her focus now.

"You're right." She grabbed her mom's hand as it dangled by her side. "I'm sorry. I should take this more seriously."

Toni watched her carefully, suspicion playing across her face.

"Really, I mean it," MJ insisted. "It is all a bit surreal to me right now, and if I think about it too much, it does get to me. In my attempt to keep the reality of it all at bay, I discounted everyone else's feelings. I know that now, and I'm sorry."

Toni sat down and hugged her again. "Thank you, MJ. I love you so much."

"I love you, too, Mom."

Edgar jumped up, trying to get between them.

Justin cleared his throat.

MJ looked up as Toni released her. "I'm still mad at you."

"Of course," he said, throwing his hands in the air.

"But just a little bit." She smiled. She needed both Justin and Toni on her side right now.

"I'll take that." Justin's brilliant smile spread across his face.

Good, thought MJ, they're both happy again.

"Well, now that we have all of that resolved, and since we all agree that I need to be with my students and colleagues," MJ said, sipping her tea again. "We need to figure out how to get me past my gatekeepers to that vigil."

"No. Absolutely not." Toni folded her arms stiffly. "I cannot be on board with that. If the police think it is too dangerous to go out, then you need to stay put."

MJ glanced at Justin. This was one time she welcomed his overprotection.

"Look, Mom. Justin will come with me. You know how vigilant he is. He would never let anything happen to me, right Justin?"

He gazed at her steadily. The raw emotion she saw there almost made her feel guilty for including him.

He spoke quietly. "I would protect MJ with my life."

Chapter Forty

Jefferson and Rory left MJ's house and headed straight to Atherton's. His property sat on the very tip of Stanton Inlet in an area of high-bank, high-dollar views hundreds of feet above the sound. The drive was not a straight shot. The highway wound around like a gray snake slithering between walls of fir trees. A few spurts of fall color still jetted out in random flashes, but the scene became a wash of various grays as the day continued to darken and the fog still danced in the headlights. Every once in a while, the trees gave way to murky glimpses of the Sound where spacious homes seemed to sit suspended above the water.

They finally pulled up to an expansive security gate. A scripted letter "A," made from the same black metal as the massive double gates, floated in the center where the two gates met. Jefferson pushed the call button on the keypad.

When no one answered, he pushed it again. After a few more impatient seconds, a female voice came over the speaker. "Yes, how may I help you?"

"Hello, we are sorry to come unannounced, but it's Detectives Hughes and Jackson of West Sound PD. We need to speak to you and your husband. It is urgent."

They heard a breath over the speaker, and for a second, Jefferson thought she would tell them to get lost.

Then the gates opened.

The smooth and clean asphalt made it feel as though the car was gliding across glass. The long driveway took them through a tunnel of fir trees created by top branches reaching across the drive to touch each other. Very little light penetrated the green mass, and the effect made it seem as if the day had completely disappeared. Soon, the tunnel emptied into a circular drive with a stone fountain in the middle. Water cascaded down a delicate balance of boulders placed one on top of the other. Only a sliver of light remained in the sky, and most of the outdoor lights were blazing around the home, giving it an even more majestic aspect.

A courtyard before the front door resembled an immaculately precise grass and stone chessboard. The creamy stone house rose like a mountain with several roof lines meeting in peaks and gables. Massive oak double doors sat beneath a stone arch with three stone columns on either side. Jefferson and Rory approached the door just as it was opening.

Amy Atherton, a petite red-haired woman, stepped out on the porch in her stocking feet. She held her arms folded tight against the cold. She looked at them with a guarded but puzzled expression.

"Can I help you, gentlemen?"

"I'm Detective Hughes and this is Detective Jackson." Jefferson and Rory held out their badges.

She examined the badges with an unusual amount of scrutiny.

When she seemed satisfied with their credentials, Jefferson continued, "Is Mr. Atherton at home?"

"No, he's not. Is it something I can help you with?"

"Would it be possible for us to come inside?" Jefferson asked, motioning with his head toward the door. "This could take a minute to explain."

She looked behind her, considering. Then she nodded. "Okay, I'll just send the kids upstairs."

A boy and a girl sat watching TV in an opulent but cozy living room. They looked up at the detectives with curiosity, but quickly lost interest and went back to their program. Jefferson guessed they were twins, maybe ten or eleven years old.

Mrs. Atherton walked over to the TV and turned it off with a remote. "Sorry guys," she said. "I need you to head upstairs for a bit. You can work on getting your clothes put away before Janie comes to clean tomorrow."

The boy, a redhead like his mom, sat cross-legged on the floor with a nimbleness that made his position look more comfortable than it should. He glanced at the detectives again, with just a hint of a glare. He clearly blamed them for this intrusion into his TV time.

The girl, her ruddy brown hair in a thick braid down her back, jumped up gracefully and without complaining. She glanced shyly at the detectives and then ran toward the stairwell. She stopped at the bottom and turned around.

"Come on, Sam," she said like a sister used to bossing her brother.

Sam rolled his eyes but got to his feet and shuffled toward the stairs. They both ascended, and the adults moved into the kitchen.

The detectives sat at an enormous kitchen island with a marble top that cascaded down the sides to the floor.

"Would you like some coffee, water?" Mrs. Atherton asked.

"No, thank you. We don't want to take too much of your time," Rory replied with a reassuring smile.

She nodded as if she agreed. Not rudely but understanding they all had things to do.

She leaned her hip against the counter and folded her arms. "So, what's this all about?"

Jefferson looked at her gravely. "We believe your husband may be in danger."

She stared at them; her face was impassive except for a slight widening of her eyes. She looked back and forth between them, her look growing more confused. "You're being serious?"

"I'm afraid we are," answered Rory.

"But why? How?"

Jefferson glanced at the family photos decorating the front of the fridge. It was important that she understood the situation, but he didn't want to terrify her.

He spoke slowly. "We believe that the man responsible for bombing city hall was a property owner in one of your husband's developments. Without going into all the details, we believe he is attempting to exact revenge on all those involved in the deal."

"I don't understand. Revenge for what?"

Jefferson paused before speaking again. "His three children were killed when the house caught fire. A flaw in the development plan meant there was no water for fire service in the development."

Her hand flew to her mouth. "I remember that. It was so horrible. Jon was devastated."

Jefferson continued, "The father blames everyone involved in the development, including members of the city council."

"The bomb." She looked at them for confirmation.

Jefferson nodded once.

She cast her eyes around the kitchen, her hand still at her mouth. Then, more to herself than them, she said, "I have to get my kids out of here." Her face had lost color and her hands were shaking slightly as she reached down and grasped the side of the countertop. "I can go to my mother, in Canada. Do you think I should? Oh, my gosh." Her eyes were growing glassy with emotion.

"Mrs. Atherton," said Rory with calm firmness. "We need to know where your husband is. Can you try calling him?"

"Yes, yes, of course."

She walked over to the table and picked up her cell phone. A tense silence filled the room as she found his number. Jefferson could feel the adrenaline kicking in as they answered more and more questions. They had to move fast. He sensed Garrison knew they were closing in after MJ recognized him. The clock was ticking.

Amy stared at the phone. "He's not picking up."

Jefferson's phone buzzed in his pocket. He pulled it out and saw that it was Wells.

"I'm sorry, Mrs. Atherton, but I need to step into the next room to take this call," he said, standing.

She nodded while running a hand through her hair.

Jefferson swiped across to answer the phone as he hurried back into the living room.

"Hughes here."

"Hughes, Wells here. Ron has pulled some magical strings, and we have the names of the investors, or at least those who received any payout from the project. Here, let me put you on speaker." After a second, he heard more voices in the background. "Alright, Ron, tell him what you know."

"Okay, well, there is Atherton, of course, but he isn't even the majority investor. Two of the payees were city council members, Silva and Cochran. They made very little, relatively speaking, small players really, and they both, unfortunately, perished in the explosion."

Jefferson heard some paper shuffling before Ron continued. "Julia found that they also both voted to allow the families to move in before the pump was installed. With the mayor's vote and Forsberg's, that was the majority Atherton needed."

"So, the mayor, Atherton, and Forsberg are the only targets still alive?"

"Ah, not so fast. There is still the biggest investor in the development who also received the biggest payout, and that would be one Jay Butler, the brother-in-law of Atherton."

"Butler? Do we know anything about him?"

"That's the thing," said Amber. "He's also the dean of students at Mariner Middle School."

Jefferson stiffened. This could be bad; very bad.

"Jefferson?"

"I'm here."

"We need to get to Butler, too. I'm sending Larson and Mendez to his house. How's it going with Atherton?"

"He's not here. We're talking to his wife. I think she is going to leave town, but if you could get that patrol car over here, I think she would appreciate it. She is understandably freaked out."

"They're on their way. Find Atherton and let me know when you do."

"On it. We'll be in touch."

He hung up and stared ahead without seeing. Why did everything always end up pointing back in MJ's direction? He rubbed the back of his neck as he walked into the kitchen.

Rory stood up. Jefferson could tell he had the information they needed to find Atherton.

"That was the station. Mrs. Atherton, there will be a patrol car outside your residence for as long as you need, until we know the threat is over or if you decide to leave town. We'll leave our cards. You can call us directly if anything changes or if you notice anything unusual."

She took their cards and sniffled. She wasn't crying, exactly, but Jefferson knew that the fear and stress would get to her.

"Oh, I've decided. I am definitely leaving town. If Jon comes back from the vigil soon, he can come too, but I'm not waiting for some madman to come and burn down my house."

Jefferson looked at Rory.

Rory nodded. "Yeah, Atherton's not answering his phone, but he's at the vigil for the middle school principal who died in the explosion."

Jefferson felt his mouth go dry. "When did the vigil start?" He asked, his words hard and even.

Rory caught Jefferson's tone, and his face became gravely serious. He knew something was up.

"It starts in 15 minutes. I think," Amy said, suddenly looking worried. "Jay, my brother-in-law, works at the school. He wanted Jon to be early."

Jefferson's eyes shot over to Rory. "We have to go. Thank you, Mrs. Atherton, we'll be in touch."

***

Rory took the wheel and flipped on the windshield siren as they flew back down the curling highway toward the middle school. Jefferson called into the station to let them know the whereabouts of both Atherton and Butler. The station rerouted Mendez and Larson, along with any available officers.

Jefferson imagined the scene at the middle school: kids, families, teachers, an entire community potentially in the sites of crazed Joe

Garrison. And then there was MJ. He hoped against hope that she'd done as Amber requested and stayed put at home.

He dialed her number.

No answer.

He dialed it again.

No answer.

He growled in frustration. He saw Rory give him a sideways glance.

"Everything okay there, partner?"

"Fine," he said between clenched teeth.

He dialed the station to find out which officers were on watch at MJ's house. It was Fogarty and Tate, and as soon as he got Fogarty on the line, he instructed the young officer to go check on MJ.

When Fogarty called him back, Jefferson could hear the shame in his tone. "She's not here, detective. Just her mother is at home."

Jefferson closed his eyes and drew in a tight breath.

"I'm sorry, sir," Fogarty said hurriedly, his words spilling out in a rush. "The only car we saw leave was her neighbor, the older woman who lives there. She said her name was Claire. Mr. Brooks was with her, and—"

"Where did they say they were going?" Jefferson asked evenly.

"Claire said they were going to the vigil, as the principal was a good friend of hers." His voice became quiet. "Ms. Brooks must have been in the car. I'm sorry, detective."

Jefferson couldn't quite put his finger on his emotions at the moment. He wasn't angry, not at the officers. Their job was to watch out for intruders, not harass or search the residents. He was more frustrated at MJ for making him feel . . . What was it he felt? Worried, he realized with disdain. He was worried about her and the trouble she might get herself into.

"It's not your fault, Fogarty," he assured the officer. "You were doing your job as expected. Stay there. We can't be sure there won't still be a danger."

"Got it, sir."

Jefferson hung up and stared ahead as they raced along the highway. He prayed they wouldn't be too late.

Chapter Forty-One

MJ sat silently in the backseat of Claire's Audi SUV, attempting to prepare mentally to see students and her colleagues. She realized with annoyance that she was clasping and unclasping her hands.

Claire glanced at her through the rearview mirror. "Are you sure this is a good idea, MJ? I can always turn around."

She shook her head vehemently. "No. I'm ready. I just need to calm myself a bit."

MJ knew this would be emotional for everyone. Going through the scene in her mind helped her visualize being calm in the moment. It was a trick she used all the time. It was one way she kept a cool head when students had a meltdown.

Justin's eyes were darting everywhere as they pulled into the parking lot. He was probably taking it too seriously, thought MJ. He seemed to go into combat mode.

He pointed to an empty parking spot. "Park here, near the exit, so we can get out quickly if needed."

MJ rolled her eyes. "We will not go running out of here."

"Just the same," said Claire. "I like the idea of being able to get out without waiting in a long line of cars."

Claire parked, and they piled out. MJ zipped up her long puffy coat and slipped her phone in the pocket. She pulled a gold MMS beanie over her ears. The temperature took a dive once the sun went all the way down. The fog had rolled away, leaving the air surprisingly crisp and dry.

The three of them headed toward the front of the school, where a vast group had already assembled. A few of the building lights illuminated the area, but a softer, shimmering light emanated from the center of the crowd.

As they approached, a lanky girl with round glasses turned to look at them. Her eyes flew wide, and she grabbed the arms of the two girls standing next to her. "Look, Ms. Brooks is here!" Then she ran over and threw her arms around MJ's waist.

MJ tentatively patted the girl's back. "Oh Olivia, it's good to see you."

The girl pushed herself back, and the other two girls came in for brief hugs as well. As MJ looked at the three of them, she could see the red skin under their eyes and tracks of tears through their makeup. She smiled reassuringly at them. They needed her to be strong.

Claire touched MJ's arm. "I see Martin Kay over there. I'm going to go have a chat with him."

MJ nodded. "Thanks, Claire. We'll catch up later."

She watched as the older woman walked briskly toward Martin, a long-time member of the West Sound School Board.

Justin leaned close to her ear. "I'm going to go run a sweep of the place."

MJ resisted the urge to roll her eyes. She figured "running a sweep" was his way of avoiding the awkwardness of following her around. How would she even introduce him? No, it was better that he just do his thing.

"Sounds good," she replied.

Justin slid away and into the crowd.

MJ turned back to the students.

"We weren't sure you'd come," said Avery, the shortest girl of the three. Her bright blonde and blue pixie cut had completely disappeared under her purple University of Washington beanie. Avery was a social magnet. Her presence always created a buzz in the classroom, hallways, lunchroom . . . you name it. She usually used her powers for good, being friendly and kind. But she was a middle schooler; sometimes even the best kids acted their age.

"I know," said MJ, nodding. "This has been hard, but I wouldn't miss being here with you all for anything. We can support each other, right?"

They nodded vigorously.

Shannon walked up to join them, balancing a cardboard box on her hip. Her eyes shone dangerously as they met MJ's. "I'm so glad you're here, Ms. Brooks."

Darn it, don't make me cry, thought MJ.

But Shannon sniffled quickly, getting herself back on track. "Do you girls have candles yet?"

They shook their heads. Shannon pulled four electric candlesticks out of the box and passed them around.

"Smart," said MJ, nodding at Shannon. You don't give middle schoolers open flames.

The girls took their candles and dashed over to greet another girl who had just arrived.

Delicate notes from an acoustic guitar floated to MJ's ears. She looked around, trying to find its source.

Shannon followed her eyes. "It's Josue Mendoza. He insisted on playing tonight. Mr. Lynden said he's been practicing a bunch of 80s tunes, Troy's favorite."

MJ felt a knot growing in her throat as she caught sight of young Josue intently focused on his fingers as they worked the strings. The unmistakable melody of Cyndi Lauper's "True Colors" floated on the air.

Oh, how she loved these kids. For all their middle school insecurities and crazy antics, they had big hearts and felt everything so deeply. Josue's musical tribute was perfect for Troy. He would have beamed with pride.

She looked around at the gathered crowd. Yes, this is where she needed to be. These were her people, and they needed her, and she needed them.

"Well, I've got to get these handed out before Carrie gets this thing started," Shannon said, handing her a candle stick. "I'll find you later?"

MJ nodded. "Sure."

"Did I hear my name?" Assistant Principal Carrie Chadwick walked up and smiled gently at MJ. "Hello, MJ."

"Hello, Carrie."

Carrie Chadwick looked like a sweet grandmother with her plump frame and silver hair swept up in a bun, but she had the demeanor of a drill sergeant. She dealt with most of the school's major discipline issues and was known as a tough cookie. MJ loved her straight-talking personality and big heart. She noticed, though, that her face looked more careworn. As the acting principal, she had a lot on her plate.

"This is going to be a tough night, isn't it?" Carrie said with a sad smile. "I miss him like crazy."

"Me too." She took a deep breath to keep her emotions in check.

Carrie patted her arm. "Troy always said you have the heart of a warrior . . . the way you fight for what you think is right. Even if it sometimes causes us administrators some heartburn." Her eyes twinkled with a knowing smile. She patted MJ's arm again. "We'll get through this. We will make Troy proud."

"I know. I'm glad I came."

"Oh, have you seen the tribute up there?" She motioned toward the area where Josue still played his guitar.

MJ shook her head.

"Well, here. Come with me."

MJ followed Carrie through the crowd. As they approached the area, MJ could see a picture of Troy on an easel. He was wearing a navy blue parka, waving to the photographer with a full-face grin.

"Maddie James took the picture for the yearbook when the science classes went to do water testing at the watershed."

"It's perfect," said MJ. It really was. The image captured perfectly how Troy interacted with his students and staff.

Hanging in front of the picture was a miniature ship's wheel. MJ leaned forward to read the inscription beneath.

"Mr. Danielson, you have been and will always be the brightest star guiding our ship. The memories of your love, kindness, and concern for the students and staff at Mariner Middle School will stay with us forever. We will carry you always in our hearts. Sail on Mighty Mariner."

MJ felt her eyes prickle, and she took another deep breath as she stood up.

"Jonathon Clark's dad made the wheel, and our ASB officers wrote the message. They also coordinated getting all these notes from students," Carrie said while motioning to the hundreds of messages surrounding the picture, "which was some task because we haven't been back to school yet."

They had also laid bunches of flowers with the notes. MJ guessed maybe a hundred bouquets were scattered among the thousands of messages. More electric candles were also intermixed, so many that the display gave off the soft glow of a small fire.

Sean Wheeler sidled up beside her. He held a dark-haired little girl in one arm. He squeezed MJ around the shoulders with the other.

Carrie smiled at them both. "Well, I'm going to get ready to start here in a minute. I'm so glad you're both here."

"Thanks for everything, Carrie." MJ squeezed her hand.

It was Carrie's turn to take a deep breath. Her eyes watered as she nodded. Then she hurried away.

MJ turned to Sean.

"It's good to see you, MJ."

She smiled up at him. He was a tall man.

"It's good to see you, too, Sean. And this must be Ella." She waved at the little girl, who smiled shyly and then buried her face in her dad's shoulder.

Sean chuckled. "She's not really as shy as she's acting." He ruffled the girl's hair. "And you remember my wife, Kayle?"

"Of course," MJ reached out her hand, but Kayle, a petite dark-haired dynamo, rushed in and wrapped MJ in a tight hug.

"We have been praying for you every night, for everyone at the school." She let go and stepped back, holding MJ's hands. "If you need anything, we're here. And I mean anything, right Sean?"

He nodded. "Absolutely."

Their sincerity touched MJ. "Thank you."

She looked out at the crowd. She noticed Justin talking to a new and beautiful twenty-five-year-old classroom assistant named Zoe Taylor.

Apparently, he'd found something interesting in his "sweep of the crowd."

"This is quite the turnout," she said, continuing to look around. A couple of students were waving at her. She waved back, forcing a smile that was far brighter than she felt.

As she rolled her eyes over the crowd again, they landed on Kevin. She felt her heart go cold. Suddenly, she couldn't breathe.

He was talking to Cheryl Lucas, a sixth-grade teacher, but he was watching MJ. He looked back toward Cheryl, put a gentle hand on her shoulder, and said a few words. He gave her a quick hug and then walked in MJ's direction.

MJ stiffened. She thought she was prepared for this moment.

"MJ?" asked Sean. "Are you okay?"

He followed her eyes to see Kevin approaching. Turning back to her, he gave her one more squeeze around the shoulders. "It will be okay," he whispered.

MJ nodded and tried to breathe normally.

"Come on, Kayle. Let's go find Shannon for some candles."

As Sean and his wife left, Kevin reached her. Without saying a word, he immediately wrapped her in an enormous bear hug. He squeezed so tightly that she had no choice but to relax. As he held her, she breathed more slowly. It was like he was trying to hug her for both him and Troy.

The crowd had gone quiet, the only sound the soft strains of Whitney Houston's "All at Once" on Josue's guitar. She realized she'd been squeezing her eyes shut. She opened them. Everyone was watching them. Tears trailed down several faces. MJ closed her eyes again and squeezed Kevin back.

When they finally separated, MJ had to mop her face with the back of her hand. Kevin was smiling through his own tears. He took off his glasses to wipe his eyes.

"MJ," he said. "I hoped you would come tonight. It means the world to me, especially after what you've been through."

She shook her head. How could he say that? What *she'd* been through?

She was about to respond when Jay Butler's voice on a microphone broke through the crowd noise.

"Hello, students, staff, families, and community members. I know I speak for all of us at MMS when I say thank you for being here. We are all grieving and trying to come to terms with not only the tremendous loss of a fabulous principal but the loss of others who were victims that day." He looked out at the captivated crowd.

He continued. "And with that in mind, I want to especially thank my brother-in-law, Jon Atherton," he gestured to a man standing next to him. MJ recognized him from the photos at the police station. She realized Atherton must not know that he was the target of a crazed killer. The detectives missed him.

To his credit, Atherton appeared shocked at being referenced. But that didn't stop Butler.

"The devastation at city hall has left our city with a leadership void, and Jon Atherton has been stepping up to the challenge."

There was a murmur in the crowd, and the discomfort of the people was clear. MJ couldn't believe Jay Butler could be so stupid.

"Jon, would you like to say a few words?" Butler held out the microphone to his brother-in-law.

Atherton, a man who obviously knew how to read a room, waved it off, declining. He mouthed something to Butler, and MJ thought she saw "wrong place, wrong time."

Carrie grabbed the microphone out of Butler's hand. He protested, but the look on her face would have made Mount Rainier run for safety. He backed away with a silent nod.

"Sorry, folks, Mr. Butler didn't think that through very well. I'm sure he will apologize later," Carrie said with her customary directness.

MJ looked at Kevin as they both fought off startled smiles. She saw similar gratified looks from others in the crowd.

That was when she saw him; a man in a black sweatshirt snaking around the edge of the gathering. Wearing a navy MMS baseball cap and a black goatee, he glided quietly around the back of the crowd. He didn't speak to anyone. One hand was in his pocket as if trying to appear casual.

MJ's heart raced, and the skin prickled on the back of her neck. She couldn't be sure without getting closer, but she was almost certain it was Joe Garrison. He'd taken some pains to disguise himself, but that face . . . she'd never forget it again.

Her mouth went dry. Fear gripped her hard, but intense, boiling anger also flowed through her.

"No!" It came out as a whisper, but Kevin looked at her in alarm.

She started moving in Garrison's direction.

"MJ?" Kevin called after her.

"I'll be back," she said, never taking her eyes off the goatee man.

Kevin said something else she didn't hear, but she kept moving.

She had no plan, no idea what she was going to do, but he would not hurt another living soul if there was any way she could stop him.

As she moved, she watched his face. He moved slowly with rabid, intense eyes set toward Atherton. It was definitely him, and Atherton did not know his danger. But MJ knew. She also knew Garrison would kill others, students, parents . . . anyone. She knew what his dead heart could do.

She pushed her way through the crowd, leaving a trail of annoyed looks behind her, but she didn't stop. If only she could run, but the crowd had condensed to hear Carrie.

She kept her eyes locked on Garrison, willing him to stop. As he moved around a couple of students, she saw that his left hand clutched something hanging down at his side. To her horror, she realized it was a duffle bag. She gasped and covered her mouth. Her breath seemed stuck in her throat. She couldn't breathe. Her heart thumped in her chest, her ears, her head.

Not again. Not here.

As if sensing her fear, Garrison turned. Their eyes met. His were calm and lifeless, full of hatred so focused he looked machine-like. He turned away and started moving faster. MJ followed, her eyes on him.

"MJ!" Meredith Hamblin stepped in front of her, blocking her view of Garrison. She wrapped MJ in a warm hug.

MJ frantically searched the crowd, but Garrison was nowhere.

Meredith pulled back from the hug. "You've got to come over and see Diana and the other kids. They've been so worried about you."

"Yes, yes," said MJ hurriedly. "I certainly will, but first . . ."

"MJ, are you okay?" The woman's eyes wrinkled with concern.

"Yes, there's just someone I have to see." She grabbed Meredith's hand and squeezed it, looking her in the eyes, trying to sound as normal as possible. The last thing she wanted to do was cause panic in the crowd. "I'm sorry. I will get over to see them as soon as I can. There is just someone I have to see before he leaves."

"Okay," said Meredith, warily, not really sounding convinced that everything was fine. "Well, we are over by the bike racks when you get a chance."

"I will make it over there soon, I promise."

With that, she moved as fast as she could toward the area where she'd last seen Garrison. When she got to the outside edge of the crowd, she stopped to look around.

"Don't move, or I'll blow this whole place right now."

The voice was low, and almost directly in her ear. Something hard, like metal, wrenched into her back.

Chapter Forty-Two

"Walk forward, toward the front. Stay in the shadows, out on the edge," Garrison said almost nonchalantly. "Don't scream, make a sound, use hand signals, or try anything else to be clever. As I'm sure you know, I don't care who gets in my way."

"You don't have to do this. The police already know everything. They can help you expose what happened, why your family died." Her voice didn't sound like her own. It was high pitched, reedy, like something was squeezing her windpipe. The bag he carried brushed the back of her legs as she walked.

He chuckled. "You're funny. I've already tried that route. The government isn't interested in real justice. Death is the only real justice for them." He pushed what she knew must be a gun harder into her back. "Keep moving."

She let out a small sound of pain. She closed her eyes briefly and tried to steady her heart. Her legs were shaking and weak, like she'd just run a marathon.

"But all these people," she said, turning to look at him.

He jabbed the gun in her back. "Don't turn around," he hissed.

She stiffened her back, trying to ward off the pain if he jabbed her again. "But they didn't do anything to you. Troy Danielson didn't do anything to you. You caused pain for other people, innocent people—the same pain that drove you . . ." She faltered, the word stuck in her throat.

"Crazy?" he finished. "Maybe. It doesn't matter. I feel nothing now. It doesn't matter to me who lives or dies. I won't live past tonight either. I'm sure of that. So other people's pain is not my concern."

As they moved closer to the front, MJ saw two figures running toward the vigil from the parking lot. She realized with relief that it was Jefferson Hughes and Rory Jackson. How could she possibly get their attention? Walking in the shadows, no one seemed to notice her and Garrison.

Carrie was still talking to the crowd, telling stories about Troy. MJ could just make out Atherton with Butler hovering near where Carrie was speaking. She had to assume Garrison intended to take her there.

"Hmm," said Garrison with a note of amusement. "I see your detective friend is here. I guess we better get a move on." He gave her a rough shove. "Move faster."

She stayed where she was. "Do you really think this is what your family would want?"

She could hear his quick intake of breath behind her.

"Don't you ever," he said with barely controlled fury, "talk about my family." His angry spittle hit the side of her face. "My wife already left this life with her pain, finding no solace or justice. I've spent every minute of every day since then planning for this. Yeah, I took the city's settlement, but only so I could become their worst enemy. I will leave this life with justice. Now get moving or I will put a bullet in the first kid I see."

MJ gazed at the crowd in front of her, the families, and her co-workers, so blissfully unaware of the danger in their midst. She closed her eyes and steadied herself. Then she obeyed and moved again.

As they walked out of the shadows and into the light, she smiled at the people around her as if all was well. Garrison walked so close behind her that it caused a few people to stare. The more attention they attracted, the more convinced she was that Garrison would do something drastic.

She looked out and located the detectives. Jefferson was standing with his phone to his ear, scanning the crowd.

Her own phone buzzed in her pocket.

"Why don't you go ahead and answer that," Garrison whispered in her ear.

She felt the need to wipe her ear, to clean his breath from her face, but she refrained. She pulled her phone out and swiped to answer the call.

"MJ!" came Jefferson's urgent voice. "Where are you?"

She tried to steady her voice with a deep breath. "I'm here at the vigil. I'm—"

Garrison suddenly yanked the phone away.

"Detective. Welcome to the party," he sneered. "Listen to me carefully. Tonight, I plan to take out Atherton and Butler, but not until everyone here knows what they've done. I also have a bomb," he said matter-of-factly. "You know what I can do, so don't test me. It's my insurance policy. If you try to stop me from killing Atherton and Butler, then you will be responsible for what happens next."

He hung up the phone and shoved MJ roughly forward. "Move!" he shouted, no longer attempting to hide the gun.

Several people near them screamed.

"Nobody move or the teacher dies!"

They were at the front of the crowd. Garrison moved slightly away from MJ and started waving the gun toward Atherton and Butler. MJ realized Garrison was after Jay Butler too. What had Jay done?

Garrison pointed the gun at both men. "You two, down on your knees."

Carrie Chadwick put her hand up in a calming gesture. "Let's all just settle down. No one needs to get—"

"Shut up!" Garrison shouted.

MJ could hear crying and shushing in the crowd. Several people were pulling their families away, despite Garrison's order not to move.

Suddenly, a shot rang out. MJ screamed at the terrific blast in her ear. For a second, she wondered if he'd shot her or someone else. Relief flooded through her as she realized he'd only shot in the air. She felt sick to her stomach. The stress of holding in the terror in her heart was almost too much.

"I said nobody moves!" Garrison shouted. "You will all hear what I have to say, and you will stay for this public execution, something that should have happened a long time ago."

Atherton was the first to move. "Okay, I'm here," he said, kneeling. "But you should let all these other people go. They have nothing to do with this." He motioned with his head to Butler that he should also kneel.

Butler's face froze in horror. MJ could see he was visibly shaking.

"Stop!" Jefferson shouted. "It's over!" He now had his gun pointed at Garrison, which meant he also pointed it at MJ.

"Oh, almost, detective, but there is still some unfinished business."

Suddenly, Butler turned to run. Garrison shot another bullet in the air, and Butler dropped to the ground as people screamed.

"You aren't going anywhere," Garrison sneered. "Get up, you coward!"

Butler stood up, turning back to Garrison.

The sound of sirens broke through the noise.

"Ah, here come the rest of the first responders." Garrison laughed. "Too late, boys. Just like the night my entire family was destroyed. You know about that, don't you?" he said, waving the gun toward Atherton and Butler. "I've waited a long time to make you pay. I hope the money you made was worth it."

Garrison turned to the crowd. "Yes, some of you may remember my children. Jonah, Macey, and Bella. My three beautiful children."

As he spoke, MJ took a few slow, small steps away. She could now turn just enough to see his face and the gun.

When naming his children, his voice was wistful, but the coldness never left his eyes. "These men sold us a home they knew was unprotected. They knew it was dangerous, and when the unthinkable happened, and fire destroyed my life, they couldn't care less."

"Drop it, Garrison," Jefferson demanded. "There's no win here for you."

"I'm not afraid to die, detective. But these two are coming with me." He pointed the gun at Jon Atherton's head.

Just then, a figure sprang up from behind, knocking Garrison's arm up so that the shot went skyward. Garrison pulled his arm back and fought to wrench free from the grip of a man MJ knew all too well.

Justin.

The two struggled for control of the weapon. Justin's elbow connected with Garrison's nose, and the man almost fell from the blow. Blood gushed from his face, but still, Garrison held onto the gun. MJ lost sight of it as their bodies twisted around.

A shot rang out, and Justin let out an angry howl.

MJ tried to run forward, but Jefferson was there in an instant. He stuck an arm out to hold her back. "No!" he shouted.

She looked up to see Justin pick up Garrison and slam him into the ground. Then he pounced on him and slammed his hand against the blacktop to release the gun. He threw a couple of punches to Garrison's face for good measure. Then he jumped up, dragging Garrison to his feet, his face a bloody mess. Blood soaked through the left thigh of Justin's jeans where he must have taken the bullet, but he didn't seem to notice.

Jefferson and Rory ran to Justin's side; Rory with his handcuffs ready. Garrison howled with laughter; it was a dark, devilish laugh that was even more sinister coming out of his bloody, disfigured face. He seemed to laugh at her, staring at her.

MJ clenched her fists. She knew this wasn't the end. But this time, he wouldn't win.

"The bag!" she screamed, trying to be heard above all the commotion and the hideous sound of Garrison's mocking laughter. Garrison had dropped it during the scuffle. She lunged to grab it.

She would take it and run. No one else would get hurt.

Just as her hand touched the fabric, it was ripped away from her. For an instant, her eyes met Jefferson's, blue and determined.

And something else. Pleading.

"Run! Get away!" Jefferson shouted at her.

Then he was gone, a blur of motion as he shoved the duffle bag under his arm and ran for the forest.

MJ watched in horror as he ran across the parking lot and disappeared into the woods. She stumbled forward, trying to follow, but hands grabbed her shoulders, pulling her and forcing her to run backward. Tears clouded her eyes. "No!" she shouted, trying to release herself. "I have to go . . ."

First the noise of the blast. Then a flash of light in the trees. Fire. Smoke. MJ crumpled to the ground.

Chapter Forty-Three

MJ and Toni hustled past the media throng to get to the hospital doors. A few reporters recognized MJ and tried to yell questions at her, but the hospital security kept them at a distance. Besides, they didn't really care about her. It was Justin they wanted to know about.

Only three days had passed since the vigil, and already every national news outlet had done a feature story on this brave, handsome soldier who captured the crazed, grief-stricken father turned mass murderer seeking revenge.

Not only that, but several women had also started social media accounts with such names as "Marry Me Justin," "Justin Brooks' Biceps," "Justin Swoon," and worse. MJ did not even know how she was going to deal with seeing "famous Justin."

When they finally made it inside, they headed straight for Justin's room. He'd already texted the room number to MJ along with his many requests that she come visit him. Not that she didn't want to visit him. He had done a brave thing, but their relationship was complicated, and this only made it more complicated.

MJ had to admit that seeing Justin grapple with that maniac and hearing a shot go off filled her with a fear she didn't know still lived inside of her. During their marriage and Justin's multiple deployments, that fear was a daily part of her life.

His work was dangerous. The possibility that he might not come home kept her awake far more nights than she cared to remember. She figured some psychoanalyst somewhere would say that she distanced herself from her feelings for Justin to experience some relief from that fear.

Maybe, and maybe not. It was complicated.

The door was propped open as they approached Justin's room. They could hear voices. Justin said something, after which a woman's flirty laughter floated into the hall.

MJ followed Toni into the room. A blond nurse was perched on the edge of Justin's bed, holding a blood pressure sleeve. MJ wondered how long it had taken her to check his vitals.

The nurse stood up abruptly. Then she looked at the sleeve in her hand. She was very pretty, with a mass of blond curls piled in a messy bun. MJ guessed her to be in her 20's somewhere.

"Alright, Mr. Brooks, keep drinking your water and buzz me if you need anything." She hung the sleeve up on the machine next to Justin's bed.

"Absolutely, Naomi. Thank you for your excellent care." He blessed her with his lights-out smile.

The woman glanced at MJ and Toni. A faint pink colored her cheeks, but she stood tall.

"I will see you later," she said with her very best professional nurse smile. Then she hurried past the two women.

"MJ! Toni! I'm so glad you came. Come sit down." Justin motioned to two chairs next to his bed.

"I see you are not being neglected by the staff," said Toni with a sardonic grin as the two women sat down.

Justin chuckled. "No, they've been great." He winked at her. "But the two people I really want to see are here now. Thanks for coming."

"We would've come earlier, but your media fans are making getting into the hospital a struggle," MJ said.

"Yeah, it's been crazy," he agreed. "I've had calls from TV shows in Germany, England and even India. Man, it's crazy how stuff gets around nowadays."

"It has gotten around," MJ mumbled. Then more clearly, she added, "But Mom's leaving tomorrow to head back to Vegas, so here we are."

Toni nodded. "Yes, I've got clients and a husband that all want my attention. But MJ has promised to come visit soon. Her dad really wants to give her a daddy bear hug." She rubbed MJ's arm. "You kids have been through so much."

Justin was quiet for a second. Then his eyes met MJ's. They were full of empathy. She hadn't expected that.

He glanced back at Toni. "My leg is healing just fine, and I'll be good as new soon enough. But I know what MJ has been through will take a little longer to heal." He turned his eyes back to MJ. "Losing friends that way . . . it takes a piece of your heart."

MJ tried to pull her eyes away, but she found herself getting sucked into their soft understanding. He probably knew, better than most, how she felt.

This was complicated.

Finally, she pulled her eyes to the window and the partly sunny sky, partly sunny by West Sound standards. People in the northwest have the amazing ability to find one patch of blue in a sea of gray clouds and consider it a ray of hope for a beautiful day. That was how MJ felt now, PNW partly sunny.

***

They visited with Justin for a bit longer before "Naomi" came and said it was time for Justin to go for another scan of his leg. He made MJ promise to come back before they discharged him.

Once out of the room, MJ turned and looked down the hall in the opposite direction of the elevators.

"Mom," she said. "You go on and drive home. I'll catch an Uber."

Toni looked at her knowingly. "Are you sure this is a good idea?"

"Why wouldn't it be? I just want to check and make sure everything is okay."

Toni rolled her eyes. "I don't understand you. Justin is such a great person."

"I'm not saying he isn't."

"You are by not coming home with me."

It was MJ's turn to roll her eyes. "It's not like that."

"Sure, it isn't," Toni scoffed. Then she took her keys out of her purse. "Fine, have it your way." She gave MJ a hug and a quick peck on the cheek. "Don't be too long. We have dinner plans before I head out, remember?"

MJ nodded. "I won't forget." Claire had made reservations for the three of them at Oyster House on the marina.

Toni gave her another mother-knows-best look before she sighed and headed toward the elevators.

MJ walked in the opposite direction.

She found him only five rooms down from Justin. His room was quiet, and as she peeked around the corner, she saw he was awake and working on a laptop.

Jefferson glanced up.

For some time, they just looked at each other. Neither seemed to know what to say.

Then Jefferson smiled, a bit guardedly, she thought.

"Ms. Brooks," he said, cordially. "I suspect you've been in to visit Mr. Brooks."

MJ nodded as she walked further into the room. "Yes, Justin seems to be doing fine. The hospital staff are being very um . . . solicitous."

"He's become quite the celebrity," Jefferson said, closing his laptop. His tone was playful, but not the least bit jealous. It was he, after all, who saved a crowd of innocent people from the exploding duffle bag at the vigil. That didn't seem to matter to him.

"I've seen your fair share of hero worship out there." She took the seat next to his bed.

He waved his hand in the air. "It's all nonsense. I did my job, just like any other officer would do in my place. But Justin," he said thoughtfully, "he didn't have to do anything. He could have run away, and no one would be the wiser. Justin took a bullet to the leg and still wrestled Garrison down like a grizzly bear." He looked at nothing, as if remembering the events all over again.

When he fixed his eyes on her again, they were deep and restless. She couldn't help but think that the blue reminded her of how the Sound could reflect the sky. The water changed the shade with every ripple of movement.

She glanced at her hands as she spread them out on her knees. They felt clammy, and she inwardly scolded herself for feeling nervous around this man.

"I . . ." she started, searching for the right words. "I need to thank you."

He objected, but she pushed on.

"No, I really do. I know sometimes I might have gotten in the way a little..."

Jefferson scoffed. "A little?" He smiled and arched his brow.

"Okay, don't exaggerate. I just know that you could have ignored me, even arrested me at certain points, so I just want to say thank you for not doing those things." Then she added abruptly, "And of course, there is the small matter of you running into the woods with an exploding bomb and breaking a few ribs." She gestured toward him lying in the hospital bed to illustrate her point.

He considered her from beneath a furrowed brow. "You helped. It took me a while to see it, but I'm not sure we would have solved this case as quickly without your insight."

"Oh, really?" she said, fighting the cheerful grin tugging at the corners of her mouth.

"I will completely deny ever saying that if you tell anyone, of course."

"Oh, of course."

"And I suspect you are eager to get back to teaching? You've probably had enough of sleuthing?"

She nodded vigorously. "Amen to that. We will go back in a week and a half. I am looking forward to it."

"And I hear the mayor is on the road to recovery. That's good news."

It was true. MJ had also heard that the other city council members were improving as well.

"And we've all needed some good news," she said.

MJ glanced around the room. There were several bouquets of flowers and a few floating balloons with "Get Well Soon" on the table underneath the TV.

"They're mostly from the station," Jefferson said, motioning toward them, seeming embarrassed. "I mean, I think there is one from SSA Wells, the chief, and one from Lisa Forsberg's family, but . . ." He let his sentence go unfinished.

No someone special, MJ thought.

She cleared her throat. "I visited Rachel. You remember her, from the homeless camp?"

Jefferson nodded. "I do remember Rachel. How is she?"

"Her parents put her in a treatment center, and so far, it is going well. She looks like a completely different person."

"That's good to hear." His expression became serious as a shadow passed over it. "Not everyone can shake those demons. I hope the best for her."

MJ felt the pain behind his statement. She would probably never know its source. She might see the detective around town from time to time, but their lives were not likely to intersect again.

She suddenly felt hollow, like a hole just opened inside of her. It made no sense to feel this way.

"Well, I better let you rest," she said, wanting to escape now, for fear the hole might swallow her up.

"Thank you for coming," he said.

Was that sadness in his tone?

She smiled and stood up. "Take care of yourself, Jefferson."

He nodded. "And you, MJ."

With that, she turned and walked out of the room.

Chapter Forty-Four

MJ straightened the desks in her room for the tenth time. She didn't know why she was so nervous about this first day back at school. She'd been looking forward to it since the district announced a return to classes. It'd been two weeks since the vigil and Garrison's arrest, and while it still felt very fresh, she knew that no amount of time would ever be enough to forget what she and her community had been through.

She took a deep breath. It was time.

She stood at the classroom door to greet students as they filtered in.

Antonio was the first. A fist bump and a smile. Then he produced a yellow rose from behind his back.

"For me?" MJ asked.

He nodded, never one for a lot of words.

Then came Avery and her bestie Kayla. Yellow roses and a hug.

MJ fought the stinging in her eyes. She'd already done too much crying, and she hated crying.

"Yo, Ms. Brooks," said Fernando, stopping at the door with a gentle high-five. He handed her a rose. "We missed you, ya know? I even kinda missed school."

"Me too, Fernando."

"So, are we going to do work today?"

She smiled. He asked this every day.

"Every day, Fernando."

He laughed and walked into the room.

By the time her students were seated, she had received an exploding bouquet of yellow roses. The last rose came in a vase with a note attached, held by a shy Ethan Lawrence. As he approached the door, he pulled his hood down from his head and met her eye.

"I'm glad to see you, Ethan."

He nodded. "I'm going to do better, Ms. Brooks. You've always been nice to me, so I'm sorry for being a jerk."

"I appreciate that, Ethan. I'm going to work on being better myself. New beginnings?" she held out her hand for a fist bump.

Ethan, with a crooked smile, put his fist up and sealed the deal with a tap.

Then they both walked into the classroom. MJ put the vase on her desk and put the roses inside. Then she opened the note and read it through misty eyes.

"You got this girl," it said, followed by "(this was the kids' idea)" and Shannon's simple signature.

Then her nerves were gone. The mist cleared from her eyes.

It was going to be a good day.

* * *

A Letter from the Author

Thank you for reading Explosion on the Sound. Writing and publishing this book has been a dream come true, but all of that doesn't matter without readers. I appreciate you!

I love Jefferson and MJ, and as I am sure you have guessed, this is not the end of their adventures together. *Deadly Deals on the Sound* will be out soon! This story will tap even closer to Jefferson's raw nerves when it comes to the drug dealers pushing their wares on the public. How does MJ figure in? That remains to be seen! And of course, the story takes place with the backdrop of the beautiful but moody Pacific Northwest, which is so perfect for the crime fiction genre. If you have never been to this neck of the woods, make it a trip. You won't be disappointed. Be sure to join my mailing list and stay up to date on new releases and free short-story downloads about the characters.

Subscribe.

Thank You

It takes a team to get to the final copy of a novel, and I appreciate the team of people who made this novel shine. Thank you for your skills, feedback, and encouragement.

Stuart Bache, cover designer

Kieran Devaney, editor

Beta Readers: Whitney Harrison and Shon Malone.

Also By Gemma Christina

Deadly Deals on the Sound
Book 2 in the *On the Sound* Series

Chapter One

Ms. MJ Brooks moved with purpose around each group of students. Her eighth-grade language arts students were in teams of four preparing for an upcoming debate.

Each group had a different side of a debate topic, all likely to get students feeling passionate one way or another: school uniforms, banning video games—things that would never happen, but brought out the best arguments.

Their task today was to find text evidence to support their claims and smash any counterclaims. So far, the students impressed MJ with their progress.

She stopped to observe a team near a bank of windows in the back. Sunlight poured in as summer lingered outside. MJ let her eyes rest in the blue sky for just a moment. This was her last period of the day.

Then she'd finish up a few things and head home to take her dog Edgar out on the Kayak. No one enjoyed being inside this time of year.

"This is a good one," said Brianna Boeser, sitting up and pointing to an article so her teammates could see. MJ listened in as she explained.

"It says that school lunches don't really—"

Thwack!

MJ's head shot up.

Jada Lausch was standing, glaring down at Cade McCann, one of her three group members.

"Shut up, you idiot!" Jada's normally placid face flared an angry red.

"Ms. Brooks," complained Cade with fake concern. "Jada threw her pen at me."

Drew Taylor, their other group member, snickered.

Jada stared at him with eyes of fire. She had another marker in her hand, likely ready to launch it. "You're lucky that's all I threw."

"You two. In the hall," MJ ordered.

Jada threw the marker down on the table so hard it bounced. Then she marched to the door.

Cade just sat there. He wore a grin, but his eyes lacked the confidence of his mouth. Whatever happened, thought MJ, Cade did not expect Jada to explode in that way.

"Cade. You too, my friend. Let's go." MJ pointed toward the door.

He got up grudgingly and followed Jada.

The rest of the class stared in silence as Cade walked out. MJ wasn't the only one shocked by this behavior.

Jada and Cade were best friends. They'd even told MJ about their families vacationing together in Mexico. It was still early in the year, but she'd never heard a bad word between them.

"Listen up, everybody," said MJ to the class. "Keep gathering your evidence. Remember, each person needs at least two pieces of evidence and a rebuttal. Make sure you know who is doing your opening and closing statements."

She knew they would most likely be talking about what had just happened, but that couldn't be helped.

MJ stepped out into the hall. Jada was standing by the door with her back against the wall and her arms folded tightly across her chest. She stared down the hall away from MJ. Cade stood awkwardly on the other side of the door, stepping back and forth.

He started pleading his case immediately.

"I swear, I didn't mean anything, Ms. Brooks. Jada just freaked out for no reason." He cast a nervous glance at the girl. "I mean, we joke about stuff all the time."

Jada continued to stare down the hall without saying a word.

"Tell me what was said."

Cade swallowed. "We have school uniforms for our topic, so I was just joking around and I said if we had school uniforms, Jada's dad would save millions not having to buy Jada's clothes." He glanced at Jada again. "I mean, she *does* have a lot of clothes. I've seen her closet."

"Shut up!" shouted Jada, turning to face him.

"Whoa, Jada," said MJ, moving between the two.

Jada locked her arms over her chest again and turned away.

This is not about Cade, thought MJ. While it was a stupid comment and insensitive, Jada would have normally laughed it off, or even been at least a little flattered. It seemed to MJ that Jada's outburst was a symptom of a larger problem.

"Cade, I think you should apologize. I'm sure you can see that, whether you meant to, you upset Jada."

"But she threw a marker at me. She missed, but still, she threw it."

"I will deal with that too, but one thing at a time."

He stared down at his feet. "I'm sorry Jada. I didn't mean to make you feel bad."

The girl's arms relaxed just a tad, and MJ caught a wave of emotion on her features before she turned even farther away from them.

"Okay, Cade, head back inside."

He opened the door but stopped and looked at Jada one more time. "Is she going to be okay?"

"Let's give her a minute. Go ahead inside."

When he opened the door, MJ peeked inside to make sure all was well and no one was climbing on cabinets. So far, so good.

Cade went inside. MJ took a deep breath. She needed to make sure Jada was okay.

Sometimes these moments lead to unexpected disclosures. A few years ago, a student revealed to her in a hallway conversation that her mom's abusive boyfriend, who had just been released from prison, was babysitting her little sister. The student acted out because she feared for her sister's safety and didn't know what to do.

MJ didn't know what to expect from Jada. They were only two weeks into the school year. She and her students were still getting to know each other.

"Jada," she said softly. "Is everything okay?"

Jada still didn't look at her. She just reached up and wiped away a tear as she shook her head.

"Can I help in some way?"

"No," she said quickly, wiping more tears. "There's nothing anybody can do."

That sounds ominous, MJ thought. Teen drama or something worse?

"Do you want to go to the office and talk to Ms. Davis, the counselor? It might be good to talk to someone."

She shook her head with vehemence. "No, I'm fine." She wiped at her face. "Are you going to write me up?"

MJ shook her head. "This is our first issue, so just a warning, but you need to apologize for throwing the marker."

Jada nodded. "Can I go to the bathroom?"

"Sure."

Jada pushed herself away from the wall and strode down the hall to the girls' restroom, her long, straight hair a salon-perfect balayage of chocolate and caramel. MJ watched, wondering what was bothering Jada. Clearly, everything was not fine.

***

When the last bell rang, MJ followed her students out of the classroom. She cautiously entered the chaotic stream of students headed for the exit, trying to avoid getting caught up in the rapid current of an adolescent damn break. There was the usual jostling, holding hands, grabbing each other's backpacks, and words the kids wouldn't say if they knew a teacher was behind them.

"Antonio," MJ cautioned.

A tall Hispanic boy turned around, throwing his head back to shift his long black bangs from his eyes.

"Oh sorry, Ms. Brooks. I didn't know you were there."

"Obviously," she said with fake sternness. "And to think, you've learned so many awesome words this week."

He shrugged, a smile playing on his face. "Habit."

His attention drifted back to his friends, and the current swept him away.

MJ shook her head. It was like shoveling in a snowstorm.

She veered away from the crowd into the staff entrance to the main office. She hoped to catch Shannon, her friend and school counselor, in an extremely unlikely moment of freedom. The month of September meant Shannon hardly had time to breathe between adjusting student schedules, registering new students, and meetings with teachers and parents.

Getting to Shannon's office meant passing the office of the principal and MJ's mentor, Troy Danielson. At least it used to be his office. It was now Carrie Chadwick's office. The school district hired Carrie, the former assistant principal, to take over the position after Troy died in a devastating bombing of city hall in downtown West Sound last year.

The room looked completely different, with fresh paint, new furniture, and Carrie's myriad of Washington State University kitsch. The changes helped some, but not quite enough.

Troy's death devastated MJ and the community. It didn't matter who was in that office. She would always feel a deep pang of sorrow every time she passed it. She missed him.

Next to the principal's office sat an empty room that housed workbooks, paper, and a new copy machine. It used to be the office of Jay Butler, dean of students. After Troy's death, Jay packed up his family and moved to Yakima to take an assistant principal position. MJ was glad to see him go. They did not get along, and Jay had the moral compass of a toad, except that was insulting to toads. He'd burned his bridges in West Sound. The district chose not to fill the dean position, and the staff gained a new storage room.

They did, however, hire a new assistant principal. His name was Adam Schwartz. MJ did not know him well, but she'd only heard good things from the rest of the staff.

Neither Adam nor Carrie were in their offices. That was not unusual. They were likely in the halls or outside by the buses during dismissal.

MJ approached Shannon's open door. To her amazement, Shannon was there by herself, typing on her laptop. She looked up as MJ's figure darkened the door.

"Oh hey, I was just going to call you."

"What about?" asked MJ.

She sighed. "New student. I think she'll be in your fourth period. Her name is . . ." she hunted through a stack of files on her desk, "Tatiana Tate."

"When does she start?"

"Monday."

"Great. That gives me a few days to get ready." MJ stepped inside the office and closed the door.

Shannon arched a brow. "What's this about?"

MJ sat in a chair next to a small circular table.

"I was wondering if you have heard about any issues happening between Jada Lausch and Cade McCann. They had a blow-up today."

Shannon glanced to the side as she thought about it. She looked back at MJ, shaking her head. "I haven't heard anything, but that's odd. Aren't they good friends?"

"Yeah, but I've got a feeling something is up with Jada that may have nothing to do with Cade. I just wanted to check with you to make sure there isn't something I should know."

"Nope. Do you want me to check in with her?"

"Maybe. Let me see how tomorrow goes." MJ didn't want to overreact, but she couldn't shake the feeling that something was going on with Jada.

"We're still on for Friday, right?"

MJ gave her a blank look. "Friday?"

"Oh, come on, MJ. You promised!"

Shannon had to attend a cousin's wedding. She'd begged MJ to go with her to avoid the awkwardness of going alone.

A wicked smile crept up MJ's face. "Relax, of course I remember."

Shannon glared at her. "Good. I can't face my Aunt Lyla alone. She's going to set me up with every single weirdo in attendance."

MJ laughed. "Don't discount it. Maybe your Mr. Right will be at our table."

"Not a chance. I know my cousin's family. They don't attract my type."

MJ stood up. "I am looking forward to meeting them. Sounds . . . interesting."

"Even if it's not, I appreciate you coming with me."

The relief in her voice filled MJ with a bit of regret for teasing her. Shannon was the first person MJ saw when she woke in the hospital after the explosion at city hall. MJ was supposed to be in the city council meeting to receive an award. She narrowly escaped dying in the explosion because she was late. Her only injuries were some bruised ribs. The explosion had thrown her to the ground as she walked up to the building. Shannon sat in the hospital all night so MJ wouldn't be alone when she woke up to find out their principal had died.

"It's not every day I get an invitation to the Fairview Valley Clubhouse. Apparently, it's quite elegant."

Shannon rubbed the back of her neck as her eyes narrowed. "I know. Don't ask me how they're paying for it. My uncle's a loan processor."

MJ's eyes widened. "Maybe we're in the wrong profession."

Shannon sighed. "I think that a lot, but it has nothing to do with the money."

MJ nodded her understanding. The school had seen a steady increase in mental health issues and anti-social behaviors. Funding from the state and the federal government did not adequately support the needs of their school. Shannon, as the only school counselor, had a shocking caseload.

MJ talked to enough other teachers and read enough articles to know that this dilemma existed nationwide. School staff members were constantly reevaluating their decision to work in education.

MJ rested a hand on Shannon's shoulder. "I'm glad you're here and don't worry, no matter who is or isn't at the wedding, we are going to have a blast Friday," she said firmly, her eyes twinkling with mischief.

Shannon leaned back in her chair and put her palms up to MJ. "Whoa, now you're making me nervous."

MJ laughed lightly as she headed to the door. "Just about time to head home. See you tomorrow."

"Yes, get out of here. I have work to do." Shannon shooed her away with a grin.

Chapter Two

Curtis wove his way around the sand trap. He loved early fall; six in the morning and the sunrise was already well underway. The sound of the mower, muffled by his giant green sound-blocking headphones, didn't interfere with his thoughts, all of which revolved around a certain girl.

A soft smile floated to his lips as he mentally replayed the moment he first took her hand during the movie last night. "I was wondering what you were waiting for," she teased, her eyes twinkling in the low light of the theater. Really, he would do anything for Izzy. The night had been magical. If it wasn't for Jerry standing by the eighth fairway pond waving his arms like a madman, he might have continued mowing in a romantic trance for the rest of the morning.

He waved back at Jerry and turned his mower toward him. Obviously, the man wanted something. Maybe his mower had conked out on him.

Once Jerry knew he had Curtis' attention, he turned to look at the pond with his hands on his hips. He reminded Curtis of the body position his dad took when he couldn't quite figure something out. Jerry always reminded him of his dad.

Curtis pulled up beside Jerry's mower, shut off his engine, and jumped down, his curiosity growing. Izzy temporarily lost her starring role in his thoughts. As he approached, Jerry turned to look at him with a sickened face. His wrinkles seemed deeper and his eyes more black beneath his well-worn Seahawks cap.

The older man turned his eyes back to the pond, motioning toward it with his head. Curtis looked down.

At first, it looked like the normal tangle of grass, cattails, and other vegetation that choked the side of the pond. Then he saw it. A hand, a man's hand, he thought. It floated in between the green cattail stalks.

He inhaled and drew back. He shot Jerry a horrified look. Jerry looked back at him, but he seemed to be dazed, like he couldn't believe what he'd found.

Curtis turned back to the pond. This time, he looked closer. He realized the hand was just the easiest part to see. The entire body was there but effectively camouflaged in the leaves, stalks, and other muck of the pond.

"What the . . . ?" Curtis choked out. "Is he dead?" It came out in a whisper.

"Yeah, I'd say so," Jerry said, taking his hat off and pushing his hand slowly through his hair. "I just don't . . ." He put his cap back on and his hands back on his hips.

"I guess we need to call the cops," Curtis said, feeling nauseous. The longer he stared, the more details came to the surface. At least he was face down, Curtis thought. He couldn't have handled a face staring up at him. He appeared to be wearing a white t-shirt, but the pond and . . . was it blood . . . had discolored it.

He turned away. Mood ruined.

Printed in Great Britain
by Amazon